GW00888644

JEFF MADISON
AND THE

SHIMMERS OF
DRAKMERE

Published by Quickfox Publishing
PO Box 12028 Mill Street 8010
Cape Town, South Africa
www.quickfox.co.za | info@quickfox.co.za

First edition 2014

Jeff Madison and the Shimmers of Drakmere
ISBN 978-0-620-61554-9

Edited by James Thayer and Maya Fowler-Sutherland
Cover illustration by Jeanine Henning

DISCLAIMER
All names and characters appearing in this
work are fictitious. Any resemblance to real persons,
living or dead, is purely coincidental.

This is for each one of you.

Meet me at the big tree

at the Dreamland gates.

Adventure awaits!

Acknowledgements

Thank you to ...

Jeanine Henning for dusting her magic all over the cover, Vanessa Wilson and the Quickfox team for their publishing expertise, James Thayer and Maya Fowler-Sutherland for bringing my words to life and making them sing.

To Mom and Dad, for opening the window of fantasy, allowing my imagination to soar. Andre, for your belief in me and teaching me to pursue my dreams fearlessly. Grant, for introducing me to the magical world of words and the secret of hiding under the bed with a good book. Angie for embarking on this wild adventure with me. How we laughed and laughed.

And Angie? Thank you for not turning me into a toad in the end ... wait ... Angie?! ... Poof.

1

The hairs rose on Jeff's neck. Something icy swept his throat, making him hunch and whip around. Long misty fingers trailed inches from his face, curling and beckoning, crawling through the air.

Behind the fingers billowed a ball of mist, like a grey cloud creeping up behind them.

"Run!" he yelled to Rhed and Matt.

The three of them took off down the narrow path as the mist continued to swirl and eddy around them. Jeff grabbed Matt by his arm, not giving his younger brother a chance to argue or run in the wrong direction.

Matt tripped and sent them both sprawling to the forest floor. Jeff scrambled to his knees and whirled around just in time to see the mist covering Matt.

The boy yelled in terror as Jeff staggered to his feet and tried to get to him. Just then Rhed came storming past and body-checked Matt with such impact that they flew through the mist and landed on the path a few paces away.

Rhed hauled Matt up, half carried, and half dragged the shaking kid down the path towards Jeff's home.

Jeff, now on his feet, stared at the mist that blocked his way out of the forest. Beyond the mist he saw Rhed hesitate and yelled, "Go, go, go!"

Not looking to see if Rhed was on the move, he darted back down the path, deeper into the forest. Looking over his shoulder, he saw the mist still coming after him. It had almost caught up.

Jeff ran, stumbled over roots and slid under fallen trunks. Twenty paces later, it felt like the forest had come alive with fury. The wind and the trees were so noisy that Jeff stopped dead in his tracks. He looked up, turned in a circle and faced the mist swirling towards him. It seemed like a twister was tearing the mist apart. He covered his eyes with his hands as the leaves and twigs slapped his face.

With the deafening roar of the forest in his ears, Jeff leapt down a side path and ran as fast as he could, trying to put distance between himself and the mist. The trees swayed and protested, and it seemed that Mother Nature had unleashed a hurricane. Jeff reached the edge of the forest and pushed through the bushes that bordered the garden of his family's home.

From where they were standing in the garden and staring at the forest, neither Rhed nor Matt had noticed Jeff's arrival. Rhed was moving from one foot to the other, as if he wanted to rush off into the forest to look for Jeff. But he was not prepared to leave Matt, who was on his knees, panting.

Jeff dragged himself to where they were waiting. He noticed that the wind had stopped as suddenly as it had started.

"Tell me you saw that too?" panted Jeff.

Rhed got a fright and promptly punched Jeff on the arm. "Don't sneak up on us, troll!"

10

Jeff did not answer, nor did he feel the punch as he looked up at the sky and asked, "What happened to the storm?"

"What storm?" Rhed swept his dreadlocks out of his face as he searched the skies for bad weather.

Jeff took Matt's hand and pulled him to his feet.

"We'll talk later," he muttered.

They ran over the back porch and through the kitchen door. Once inside Jeff sank to his knees so that he was eye level with Matt. "Matt, you okay? Did you get hurt?" he asked.

Matt shook his head and whispered with a lisp, "It was just scary. I thought I heard voices in the mist."

Jeff studied Matt, who was chewing on his bottom lip. He was a small for a six-year-old, his sandy blond hair spiked up in a messy style. He absently rubbed his button nose with a finger. Although Jeff was only twelve, he stood tall against his younger brother.

Jeff had always looked out for Matt. Yes, there were yells and fights, especially when Jeff found Matt in his room messing about with his things, but they had fun too.

Jeff and Rhed were huddled in the loft in Jeff's room, talking about what each one had seen, and trying to make sense of it.

"That ball of mist was after Matt, for sure. He was the target." Rhed stabbed his finger in the air as he spoke.

"Yes, it did look like it was attacking Matt. And it only came after me when it couldn't get to Matt. Good thinking, tackling Matt out of the mist."

"What were the voices Matt seemed to hear in the mist?" Rhed wrinkled his nose as he pushed his glasses up. "And why was the storm only in the forest?"

Jeff's mother, Ella, called the two youngsters to set the table and then went to fetch Matt.

Jeff heard her footsteps on the landing, and then she was calling for Matt. From the sound of it, he was not in his room playing. Her footsteps moved further up in the house, going from room to room and finally headed towards Jeff's room.

And then came the heart-rending shriek.

"Maaaaaatt!"

Both boys dropped everything and raced upstairs. They found Jeff's mother holding Matt's face in her hands, trying to make eye contact. Matt was sitting in front of the glass door they called the moonglow doorway, his mouth open and drooling. His eyes were vacant and staring at the moon shining through the window.

It was like he was watching a play and Jeff was sure he saw a flicker in Matt's eyes – he was there the one minute and then in the next instant he was gone, his eyes glazed over.

A few days later Jeff and his mother were sitting with Matt in Jeff's room again. Although the younger boy was still in a daze, he seemed happiest in front of the moonglow window.

"Mom, what's wrong with him?"

Matt had been like this for days, not talking, not smiling, just staring into space.

"How is it that he seems asleep when he's actually awake?"

"I don't know, Jeff. He does what I ask him to do. He sits where I put him, but ..."

Jeff knew what that "but" meant: Matt, normally so lively, hasn't done a thing on his own since that day.

Jeff's mother put her hand up to Matt's forehead and clicked her tongue. Jeff had done this a few times himself by now, but no, no fever.

"I'm really worried, Jeff." She paused, her frown deepening. When she spoke, the words came out slowly. "Did anything

12

odd happen, in the forest, at your hideout?" Then she spoke more quickly. "Or was Matt angry or upset about something? Was he being bullied at school? Anything you can think of, anything at all?"

Jeff stared at his mother. Why would she ask about the forest? And lately she was always muttering to herself about the forest and … fudge, of all things.

Jeff felt guilty about keeping this secret from his mother but he knew that what had happened in the forest did not make any sense.

They were on their way back from their visit with Dr Swanson, the psychiatrist their GP had recommended.

Jeff stared out of the car window, trying to count the rain drops as they hit the pane. His mother had slowed down to guide the car more smoothly around the slippery corners, winding along Route 647.

The road curled between the mountains towering on either side, thick with forests. They passed a dilapidated, weather-worn sign that read "Little Falls 38km". Home sweet home.

Jeff screwed up his eyes, trying to see through the trees. They were dark green, huge, and overbearing.

How dark can it get in there? The blackness of the forest between and beyond those huge trees looked unforgiving, yet almost inviting. It was like the darkness was knitting the trees together, shaping them into the black void. The forest looked menacing and dangerous. He had never felt that way before, but things had changed since they were attacked by the mist.

Jeff tore his gaze away from the forest glaring at him to his little brother sitting quietly next to him on the back seat. The kid was staring out of the window, his sky blue eyes unfocused. Jeff was not sure he was seeing anything beyond the drops on the window pane.

Matt, how do I reach you? Should I take you back to that place in the forest?

Matt absolutely loved his older brother and would trail him everywhere. And although he normally irritated the daylights out of Jeff, he missed the kid.

"Some rain, huh?" Jeff's mother said to him over her shoulder. Jeff tore his gaze from his brother and leaned forward to talk to her.

"Not far now, saw the sign a little way back."

The rain stopped as abruptly as it had started as they passed the 'Welcome to Little Falls' sign. The village had a glistening glow around it from the sun shining through the moisture in the air. *How weird, the rain stopping just like that.* Jeff turned around on the back seat and stared out of the window, frowning at the sheet of rain that was still visible behind them. *What is happening here, the forest, the rain … Everything is just going weird. Does everyone see it or is it just me?*

Jeff whipped his head left and right, trying to see if any of his friends were riding their bikes on the streets. It was so much fun to bike through the puddles after the rain, skid in the mud and splash through the water in the gutters. *I wonder how much chance I have of getting my bike out, hitting the streets … Wonder where Rhed is.*

Rhed and Jeff had been friends since they were six. Rhed had skinny legs with knobbly knees and long dreadlocks that looked like noodles. They met the time they got into their first mud fight. It ended in gales of laughter with more mudslinging and plastering each other with mud than actual fighting. From that day on they did everything together.

They arrived at the house that Jeff had been living in since he was born. It was a huge double storey, with large windows framed with star jasmine. The front garden was crowded with red tulips, yellow daffodils and tiny grape hyacinths. The two large trees were surrounded by lavender that also hedged the pathway. His mother loved to work in her front garden.

Mom can have the front but the back is all ours.

The garden at the back of the house was dark and mysterious just as the woods surrounding the town of Little Falls were. The back garden was an unusual circular shape. Lining the circular patch of lawn were thick shrubs and bushes, melding and weaving into each other.

Over the years Jeff, Rhed, and Matt and some of their friends had opened passages in the shrubs making secret pathways to their hideouts. No sooner had they made a pathway, than a grass patch would sprout up behind it. The garden was ever expanding into a maze of thick bush and little patches of green grass.

While holding Matt in her arms, Jeff's mother pushed the door open over the huge entrance hall. The family room was off to the left and was double the size of the entrance hall. She put Matt down on the sofa and phoned Jeff's father, who was away on a business trip. She gave him an update on the doctor's appointment. The doctor wanted to have Matt admitted for tests and so arrangements had been made at the Angel Wings hospital for two weeks later.

Jeff grabbed some juice from the fridge and headed upstairs. His room was large and every time he got home from a long trip, he always felt like he had just returned to his own personal haven.

He turned, taking in the slanting roof that gave the room character. There was a bay window which looked out towards the green garden and the forest beyond. To the left was another door where a narrow wooden spiral staircase led to the loft.

Jeff made his way up to his loft. The room was half the size of the one below, squarish, but big enough for two chairs and a sofa. This was his favourite hangout.

The room was attic-like and just had a large oval-shaped glass door. The glass was milky in colour with strange patterns and sometimes it looked like it was providing a doorway to the dark forest outside. This window-door led to a narrow balcony that pushed right up against a large tree of the back of the house.

"This is so cool. I love the attic with your own door," Rhed gushed when he first saw this room.

"My mom calls it the 'moonglow doorway'. It sounds like a lame name, if you ask me."

"Sounds odd alright, probably a girl thing. It should have been called 'Stargate' or something like that."

"She said that she has always known it as the moonglow doorway, but she couldn't remember who told her the name. Probably my grandpa, before he disappeared. She doesn't like to talk about it. Anyway, he disappeared long before I was born."

Jeff flopped down onto the sofa and gazed at the moonglow doorway.

He grabbed his phone and dialled Rhed's number. His friend answered on the second ring.

"How's Matt?" Rhed asked.

"They want to run tests but that will have to wait until week after next when they can admit him to that kids' hospital. Mom is going to take him and stay there for a few days while they do the tests."

"Man ... that sucks."

"The psychiatrist, Dr Swanson, said he couldn't explain it. He said the problem was not medical, it's in his head. He even asked my mom if something had happened to Matt to shock him into this silent shell."

There was a loud inhalation on Rhed's side. "Jeff, I was thinking, maybe you should tell your mom about what happened that day in the forest."

Jeff paused. "And how do you think that will go? 'Mom, we were attacked in the forest by mist, it was scary and I think that turned Matt into ...' Huh?"

Rhed sighed and agreed. "It does sound thin. You'll be on the couch next." He spoke in a deep voice, imitating a doctor: "Tell me, when did it first appear?"

"And how did it make you feel?" finished Jeff with a snort. "Then my mom will go on and on about how many times she has asked us not to play in the forest."

Jeff changed the subject. "There is no chance of biking in the park today. We got back too late, but we can probably still catch some mud tomorrow."

"Hey, Jessica was looking for you this afternoon. She said she had your history book."

There was silence as Jeff imagined Jessica, smiling ... at him.

"Jeff?"

"She's borrowed my history book, nothing else, Rhed."

'Whatever, gotta go. Let's chat later."

Jeff sighed. Rhed also liked Jessica. But the knot in his stomach soon pushed the thought of girls aside. Maybe Rhed was right. Maybe he shouldn't be keeping this secret from his mother.

Then he remembered the cold tendrils of the mist on his throat. He shivered. He couldn't put his finger on it, but he was starting to think there was something unimaginably bad behind whatever was wrong with Matt. And that it might just be his job to find out what that was.

After dinner, Jeff flicked on his PC so that he could message Rhed.

"Yo, my man," the message blinked in orange.

"When is your dad back?" typed Rhed.

"Should be here tomorrow." Jeff's father had been gone on his business trip for about four days now and Jeff was missing him.

"Matt was acting odd tonight at dinner," he typed.

"What do you mean?" the response popped up.

"Well, he moved his head to the side. As if he was straining to hear something or someone."

"Jeepers, you think that mist thing is there again?"

"I checked, but nothing, and then, just like that – Matt was quiet again."

"Did your mom see him?"

Jeff sighed to himself.

"Don't think so, but she has been acting strangely too. Talking to herself about the forest and making fudge all the time."

"Jeff, honey!" His mother called him to the landing.

"I'm heading to Aunty Alena to chat to her about Matt. And to give her some books and fudge. I should be back in about two hours."

"That's cool with me, Mom," Jeff called, leaning over the railing to see his mother's green eyes peering up at him from the bottom of the stairs. Her long brown hair was in a loose knot on the top of her head, she was slender and wore blue jeans and a simple white T-shirt.

"Matt's in his room."

"OK, I'll fetch him and keep him here with me, Mom. He can sleep on the sofa."

Jeff stayed where he was, not moving, but counting down under his breath: "Aaaand ... three-two-one-and?"

His mother's head popped into view again. She smiled as she continued with "don't get up to anything ... Nothing ... nada!"

"Nada," mouthed Jeff at the same time in answer to his mother's smile.

"You're a good kid! Bye, honey," she called as she closed the kitchen door and made her way to the car in the driveway.

Jeff headed to Matt's room. The kid was sitting in his play area, probably where their mother had left him, holding a truck and staring into space. Jeff ruffled Matt's hair, took him by the hand and pulled him up.

"Come on, kiddo. Let's go to my room." Jeff hoisted Matt over his shoulder, and with a pang he remembered how Matt always used to squeal with delight when he did this.

Jeff settled Matt onto the sofa but almost instantly Matt was fast asleep, looking very small as he curled up against the cushions. He had his aeroplane-patterned pyjamas on. His face looked peaceful as he slept, his rosy cheeks made him look flushed.

Jeff headed back down, not worried about the noise he was making as Matt normally slept so deeply that wouldn't notice a tornado. Jeff sat by his computer again to carry on chatting with Rhed, who was impatiently sending him "What's up, man?" messages.

They talked about the school dance coming up and if it would be cool or un-cool to go, and if they did go, did they *really* have to ask a girl? Maybe Jessica would go with one of them, maybe she had a friend.

Jeff was just about to tell Rhed about his new idea for their camp in the woods when he heard an odd tinkling noise from upstairs. It was a soft musical sound, yet it sounded more like broken glass in a bag, and it was coming from where he had left Matt. Jeff's heart lurched. He jumped up and started scrambling up the stairs.

3

The sight that greeted him as he hit the landing stopped him in his tracks.

What the heck?

The bright green light was shining through the *unbroken* moonglow doorway, with a green beam shining directly onto Matt, who was . . . floating.

The light glittered and sparkled around him, a light greenish mist swirling around him. Matt was floating and slowly rotating. He turned full circle to face Jeff, who realised with a shock that Matt was awake, truly awake and he was looking around him in wonder. His eyes lifted and locked onto Jeff's eyes.

Yes, Matt was there, displaying the childish wonder and excitement of the moment. Just then the reality of floating hit him, and he reached out to Jeff.

Jeff shook himself out of his shock and reached out to Matt. He had to take a few steps towards him as Matt was floating closer and closer towards the window. Just as their fingers were about to touch, the glittering haze glowed so brightly that Jeff had to shield his eyes from the glare. He could just make out Matt in the haze but the light was too bright for him to look at it directly.

The room was illuminated in green, giving it a creepy, eerie glow. Just as he was about to reach out and grab his brother regardless of the consequences, there was the splintering, shattering noise of glass breaking. Jeff's eyes were watering from the brightness as he darted towards Matt's shadow. It was then that he saw the glittering haze had moved Matt outside, beyond the window.

"Maaaatt!" Jeff yelled.

He raced to the moonglow doorway intending to jump through the door, but he bounced back against the glass. Moving his hands over the glass, he realised that the glass was not broken or open. The glittering haze was still holding Matt in its grip and was slowly lowering him to the grass below.

Jeff gripped the handle and yanked, expecting the door to be sealed by magic or by the green light somehow, but it opened as if it was just normal door. He raced along the short balcony, almost diving onto the branch closest to the rail, slipping from one branch to the next in his desperate rush to get to the ground.

The branches whipped at Jeff's face and tore his clothing. His hands burnt from the roughness of the bark and the splinters, but he did not care. His only aim was to get to the ground.

Matt and Jeff reached it together. This time Jeff did not hesitate, but rushed at his brother intending to tackle Matt right out of the strange glowing haze, just like Rhed had in the forest with the mist. Matt was still floating in the air surrounded by this strange glittering light. He did not look scared but his head was tilted to one side as if straining to hear something, and his eyes were on Jeff as if he were fully trusting his brother to get to him.

Jeff was about two steps from Matt's outstretched hands when he was tackled from the side. The air exploded out of his lungs from the forceful change of direction. He landed heavily on the grass, rolled twice, and stopped with his face pressed into the sweet-smelling grass.

Jeff's mouth gaped like a fish's and he blinked repeatedly as he gasped for breath, having no idea what or who had hit him. He pushed himself off the ground, turning around at the same time toward the glow which held his brother captive.

Standing between him and his brother was a dark figure with a billowing cloak. He was the same height as Jeff and standing with his back to him, facing Matt. He was whispering to Matt but his voice was too low for Jeff to hear what he was saying.

Jeff's heart was thumping in his chest and his mouth was dry, his breathing came out in rasps as he lunged towards his brother. "Maaatt," roared Jeff, intending to force him out of the glow and away from the stranger, but the minute his fingers were about to touch the glow, the man put his hand out and grasped Jeff by the arm – halting him in mid flight. As the man held him aloft with one hand with unbelievable strength, Jeff pulled madly but could not break the steel grip on his arm.

"You cannot save him," a voice whispered. "Let him go."

"No! Are you mad? Let me go!" Jeff struggled.

The man abruptly let Jeff go, and he started stumbling towards the light, yelling for all his worth. Matt had that same peculiar face again as if he were listening to something or someone that was whispering to him inside the glow.

Jeff dived into the glow and grabbed wildly for his brother, but then the glow and mist were gone, taking Matt with it. Jeff turned around in a circle with his eyes wide. The sudden darkness was as blinding as the bright light had been.

"YOU!" he yelled at the man. "You stay there!" Jeff tore back into the house, racing for the loft, hoping that somehow Matt had been taken back there.

"Please let this be a dream, please let this be a dream, please let me find Matt asleep on the sofa!" he begged to no one in particular.

He reached his room. No sign of Matt. He raced upstairs to the loft; the room was as he had left it: the moonglow doorway unbroken, and no Matt. He raced to Matt's room, checked his parents' room and then dashed into each room of the house. Matt was not there. Racing back outside, breathless and terrified, he was surprised to find the man had not moved.

"Where is he? Where is my brother? Who are you? Where is my brother?" the questions streamed out.

The man shook his head and in that same low voice he said, "Matt has been taken to Drakmere."

"What? Where?"

"Many questions I am not able to answer right now. I need to head back to the elders to advise about what transpired tonight."

"You don't need to go anywhere right now," Jeff growled. "You need to tell me what you know and where my brother is!"

Jeff's fingers shook as he swiped his fringe from his eyes as if this would enable him to see the man better but his face was in darkness. He could barely make out his features. The man turned a little and Jeff was struck silent by the glowing purple eyes. He stumbled back and rubbed his face. How could this be real, how could eyes be glowing that bright, and purple? He felt he was in a scene from a horror movie.

"Time is of the essence. I need to get into council with the elders immediately, although they probably already know." The man sighed and raised his shoulders. "But I will return. Please wait for me and I will explain what I can when I get back."

"When you get back? What is happening? What elders? Who are you?" demanded Jeff, breathing hard but keeping his distance from him.

The man continued as if Jeff had not spoken. "And do not tell anyone what has happened here tonight. Be ready to leave at a moment's notice when I get back, as we will only be able to find the doorway in the full moon. We have to leave soon if we have any chance of finding Matt."

"Who are you?" whispered Jeff.

"My name is Madgwick."

And with that, the cloaked man reached into his pocket, with a single upward movement he tossed a small handful of silver stuff that looked like glitter into the air. The glitter floated up and as it rained down over him, the man vanished. Jeff sank to his knees, staring ahead into the darkness. And he whispered his brother's name.

4

Elder Galagedra gazed at the white, glowing globe, unconsciously breathing in time to the light that pulsed from it. The rays danced as they reflected against the stone walls of the circular room.

The globe hovered in a stone structure standing in the middle of the ancient room. It was held in place by old magic. Although the room was large, it seemed small in comparison with the overwhelming globe. It was the heart of the Sandustian kingdom; the elders were the watchers of the moon globe.

The globe watched over the children of the earth and displayed their dreams. Mostly the dreams were pure and delightful and funny: wonderful dreams were important for a healthy, happy child.

Now and then a shimmer of darkness would find its way to a child and the nightmares would torment him or her. The shimmer would float across the globe and the elder on watch would alert the warriors, who would vanquish the shimmer and chase the nightmares away back to where they came from, an evil place called Drakmere.

Tonight was Galagedra's turn to watch, and towards the top right of the glowing globe he noticed a maremist floating. Quickly he noted the time and place and then he went rigid with shock as he recognised the name.

It was no coincidence that the maremist had appeared twice in a row in the same place: the town of Little Falls. No, there was trouble in the air and they had to act before it was too late.

After reaching into a jar of silver moondust, Galagedra tossed a pinch of the dust into the air. The silver specks hung above him, circling, and as it drifted down, caught in his grey hair, which was tied in a neat ball in the nape of his long neck.

"Elders," he called, his normally soft voice booming and echoing around the chamber. The magic of the globe carried the soft yet powerful request to all the elders. It was an urgent message that only the elders would hear.

He again threw a pinch of silver dust into the air.

"Warriors," he called again.

Sitting back with a heavy heart, Galagedra waited, knowing that the calls would be answered immediately. As the dust drifted to the chamber floor, the elders began to appear, carried through space and time by the dust to take form and take their seats. Their faces were grave. It was not common to be summoned in this way and it was only in dire circumstances that the elders were called to gather.

* * *

Madgwick took form in the village market. A quick glance confirmed that no one had noticed his arrival.

Just as well. I don't really have time for chit chat.

It was twilight. The sky danced with the golden glow of the receding day, the orange fading to the pale yellow, shading into the blue. Purple turned to black as the night snuck across the sky.

The Sandustians were bustling around the market square, the busiest part of the village.

The stalls were draped with the vibrant colours of sunset. Whether the stallholders liked it or not, these stalls loved to move around all by themselves. They moved around at random and once a stall was in motion, a mist would swirl inside until it had chosen its next position. The Sandustians would laugh and have a moon juice while they waited for the stall they were looking for to either reappear or for the mist to die down so that they could leave the stall they had been caught in when it decided to move.

"Top of the day to everyone! Toffee apples?" a villager beamed. "Toffee apples for the children?"

"Oh Roger, those look tastier than last month's. Were they created during the full moon?"

"No, Agneslys, these were done in a *blue* moon, and left to ripen. The kids will love them, and they'll make their tongues blue too."

Madgwick watched a crowd of villagers gathered around the stall, all talking at once and all about their children. It was a pleasant, comfortable chaos.

The talking and laughing villagers opened a pathway for an oncoming elder so that he could pass through. He was on his way to the Chamber and seemed to be in a rush.

Agneslys smiled and waved at the elder and received a smile and a nod in return.

"I wonder what is happening in the Chamber," Agneslys asked, sipping a moon juice. "I was just talking to Elder Jozephus but he suddenly heard a call and left in a hurry. He didn't even walk, just ... dusted!"

"Must have been something very important," answered the stallholder, his brow creased. "If the elders are on it, it's urgent, isn't it?"

Agneslys finished her juice with a "Hmmm," just as Madgwick set off for the Chamber.

* * *

The elders continued to watch over the children of the world through the moon globe. Most of all they stayed on the lookout for the shimmers of darkness that slipped through from time to time to create havoc with dreams.

Apart from the elders, there were the warriors, like Madgwick. The Earth children had a different name for them, a name that has travelled through time from legend to myth and finally into fairytale: the sandman.

Because as all Earth children know, when they are ready to go to sleep, the sandman sprinkles sand dust into their eyes to make them sleepy, sending them on their way to happy dreams.

* * *

Madgwick hurried through the market, dodging between the stalls on his way to the Chamber. He carried his trusty satchel over his shoulder. He never went anywhere without it. He waved back at stall owners who shouted greetings, but he pressed on.

When he heard the call from the elders, the urgent whisper of "warriors," the call so strong that his hair ruffled as the wind carried the sound through the market. But because only warriors could hear this call, the folk in the market carried on as normal.

He was mid-stride when a hand gripped his wrist, stopping him in his tracks. He looked sideways to see Angie, the witch, clutching his arm while she pulled her shawl closer around her shoulders with the other hand.

"It has begun again, Madgwick! Remember that they don't like water …" She squinted at Madgwick through her curly hair.

Madgwick pulled up short. "Angie," he answered. "What has begun?" He frowned. "Who does not like water?"

But Angie had released his arm as suddenly as she had grabbed it, and was turning away muttering. No more words would Angie speak. She was already on her way.

Okay, that was just weird, but I better remember her words, even if I don't have a clue what she means, Madgwick made a mental note. It was not often that Angie offered wisdom and it would be very silly to ignore any advice the witch chose to give.

Madgwick watched Angie go. She had curly hair that tumbled over her shoulders. It was a hazelnut brown with streaks of fiery red. She had high cheekbones and her large eyes were emerald green. Angie had a wide mouth with full lips and a long and slender neck. She was tall, and she would often glare down at someone, which tended to make them quiver.

Not only was Angie the most powerful witch in Sandustian, she was also the crankiest. Give her the wrong look and you were bound to be turned into a toad. The worse the offence, the more warts she would give the toad. Although she had the power to, she never used spells that the spell-weavers could not easily undo and it was common to see a warty toad or two hopping to find a spell weaver after a run-in with Angie.

Madgwick ran up the last few steps towards the oak doors of the Chamber. The wood was carved with the magical moon runes, which moved and changed constantly, sometimes advising on events still to happen, sometimes recalling past events.

The keeper of runes sat by the door, noting all the changes as they appeared and disappeared. He looked up at Madgwick, his mouth turned down and his eyebrows lowered.

"The runes foretold of your haste. Enter, they await," he said and stepped aside leaving the doorway open for Madgwick.

Behind Madgwick the chamber door opened once more. Hearing the footsteps behind him, Madgwick looked over his shoulder. He grimaced as the warriors filed into the chamber and took their seats in the rows behind the seated elders. It was not often that the warriors were requested to gather in the Chamber.

Madgwick made his way down the wide staircase that led down to where the globe was still pulsating and glowing. He glanced up at the high ceilings with their archways: windows of the night. The stars and planets twinkled brightly, it was always night time in the Chamber of Sandustian.

Inside, the Chamber was a pearly white colour and the air itself sparkled and glittered, splashing prisms of colour onto the walls. Silver moon-shaped cushions floated inches above the benches. The cushions took whichever form they wished, full or half moon and sometimes even a sliver of a crescent moon.

There was a musical hush to the room and Madgwick could always smell the distinct scent of pine and cinnamon. No one experienced the same sound or smell. The magic of the Chamber affected everyone differently.

Madgwick strode silently down the aisle until he reached the front row where the globe hovered. He noted with a shock that all twelve elders were already seated and talking quietly among themselves.

Madgwick watched while the warriors filed down and took their seats while some of the cushions, being in a playful mood, darted away from some of the younger warriors and started cushion fights, forcing them to duck and dive, as they tried to catch the cushions while being pelted from all sides.

The warriors were all shapes and sizes, some tall, some short, some thin and others hefty. The younger warriors, like Madgwick, looked like teenagers and some appeared decades old with sun-kissed faces that were lined with wrinkles. But all the warriors looked brave and all had purple eyes.

The depth of purple of their eyes indicated the level of experience of each warrior. New warriors had very light eyes while the oldest warriors' eyes had already turned deep purple.

Each warrior had a role to fulfil but not every warrior's duty included fighting with shimmers.

Once all the warriors were seated, Galagedra lifted his arms and a hush fell over the room.

Galagedra's square face was brushed with wisdom. Deep grooves ran from his cheeks down to his chin. Unlike the warriors' purple eyes, Galagedra's were a deep shade of blue, and were surrounded by wrinkle lines that criss-crossed and deepened when he smiled. He looked stern but when he laughed his face softened and his eyes brightened and glowed.

Like most of the elders, Galagedra was tall and slender, and his movements were graceful and purposeful. He wore the Sandustian elders' robe of midnight blue and a bright yellow sash around his waist.

Madgwick watched Galagedra's eyes roam over the warriors. He could sense this sent a shiver up many a warrior's back. The elders were formidable and not to be trifled with.

"Welcome, our great elders, welcome, our strong warriors," began Galagedra, his voice booming.

All eyes locked on him.

"Recently a maremist entered through a crack in our defences and attacked a young child. Inside this maremist, a trance spell was hidden." Galagedra cleared his throat. "The spell was completed when the child was touched by a full moonbeam. This child has found himself in a moontrance ever since."

There was a collective gasp from the warriors.

"Our spell weavers have been working frantically on a spell to release the child from this moontrance. However, the spell is complicated, as it needs to be cast and woven in a full moonbeam. This means we have tonight only!"

Many pairs of eyes darted around the room, and Madgwick felt his mouth go dry.

"We had hoped that perhaps the child had wandered unknowingly into the path of the maremist. We, however," and he nodded to the elders, "knew there was a chance that this was something more, something we have been vigilantly watching for over the years."

Galagedra paused. He closed his eyes a moment. He raised his head to look at each of the elders, who were watching him gravely.

"Elders."

He began again, steeling his voice. The sooner the facts were told, the sooner they could start working on the best plan to save the child.

"Elders, the maremist returned to the town of Little Falls tonight. Not more than a few moments ago, the child that was caught in the moontrance ..." He dropped his shoulders, his voice cracked as he took a deep breath and then softly continued, "this child has been taken by the darkness. Our fears have been confirmed that the child has been taken to Drakmere."

The gasp was audible and the muttering renewed, and a few elders cried out in horror. When the muttering became louder and louder, Galagedra lifted his tired hands to call for silence.

"Madgwick the Warrior was in Little Falls when the maremist passed. Once we have heard his tale, we will decide on the best course forward."

Galagedra fell silent as around him the muttering and humming started up again, filling the Chamber as all the elders started talking at once, some to each other, some to no one in particular. At the same time it seemed to Madgwick that a hundred pairs of eyes were locked on him.

Galagedra spoke up. "Madgwick, would you please tell us what you witnessed?"

Madgwick drew in a deep breath. It was overwhelming to see all the elders in their places and the warriors seated behind them, faces all grave, watching him. Madgwick lifted his head. Staring ahead but not looking at any one elder directly, he began.

"I was in the forest that surrounds Little Falls. Twilight was approaching, bedtime stories were being read and children were preparing for sleep. But then suddenly I felt uneasy. There was a flutter in the air. At first I thought it was the aftermath of the rain."

Madgwick took a deep breath.

"There is always a flutter when the sunbeams touch the raindrops on the leaves. This happens in Little Falls especially, because the forest that surrounds the town is enchanted." He paused.

"At first I was bewildered because I couldn't understand what I was feeling. It was more than just a flutter in the air. And the last time a maremist collided with a moonbeam, I was not in the field yet, so I didn't know what to expect or to feel."

Madgwick's feeling of failure settled securely in his chest and his explanations felt and sounded incredibly lame to his own ears. He was cringing at what the elders were thinking of his failure.

The elders nodded to each other. Madgwick had still been a child when the last maremist came through. It was not likely that he would know what to expect.

Madgwick's intense misery increased as he misinterpreted their nodding. But he ploughed on.

"I was looking around, trying to find the cause of my unease when the trees started to whisper to me, 'Run Madgwick, run to town …' I started to run but I did not know exactly where to go."

He stopped to catch his breath, as if he had been running again.

One of the more experienced, a warrior called, Upijer, spoke up: "I would have made straight for town. The trees never issue warning unless it's urgent!" Warriors on either side of him bobbed their heads in agreement.

Madgwick nodded, then continued. "I followed the trees and they led the way, whispering and swaying. I could tell they were anxious and that there was much danger and evil in the air. Suddenly I knew. The trouble was the child caught in the moontrance. So I threw dust in the air and when I appeared in the garden, the boy was already trapped in the moonglow. And the elder boy was running towards it."

"No!" cried a couple of the elders in alarm, their hands stretched out as if they could stop the child from touching the moonglow. "Did he touch it?"

Madgwick shook his head. "I managed to stop him from entering the moonglow, but it hovered and then vanished, taking the boy with it."

Madgwick stopped to catch his breath.

"The elder boy struggled to get free and it took a lot for me to keep him out of the moonglow, at the time and even now! I feel like I should have, or could have pushed the child free of it. There was time ..."

Galagedra stood up and everyone's gaze moved from Madgwick to Galagedra, who had been watching the young warrior carefully as if he could tell that Madgwick felt responsible for the child's entrapment in the moonglow.

"You did well to save the older child," Galagedra reassured Madgwick. "It would have been a catastrophe if both children had been trapped in the moonglow. We still have a chance of saving the young boy."

Galagedra took a deep breath and then continued.

"Madgwick, we know you feel responsible. However, I need to explain that no blame lies with you. This maremist was beyond our control once the child was captured in the moonglow."

He looked at Madgwick and blinked slowly. "You did well to keep the older boy safe. I know your instinct was to leap into the moonglow to rescue the child but, Madgwick, had you done *that*, then you would have been lost to us too."

Madgwick took a deep breath, but despite Galagedra's words, he still felt the weight of the day's events.

"That you kept yourself and the older child from leaping into the moonglow showed bravery beyond instinct."

The elders nodded.

The warriors were silent. Being caught in between a maremist and a moonglow was a rare occurrence, but it had happened before. And the last time it happened the results were disastrous. This time was remembered with great sorrow by the Sandustian people.

Madgwick, finished with his tale, was suddenly weary.

He climbed the steps to where the rest of the warriors were seated, took his place and waited. One or two of the warriors caught his eye and gave him stiff nods of support.

Madgwick's shoulders relaxed at the gestures from his friends and fellow warriors. Rising voices hummed as the elders started muttering to each other. The din grew as Galagedra took his seat, lost in thought. There was plenty to consider and discuss, and not a lot of time to do it. The longer they delayed the more danger the child would be in.

Galagedra got to his feet and brought the humming down to silence with a single wave of his hand.

"As this has happened once before, we know that the child has been taken into Drakmere. We know that the child will survive … for a time."

The hum started up again and Galagedra waited for the crowd to settle.

"And what is of greatest concern, is that we know who the child is."

Some of the younger warriors looked at each other in confusion and with raised eyebrows. The elders stared at Galagedra. They knew what he was referring to.

Galagedra continued. "For many years we have watched the town of Little Falls. We have kept watch remaining wary, as the doorway to Drakmere was first opened there.

Again the crowd started up, and Galagedra waited.

"This doorway, to be found in the town of Little Falls, has a purpose, namely to provide us with a safe way of entering Drakmere."

A nervous twitter fluttered through the room.

"The worlds are deeply bound by this magic passage. The first child taken into Drakmere by a moonglow also lived in Little Falls many years ago. She was a dream catcher."

He paused to allow the younger warriors to make sense of this point.

"Our warriors went through the doorway and fought a brave battle to bring that little girl home. Although we triumphed with the safe return of the child, our hearts were heavy, and we wept with sorrow as we lost one of our brave warriors to the evil in Drakmere."

Galagedra stopped, the pain of the loss still as fresh as all those years ago.

Jozephus, a short, slender elder with cropped hair, continued in his soft voice where Galagedra had left off. "With the assistance of our elders, we weaved a powerful spell to entrap the terrible memories that could harm the young girl so that she could live a normal life without the terror of Drakmere chasing her in every dream. To this day the spell lingers, protecting the child who is now all grown up with a family of her own. Our spell keeps her memories and dreams blocked from evil."

Galagedra took over from Jozephus as if they had timed their speeches.

"As strong and skilful as our spell weavers are, the child who was taken tonight cannot be brought back with our magic."

He was met by a sea of concerned faces.

"We cannot bring him back as the crack has already been woven closed. No magic can get through unless we reopen the crack. And this we cannot risk. We will not be able to stem the tide of shimmers. The shimmers of darkness just waiting for a slight gap to float through and force their way into the dreams of the sleeping children."

Another elder, Torledo, tall and slender with long silver hair hanging to his waist, stood up. His face was smooth with rosy cheeks. He turned toward Madgwick and spoke in a gravelly voice.

"Madgwick, my boy."

Madgwick winced at the term *my boy*. He was a warrior, a good one, and had been one for a long time, but the elders saw everyone as the youngsters, so it was hard to be annoyed at the affectionate wording.

The elder continued. "How much did the older boy see, this boy Jeff, is it?"

He looked around at the other elders for confirmation of the name. Then he turned back to Madgwick with a raised eyebrow.

Madgwick got up and spoke loudly so that all could hear. "Torledo, the boy Jeff, saw his brother Matt trapped in a moonglow, saw him going through the window, being lowered into the garden and then in the garden he saw his brother disappear. He did not see me appear and I had to tackle him from the side to stop him from touching the moonglow."

"I am interested to know how he reacted to all of this," the elder said.

"He was shocked and that is understandable. He was angry and he wanted to know where his brother was."

"And you told him?" Jozephus asked.

"I told him the boy had been taken to Drakmere, that he was not to tell anyone what happened and that I would be back to explain. And I told him we would be able to find his brother. I know I should not have told him anything, but he was so distraught I had to say something."

The muttering started up again among the elders and warriors. It became louder from the ranks of the warriors, until the words became clear: "The boy cannot go into Drakmere, unthinkable, no way, can't happen!"

Madgwick cleared his throat to make sure his voice would rise over the muttering.

"I have been watching this family since the child got caught in the moontrance and I know Jeff will not be left behind voluntarily. He is a strong boy and this is his brother."

The room was quiet, then Galagedra stood up. All faces turned to him as he spoke calmly. "I too have been watching this family and I am sorry, Madgwick, but the boy may under no circumstances enter Drakmere. We have to leave the brother at home, as far away from Drakmere as we can, yes. Being in Drakmere would put them in grave danger. These boys are dream catchers just as their mother before them."

A gasp floated around the room. Rubisid, a short warrior with grey curly hair and a lined face that looked like a jigsaw puzzle, stood up, spreading his hands. "All known dream catchers have disappeared over time. Most of our warriors have never even seen or met a dream catcher. How were they found?"

Jozephus dropped his head. "Drakmere is ruled by evil. With the right spell it would not be hard to find a dream catcher if there were one to find."

"We must choose carefully as to who will be going into Drakmere," said Galagedra. "Yet again, we must brave the horrors of Drakmere and enter the world of nightmares to bring back a child."

There was a rumble in the room as Madgwick and all the other warriors leapt to their feet, all volunteering to fetch the child, ready to rush off at once.

Galagedra bowed in gratitude and addressed the standing warriors.

"The time of choosing who will do this brave deed will come soon enough my honourable warriors. For now, please be seated."

Madgwick stood silently as he waited for permission to speak. Galagedra nodded for him to talk.

"Elders, the boy Jeff saw me this evening and is waiting for an explanation as to where his brother has gone, and I told him that I would be back to explain. I ask that I be chosen as one of the warriors to enter Drakmere to bring the young boy home."

Madgwick sat down, feeling the gaze of every warrior and elder on him for making such a bold request, but not really caring what they thought.

Galagedra turned towards the elders and there was a rush of whispered muttering between the elders.

Some of the warriors leaned forward, anxious to hear what had been decided, but to no avail: it was impossible to catch even one word between them.

After some minutes, the mutterings and whispers ceased and Galagedra turned back to the warriors.

Galagedra spoke again. "The task will fall to you, Madgwick. You have already made contact with the boy."

Horrigan, one of the older and more experienced warriors, stood up. He was a little taller than Madgwick, with dark purple eyes that showed his years of experience. His taut face had a dagger tattoo down the side. He looked tough and his head was shiny and bald.

He cleared his throat and said, "With all respect, Madgwick is a fine warrior, but he lacks the experience to enter Drakmere. We should send older warriors to bring the child home."

He glanced at Madgwick with raised eyebrows but seemed determined in his statement.

Galagedra gazed up at the Warriors, many of the older warriors nodding in agreement, while the younger warriors scowled.

He raised his hands to once again silence the room and said, "Yes, a more experienced warrior is a consideration. However, in this case, we," he swept his hands over the elders seated behind him, "feel that Madgwick has the necessary qualities to complete this task.

Galagedra let the information sink in.

"We believe he can guide the child through the dangers of this terrible world. We also agree that a warrior with experience must accompany Madgwick. We must keep the rescue team small to escape unwanted attention. We therefore suggest that only one other warrior accompany Madgwick."

The room was enveloped in a hush.

"The elders and I choose warrior Rig to take on the burden with Madgwick."

This time the whispers and the mutterings came from the warriors, and everyone glanced at the silent warrior called Rig who sat with his head bowed, staring at his hands.

Galagedra spoke again, causing the mutterings to stop instantly.

"We believe that Rig has the experience as he alone has been to and returned from Drakmere. He understands the dangers that lie within Drakmere better than any other warrior in this chamber. He also understands why this particular child was taken. And I think he has earned the right to go and avenge his loss."

Some of the younger warriors, including Madgwick, looked curiously at Rig while the older warriors merely nodded at the choice. Rig got up, and then, speaking in his bass voice, said his first words since entering the chamber.

"I accept this task."

Galagedra gazed at Rig for a second. He spoke softly.

"Thank you, Rig. I understand the pain this decision must cause you. The child's life lies in both your hands."

He paused. "The elders will prepare dust for you to travel with. You must go tonight, as the doorway can only be revealed in a full moon before it reaches its full height in the night sky. Please prepare yourselves and meet back here at the chamber in an hour."

Madgwick stared at Rig and felt delighted and a little intimidated by the choice.

Rig was a fierce and bad-tempered warrior, the warrior most feared by foes of Sandustian.

He had long, sleek black hair, which was tied in a ponytail that ended halfway down his back. His eyes were the sharpest colour of blue-purple Madgwick had ever seen. There was a sadness about him that often reached his eyes.

Rig was not unfriendly but he did not mix with the other warriors, preferring to keep to himself or to stay out in the field. He was good looking but did not even notice when the girls in the village blushed if he nodded or smiled in their direction.

And he himself did not smile much. He was about as tall as Madgwick, but had a stronger body from all the years in the field. He had many years of experience over Madgwick.

Had he really been to Drakmere? And what loss were the elders talking about? Madgwick wondered.

Galagedra raised his hands to all. The meeting was done and so the elders, with the use of their dust, popped away in a blink of the eye.

Each elder had his own special preparations to do before Madgwick and Rig left.

Some of the elders would assist in preparing the magic dust that would go with the warriors while other preparations were more behind the scenes: the magic that would open the doorway to bring the child home when it was needed.

5

Madgwick made his way from the chamber, hearing the buzz of voices as the warriors started among themselves. The drone grew until he felt like it was pushing him along the chamber aisle.

The humming was silenced with the dull thud of the door closing firmly behind him. Down below he caught a glimpse of Rig who was already at the end of the market. *Drat,* he thought, *I didn't even see him leave. I would have liked to talk to him.*

Madgwick sighed and sat down on the carved stone bench just outside the door. It looked out across the village.

He was relieved that he had been chosen as the warrior to go to Drakmere. He thought he would have a hard time to convince them.

Madgwick winced at the thought of his mother's face when he had to tell her he was going to Drakmere. Oh, she was immensely proud that he was a warrior but she would have been even more delighted if he had had a different calling, such as watching over the vegetable garden or something equally dangerous, like attacking tomatoes.

He also wanted to find Angie. She might be able to give good advice … or not. As long as she did not turn him into a toad. He did not have time for that right now.

"Madgie! Madgie!" his six-year-old sisters chanted as he opened the door to his family home, and before he could utter a word he was grabbed around his legs by four little arms.

Laughing, he ruffled their golden locks and then promptly lifted them each over a shoulder and carried the giggling twins to the slide as they went looking for their parents. Madgwick adored his sisters, Lori and Penni. He thought they were the prettiest little girls in the whole of Sandustian.

They had matching cheeky dimples that popped up when they laughed, which was very often. And they constantly bobbed up and down with endless energy.

Like all Sandustian homes, Madgwick's family home was intertwined with a large tree. There was a bright orange slide that ran throughout the home, and it was activated when someone sat or stepped on it. The slide went in all directions, up and down, around and around and was the quickest and most exciting way to move around the tree house.

Together, Madgwick and his sisters slid around the house. The girls squealed as Madgwick stood on the slide while they were dangling on his shoulders. He was an expert at navigating the slide standing.

Finally they found themselves in the kitchen where Madgwick gently set them upright on the floor and winked at the animated faces gazing up at him. Then he looked into his parents' faces.

Madgwick's mother, Anny, had short, curly golden hair like the twins and although she also had dimples, they were not as pronounced as the girls'.

His father was tall and skinny and had to wear braces to keep his trousers up. His hair was thin and black with streaks of grey running down the sides. He was always laughing and telling jokes and to the delight of the twins, when he laughed, his ears wiggled.

Madgwick inhaled deeply and in a gush of words told his parents about the crack, the maremist, and about the child that was captured in a moonglow.

He finished with the biggest news of all.

"I have been chosen to go into Drakmere and bring the child home," he told them.

Madgwick paused and waited for the explosion. His mother did not disappoint, and burst into tears covering her round face with her hands.

Madgwick looked at his father with a crooked grin. "Dad, did I tell you the elders chose Rig to go with me?"

He knew the news would ease his mother's fears.

"Really? Rig is going with you? Oh, I feel so much better."

His mother's voice came out muffled as she spoke through her tissue. Madgwick rolled his eyes and said "Thanks, Mom."

Five minutes later, after hugging the girls and his still-sniffing mother and shaking his father's hand, Madgwick bid his family farewell.

* * *

Madgwick's mother felt her heart contract as she watched him go. She would miss that crooked grin and the way it showed his dimples, not to mention his tendency of raising one eyebrow when trying to make a point. These were just some of the things that made everyone like him.

She glanced at her husband who was also standing there, watching Madgwick go.

She sighed. She knew her son was not as strong as the older warriors, but he had only been in the field a few years. In time, his strength would develop and his body would transform the way she had seen it with other warriors. But in the meantime, she hoped his young powers would prove strong enough for the danger ahead.

* * *

Squaring his shoulders, Madgwick headed back towards the village, intending to find Angie. He searched and searched and was starting to stress, because he did not have much time left and there was no sign of the witch.

Disappointed, he turned to head back to the Chamber, but as he rounded a corner a cheerful voice spoke up.

"So, my boy ... You're heading into Drakmere. Do you think that's wise?"

"Angie!" exclaimed Madgwick. "I have been searching for you everywhere! What did you mean earlier? What do you mean now? Of course I have to go. How can I not go?"

Angie glared at Madgwick.

"Mind your manners boy, one question at a time, or you may be croaking your next question. Hopping your way into Drakmere will not be fun."

Madgwick reined in his relief at running into her.

She cracked Madgwick a rare grin. She had a very soft spot for the young warrior.

"What I meant earlier you will still find out, and what I mean now is that it is never wise to enter Drakmere, urgent mission or not, and yes you have to go, now run along. You're late!"

She whirled around and walked away, leaving Madgwick with his mouth open. He was flabbergasted. She had been no help, no help whatsoever.

He turned away towards the Chamber when Angie called. "Madgwick?"

He hesitated before turning around. The witch was half turned back to him. "I will be watching your adventure and interfering now and then. And if you come across a moonaisy, will you bring it for me?" She hurried down the lane in between the people.

Madgwick watched her hurry away, and started when she yelled without stopping or turning around. "TOAD. Madgwick, if you're late I will zap you into a toad! Toooooooaaad!" Her voice faded out.

Madgwick laughed as he hurried towards the Chamber.

On entering, Madgwick glanced around and noted he was alone. Rig was not there. He was disappointed as he had been hoping to discuss their plan.

With nothing else to do, Madgwick caught a cushion and sat in the front row ahead of the pulsating globe, mesmerised by the eerie glow. For the second time in a day, Madgwick started when a voice spoke right next to him.

"Madgwick, you must take utmost care once entering Drakmere. We will watch your journey but there is much we will not be able to see. You will have to rely on your wits and bravery, something I happen to know that you gave an abundance of," Galagedra finished with a smile.

Dropping the smile, he added, "We do not send our warriors into Drakmere with an easy heart, Madgwick."

The elder's face was grave. "The dangers are so great that we shudder at the thought. But this child, he is too young and he will not survive Drakmere on his own. This child, Matt, possesses the quality to infiltrate the dreams of all children. The king wants this child, but make no mistake, Madgwick, that the king will grab either child, the younger or the elder!"

Madgwick gasped. Keeping Jeff out of Drakmere was an even greater priority than he had realised.

"Either one will serve his evil twisted purpose, as both boys are dream catchers," Galagedra continued. "With an enchantment or spell, their dreams can be manipulated to catch the dreams of all other children."

He paused to let Madgwick absorb the information.

"If the king, by some inconceivable series of events, manages to keep either child, that child will be lost to us forever, and the dreams of the children of the world will be open to nightmares and terrors forever, without any way of stopping them."

Galagedra sighed. "You must bring the child back. And for all these reasons the brother, Jeff, cannot go with you into Drakmere."

Handing Madgwick a brown leather bag heavy with dust, Galagedra said, "Take this dust the spell weavers and elders have prepared for you. It should last a while, but use it with caution. It is very powerful. And Madgwick, listen to Rig. He has been there before and will lead you through many dangers.

Galagedra smiled. "He is not easy to work with, this we all know, but he is the best warrior to have with you in Drakmere."

Then Galagedra paused before adding, "You will have to help the child. There may be tears."

Madgwick nodded. "Galagedra, I will not return without the child. And ... I was hoping to meet Rig here."

Elder smiled, and said lightly, "Go Madgwick. Rig will catch up to you before you enter Drakmere."

Madgwick nodded once more. It was more or less as he had expected. Rig had his own ways of doing things. No one really told Rig what to do. He just knew what to do and how to do it. The younger warriors all looked up to him, trying to imitate his fighting style.

Galagedra stood and Madgwick did the same.

There was so much more he wanted to know, needed to know but there was no time for questions. With so much happening so quickly, now when it was time to act, he was not really sure what to do next. Find the doorway, go through and look for the boy Matt, he supposed.

Madgwick smiled briefly at the elder and started towards the door, then asked, "Galagedra? What is a moonaisy?"

Galagedra laughed. "Angie caught you, did she? It's a flower, a daisy bewitched by the moon, very rare and sought after. The magic of a moonaisy is powerful, and only the very skilled can use its magic successfully. You will be lucky indeed if you find one of those."

Galagedra sighed and sat down by the globe, watching the glowing orb.

Madgwick watched for a moment, then squared his shoulders and walked to the Chamber doors. The runes were moving and recreating themselves, no doubt rewriting tales of adventures to come.

Madgwick stepped out of the Chamber and the door swung firmly shut behind him.

J eff stayed on his knees for about five minutes, his mind going over Matt's vanishing. He remembered Matt floating, the glow, and then, gone! How was it possible? Still in disbelief, he pushed himself to his feet. He felt windswept, like he had just been through a storm.

Jeff reached his room, where his unanswered messages from Rhed were still flashing impatiently. He bent over the keyboard, not bothering to sit.

"Matt gone," he typed and hit enter. He decided to do another sweep of the house. What had happened could not be real. Surely Matt was just asleep somewhere, and Jeff was in serious need of some sleep too. He was so tired, in fact, that perhaps he had imagined the whole thing. *Yes, that's it.* Jeff half laughed at himself for a second before he was jolted back to reality.

Starting at the bottom of the house, Jeff started going through each room and each cupboard a boy might crawl into. He checked the washing machine, the dryer … nothing. Jeff just reached his room when he heard the squeal of bicycle tyres. Rhed!

Rhed rushed up the stairs two at a time.

He had been best friends with Jeff forever. Matt was just a baby when he and Jeff met, and Rhed was there for all the firsts. Like the first time Matt fell out of the tree, and the time they taught him to ride a bike.

When those two words flashed on the screen, Rhed bit his lip as if he knew this was serious. This was trouble and Matt was in the middle of it. Jeff would not joke about this.

"Matt gone" must have meant Matt was not in the house and not in the garden. And that left only the forest. There was a lot of ground to cover.

"Jeff! What is going on?" Rhed's shoes squealed in protest as he bolted through the sliding door.

He stepped into Jeff's room, dropping his bag in the corner.

"What do you mean Matt is gone? Gone where?"

Jeff cleared his throat then looked Rhed in the eye. "I'm not sure where he is, but he's gone. I've searched the house, every room. He isn't in here. Just … something weird happened tonight and I don't know how to explain it." He rubbed his eyes. "I think I'm going crazy."

Rhed looked at his friend with raised eyebrows. "What the heck is going on?"

"Matt was asleep on the couch." He hesitated. "Next thing there was the sound of breaking glass. And then he was floating!"

"Whoa, did you just say floating?"

"Floating! Then he went straight through the window …" Jeff moved to the moonglow door, stretching his hands over the cool glass, trying to feel cracks that were not there.

Rhed's eyes narrowed as he examined the glass looking for cracks.

"I raced after him." Jeff held up his hands to show the evidence from his hasty tree descent.

Rhed narrowed his eyes again. "Geez, that looks rough."

"When I got to the bottom, I tried to tackle Matt out of ... whatever it was. But I was stopped by some dude who seemed to know what was going on, and then Matt disappeared, the dude also disappeared but he said he would come back!"

Attesting to true friendship, Rhed did not laugh. He did not even snort in disbelief. Then Jeff turned toward Rhed with a frown, not sure what kind of look he was going to be facing. But Rhed merely appeared thoughtful.

Rhed glanced at the moonglow door again and asked, "Okay, so if it all ended outside, then it makes sense that Matt could be in the forest somewhere."

Jeff's eyes widened. He whirled around and then, without a word, both boys rushed out the door, shoving each other in their attempt to reach the stairway.

Jeff raced to the kitchen drawer, grabbed two torches and ran to the back door to catch up with Rhed.

He stopped on the grass, not sure on where to go next. The full moon, lying low on the horizon, gave off an eerie golden glow. Jeff doubled over and planted his hands on his knees, as if he had a stitch.

"How come you believe me?" he asked Rhed.

Rhed was turning in a circle, staring into the darkness. "It's you, bud. You don't tend to exaggerate. Besides the fact that I saw the mist attack, you'd kick my butt!"

"Well, maybe I have lost it," Jeff muttered before yelling his brother's name into the night.

Jeff strode towards the path on the left side.

"Rhed, you head on down that path on the right," he said over his shoulder. "These paths meet in the middle. If Matt is in the forest then we should find him." He paused. "That is, if he has not wandered further than the brook."

Jeff did not need to wait to see if Rhed had started moving. He knew his friend was already heading that way.

The forest felt angry. There was just a slight breeze and yet the branches were rustling restlessly.

Jeff kept on the path heading all the way to the brook, although it was unlikely that Matt would wander all this way by himself: he was afraid of the dark.

Jeff shone his torch up and down in frantic jerks. He stopped at all Matt's favourite trees where the kid liked to play or hide. His heart was sinking. If Matt was not in the forest then how was he going to explain what happened to his mother or the cops? To anyone, for that matter.

Jeff and Rhed met in the middle where the two paths joined. Rhed shook his head.

"Damn," said Jeff. "I think it's time to call the adults and explain …"

He stopped, dreading finishing the sentence. His parents thought he was so responsible for his age and he hated that they were going to be disappointed in him.

Rhed muttered, "Of course, it would not be a good idea to mention the floating-through-the-door thing."

Jeff stared into the darkness. "You believe me, right?"

"Aw, man, you have to ask? Of course I believe you," replied Rhed.

Although the two boys were still swinging the torches side to side, calling for Matt and muttering back and forth, the cloaked figure watching them from the shadows went unnoticed.

He was standing in the darkness, blending in with the shadows of the forest when the kids passed him. Even the light of their swinging torches did not reveal Rig. Their hushed voices floated in between the trees, and their fear for the little boy was very apparent. Even the forest felt it. Rig bit his lip to stop a small smile escaping as if he were glad Madgwick had been chosen as part of the rescue team. Madgwick was good with kids and would be well equipped to handle the little boy: his runny nose, the possible whining, the probable crying.

His lips pulled up in a sneer as he thought of going into Drakmere. This was his big chance. Rig had unfinished business in Drakmere, and he was prepared to create some havoc of his own there. He pushed away from the tree and followed the boys towards the house.

Rhed was asking Jeff details about the cloaked man he had seen earlier.

"So, he physically stopped you from grabbing Matt?"

"He stopped me in my tracks. It was like walking into a concrete wall. I couldn't move. He said that he had to talk to what he called elders. Then he would be back and we would go and find Matt."

"Do you believe him, Jeff? That he is coming back and that he knows what happened to Matt?" Rhed asked.

"I can't explain it, Rhed. It felt like I had known him for years, although I have never seen him before. Like he was an old friend. He felt real. Deep down I felt a connection. It was weird."

The garden was coming into view, and they were about to step onto the grass when a shower of silver glitter exploded into the night.

It came as such a surprise that both boys instinctively crouched and grabbed each other's arms. As they straightened, the shower drizzled down to the ground and a cloaked form took shape.

Jeff and Rhed stumbled forward in half-steps, both speechless. The cloak fell back and revealed the man Jeff had seen earlier, the man who said his name was Madgwick.

Rhed nodded towards Madgwick, and asked Jeff, "This him?"

"I think so, yeah." The relief was evident in his voice. He was not losing it after all, he had not just imagined the whole thing, and the couch was not waiting for him in Dr Swanson's rooms. And here was the link to his brother's whereabouts.

7

The cloaked man in front of them was of average height with short black tousled hair that made him look like he had just stumbled out of bed. His eyes were a shade of purple a little darker than lilac. He was wearing a white loose shirt with a light brown leather waistcoat laced up with thin blue rope and a deep purple cloak that dropped to his ankles. His trousers were light brown and his dark boots were scruffy and comfortable-looking.

Madgwick blinked rapidly as if he was surprised to see the two boys staring at him. He was not unhappy to see the friend. It would make it easier to leave Jeff behind if he was not on his own. The last time he left, Jeff was sinking to his knees in despair.

"Jeff, Rhed," Madgwick nodded to the two boys.

Madgwick paused for a second to absorb Jeff properly in the dim light. The boy's short brown hair appeared sun-bleached and straight and he kept tossing his head to flick his fringe back. His eyes were dark green, his nose and cheeks speckled with freckles.

Madgwick stepped forward. The boy called Rhed had a very puzzled look on his face, as he pushed his glasses up on his nose. His hair, Madgwick noticed, was pulled back in a band wide enough to hold his dreadlocks. He had a large nose that supported his heavy framed glasses; his brown eyes had thick eyebrows and lashes. And his knobbly knees were sticking out from beneath his long baggy shorts.

Jeff moved closer, watching Madgwick. He was a little taller than them, with thick black hair that looked like it had just been through a whirlwind. The purple of his eyes was a startling purple. He had a smile that made him look friendly, but he also had a deep frown knitting his eyebrows together. He had a look of determination in his eyes. This was not a social visit.

If it were at all possible, Jeff's heart sank even lower. "Where is my brother?" he blurted out.

"I am sure there is a lot that you wish to know, but we have limited time, so I will explain what I can now." Madgwick bowed his head as if trying to decide on where to start, and then continued.

"We are the guardians of dreams, or as your myth and fairytales like to call us, the sandman. We ensure the dreams of children are beautiful, full of colour and full of laughter. We sometimes use magic sandust to send the children to dreamland."

He stopped to check that they were with him. "We watch and protect them from nightmares. When the nightmares arrive, we are the warriors who fight against the evil that tries to destroy the magic of dreams. Your brother, Matt, has been taken into Drakmere, the land of nightmares."

Jeff let out a little sound.

"We know that for now he has not been harmed, but we need to act quickly to bring him home. The longer he spends in Drakmere the bigger the chance of Matt being hurt. We need to go and get him back – tonight."

Jeff and Rhed were opening and closing their mouths. Jeff had hundreds of questions but somehow could not form them.

The two of them exchanged a look that said, *did he just say the sandman – guardian of dreams?*

"Okaaaaaay, why don't you just sit tight, hang around and we'll get someone to help you," Jeff said. "No worries, you're safe with us."

Jeff forced himself to speak in a soothing voice, but out of the side of his mouth he muttered to Rhed, "I will distract him. You get help."

With his hands spread out in front of him, showing that he meant no harm, Rhed started to back away one step at a time in the direction of the back door.

"Ugh, of course you don't believe me," Madgwick said, shaking his head. "Come on Jeff, search your heart, you know me, you know the truth. I have been sprinkling dust in your eyes since you were a child."

"You have not!" Jeff put his hands on his hips. "I have never seen you before tonight, and you expect me to believe that you are a, what? Sandman? *The sandman* they tell little kids about? I may be young, but I'm not dumb."

Jeff stopped to take a breath. "Now what have you done with my brother? How long have you been watching us, and how do you know our names?"

Madgwick sighed and stared past the boys towards the forest behind him. "I have to dust them."

"You will NOT dust them. They do not need to know!" said a gravelly voice from the edge of the forest.

Both boys whirled around at the voice behind them. *Oh crap, there were two of them!* Jeff thought in a panic.

Madgwick was determined. "I have no choice, and if the elders want to be angry then they can take it up with me when I get back.

The boy needs to know. We can't expect him to understand. He has seen too much!"

"Are you mad?" the voice asked. "You can't just dust them and open their minds! Send them to their rooms, send them to sleep, but no dusting! I forbid it!"

The voice was low and furious.

Jeff puffed up his cheeks before letting all the air out. It was all becoming a bit too much for him.

"I have seen some weird stuff tonight," he said, "and I don't know what to believe. My brother floated through a glass door and then disappeared in front of me. Now you tell me he's been kidnapped, taken to this place called, what? Draksomething? And that you are the sandman, or something!"

Jeff rubbed his temples, suddenly longing for a couch, even if it was Dr Swanson's.

Madgwick took one step towards the boys and without warning tossed a handful of silver dust in the air. It glittered as it floated down over them, and they gasped.

Rhed swiped and swatted at the glitter as if he was totally disgusted. What self-respecting boy would be caught covered in glitter, irrespective of the colour!

"What are you playing at, tossing glitter at us? Is this supposed to be a party now?" yelled Rhed, turning to Jeff. But Rhed stopped in his tracks as he looked into Jeff's face.

Jeff was speechless. His mouth was hanging open but his eyes were shining.

"It's true," he whispered. "They're telling the truth, the sandman does exist!"

He turned to Madgwick who was anxiously looking at the slow moon rising into the night sky.

"What is that stuff?" asked Jeff, eyes still wide open.

"It's called moon dust. It reveals the magic around you, and I am probably going to get into a huge amount of trouble for dusting you, but really, I am running out of time. We have to find the doorway and it must be found now."

Jeff's mouth hung open.

"I do not have the time to try and make you understand or see what you do not want to see. The dust reveals the magic to your mind."

Glancing at Rhed, he continued. "It may take a bit longer with your friend. He has not seen all you have."

But already Rhed's mouth was still making like a fish as if his mind was opening to the truth of the magic.

Rig stepped from behind the two boys, and spoke in his gravelly voice. "Nice, Madgwick. I asked you, no, I told you not to dust them, but you did it anyway." He turned to Jeff, glancing at Rhed who was still gaping in the background.

"We have been appointed to enter the dark world of Drakmere and bring Matt home." Rig nodded to the two boys, then looked at Madgwick. "You and I have to start moving, and yes, you are in so much trouble for using the dust!"

Madgwick held his hand out to the boys. "And with that, may I introduce Rig. He is the best warrior there is. He has been to Drakmere before. He knows exactly what to do to find Matt and get him out of Drakmere."

Rig's words "you and I" shook Jeff back to the present. "Give me a few minutes to get a few things, then we can go."

Rhed's head whipped towards Jeff. "I'm coming too, not sure where, but I'm coming!"

Jeff shook his head. "I don't actually know where we are going, but it sounds far away. And besides, your mom will kill me if you got lost too."

"Cool," Rhed said. "Like your mom is going to love the news that both her kids are missing. No way, man. I am not staying behind to explain *that*. Also, he is as much my brother as yours, and then if you really haven't realised it by now, you need me, 'cos I'm the brains in all of this. It's always my ideas that work when we build something, and besides, my mom can't kill you after your mom kills you!"

Jeff glared at Rhed. Whatever he was going to say disappeared when Rig spoke up.

"*Neither* of you is joining us on our journey to Drakmere."

Jeff pushed himself taller. "Just wait a minute. I *am* coming with you! *He* said I could!" He was staring at Rig but pointing an outstretched arm at Madgwick.

"It was not his place to promise. You are *not* coming and I will not waste time on this any further." Rig's tone was very final, and Jeff's whole body buzzed with rage.

J eff whirled around to Madgwick. "But you said ..."

Madgwick's brow was furrowed and his lips pulled into a thin, tight line. "I am truly sorry, Jeff. I tried to talk the elders into letting you come along, but they have forbidden it, and they are right. It is just too dangerous to have you in Drakmere. You have to stay here."

Jeff's teeth ground together. "I don't care what these so-called elders say, this is my brother and I am going to go and look for him!"

Rig, who was watching the forest with his back to Jeff, turned back slowly to face him. His features were like stone. Jeff swallowed and stepped back.

Rig's voice was hard. "Little boy! It is dangerous enough to go into Drakmere to rescue your brother. Do you have any idea how difficult it will be to bring out *two* kids, never mind three! You will both stay here."

He turned away from the two silent boys, almost dismissing them.

Then he spoke to Madgwick. "The moon will soon be high. We have to find the doorway or miss the entry completely. We can't afford to waste more time."

Madgwick turned to Jeff. "I am sorry, Jeff. We have to find a secret doorway. This is the quickest and only way to get into Drakmere tonight. If we don't get through the doorway tonight then we will have to wait until another doorway is opened by the spell weavers."

Jeff blinked.

"That means that Matt would be in Drakmere a while before we could try to rescue him. We don't know what state he will be in by then or what they will do with him."

With that he left Jeff and Rhed and walked to where Rig was standing holding his hands out towards the forest.

Jeff hung his head. Weird things had happened, and not just that night.

There was the ball of mist chasing them through the forest, Matt floating through glass, the silver showers of dust, and people disappearing and appearing in a blink of an eye.

None of this could be explained logically, but the fact was that Matt had disappeared.

He was gone, these two Sandman dudes knew where he was, and they were worried about him. It also sounded as if they had a deadline to find this doorway place.

Jeff did not know what to think. But again he felt the truth around him. He felt like he had known Madgwick forever, even though he was sure he had not seen him before.

Jeff could reject all this weird stuff, go inside, and call his mother and the cops. Or he could accept what he had seen with his own eyes, even if he didn't understand it.

Something magical was happening. Jeff still had enough imagination in him that he could turn his back on the logical and move towards Madgwick and that unfriendly guy Rig.

"Okay," Jeff said, coming up behind the two. "What exactly are you looking for? We could at least help you look."

Rig shook his head. "How about you go inside and watch that flashing talking box thing. You're interrupting us!"

Madgwick put his hand on Rig's arm to silence him. "No, they can help. We don't know where the doorway is, Rig, and I don't know about you, but I am starting to get worried. If we don't find that doorway within the next few minutes then we will be lost before we even started."

He turned to Jeff and Rhed. "We are looking for a doorway that is activated by the moon, and only by the moon and then only once a month."

Madgwick swept his hand over the forest. "The doorway could be anything, from a shape to a tree, anything."

"How come you don't know what the doorway is?" Rhed asked. He turned to Jeff and continued. "Isn't it strange that these guys are the experts but they don't know what they're looking for."

Rig glared at Rhed. He pursed his lips as if he was highly annoyed that their knowledge was being questioned, but answered anyway. "The doorway was last used many years ago, long before you were born, and to ensure that no one could open it again, the magic of the forest hid it from view. That is why!"

"Oh, the forest hid it," said Rhed, nodding at Jeff. "Yes, that makes perfect sense."

Jeff hid his smile. He did not like Rig either, but he was preoccupied. The word "doorway" was playing in his mind. But the answer danced just out of reach.

Rig and Madgwick stood on opposite edges of the garden, hands outstretched, muttering in some strange language.

Rhed grabbed Jeff's arm. "Hey don't you guys call that door upstairs …"

"The moonglow doorway … but that's inside, not outside in the forest," replied Jeff.

Rig turned around at their talk. "What doorway, what are you talking about? Madgwick! What are they talking about?"

Madgwick turned to Jeff. "What doorway are you talking about?" He smiled to lighten the harshness of Rig's tone.

"Well, I'm sure it's nothing," Jeff said.

"Then why bring it up?" growled Rig.

Ignoring Rig, Jeff spoke directly to Madgwick. "My mom told me it was called a moonglow doorway."

"Your mother called it a moonglow doorway?" asked Madgwick. His eyebrows shot up. "Who told her that it was called a moonglow doorway?"

"She always said she couldn't remember who told her, but she has been living here since she was a baby. So maybe it was my grandpa who told her, but it's nothing, just some stained-glass door."

Madgwick and Rig stared at each other. "What better place for the forest to hide the doorway than …" whispered Madgwick.

"With humans having lost their imaginations, the door would be safe! No-one would know, understand or believe what it could do," finished Rig, his purple eyes shining.

Jeff looked at them, his eyes darting from face to face. "What do you mean? Is this the doorway we're looking for?"

Then it hit him. He grabbed Rhed's arm. "Matt was sitting in front of that window when he became sick, remember?"

"Yes, your mom found him there!"

"And tonight he was asleep on the couch when I heard the breaking glass," Jeff finished.

Madgwick and Rig stared at them open-mouthed.

"What breaking glass?" Rig sputtered.

"Matt was asleep on the couch, then I heard glass breaking. When I got upstairs, he was awake but floating in a green light. And this light brought him down to the garden."

Rig turned to glare at Madgwick, who shook his head. "I got here when the boy was already in the glow right here, where we are standing."

Rig's glare switched to Jeff. "Wait a minute, did you just say broken glass – that the doorway is broken?"

Rig muttered to Madgwick. "If the doorway is broken then it may cancel the entry tonight. The weavers would have to find another way. Maybe the witch, Angie, could help. She tends to go where she pleases."

He looked up at the moon. "Maybe this is not even the same doorway. And how would these two kids know anyway?"

Jeff was already shaking his head, not noticing the emotions playing on Rig's face. "That's the strange thing. I heard the glass break, but when I got there it wasn't broken."

Madgwick turned towards Jeff. Behind him the air whooshed out of Rig in relief. "Jeff, can you show us this doorway?"

"Heed the moon, Madgwick," said Rig. He pointed at the moon, which had risen higher into the sky, the glow becoming white.

"The doorway is in my room," said Jeff, turning on his heel and heading for the back door.

He pulled the door open and stepped back to let Rig and Madgwick enter ahead of him, but only Rhed was behind him.

Jeff craned his neck to look behind Rhed to see where the other two were.

"They went poof," said Rhed.

The glittering of silver dust lingered, drifting to the floor where Madgwick and Rig had been standing a few seconds before.

When the boys reached the room, both Rig and Madgwick were already there, running their hands over the moonglow door. They were grinning widely. This was the doorway, hidden away for many years. This was the entry point to Drakmere, they had found it!

"You know, the elders could have just told us that the doorway was here," mumbled Madgwick to Rig.

"As I understand it, the forest surrounding Little Falls is powerful, and the elders may not have known exactly where the forest hid the doorway," explained Rig, his mood vastly improved now that the doorway was found. Now they just had to wait for the right moment to open the doorway, and that was meant to happen within the next few minutes.

"How will you find my brother and how long will it be before you come back? Will the doorway stay open until then?" Jeff wanted to know.

Rig rolled his eyes but Madgwick understood Jeff's fear for his brother. "We think he will be held in the king's castle. We are not sure how long we will take, but time in the land of nightmares is much longer than here. A few hours here could be days there. We have some magic dust to open the doorway from the other side."

Madgwick paused then pre-empted Jeff's next question. "The magic dust will only open the doorway from the other side. It will not work on this side of the door."

"Why would they take Matt?" Jeff asked.

Rig and Madgwick were both staring at the moonglow door, not wanting to miss the sign, but Jeff did not miss the quick glance Rig shot Madgwick and the slight nod from Madgwick in return.

Then Madgwick answered. "We do not know for sure, but we think that any child could have been taken. Matt was just in the wrong place at the wrong time."

Jeff's eyes narrowed as he listened to their answer. Something did not sound right. He could not pin-point it, but they were definitely brushing over that answer. There was certainly something they were not saying.

He opened his mouth, about to argue the point when the path of the ever-rising moon must have aligned into place. A moonbeam came straight though the centre of the moonglow door. The beam was concentrated on the centre but as the moon moved into place so the radiant light travelled through the rest of the door, lighting it up in a brilliant silver glow.

It was so bright that their eyes started to water. Then it started to dim from the inside towards the rim, revealing a room that looked like Jeff's room except there was no furniture, just an empty room. The same dimensions, the same window, but just empty. Jeff gaped at the identical room and then turned back to look at his own room.

Rig and Madgwick straightened up. Rig glanced at Jeff and stepped straight into the room.

And bye to you too, thought Jeff as Rig stepped past him.

Madgwick turned to Jeff, "I will find Matt and bring him home. You have my word."

Jeff nodded. Then, without giving Jeff any chance to talk or try to ask to come with them again, Madgwick stepped into the room beyond.

Rig and Madgwick crossed the empty room to another door, opened it to reveal another identical room. They moved into that room and so proceeded from room to room, getting smaller and smaller the further they went. Finally they opened a door far away and that was it, they were gone.

Jeff stared into the room and the rooms beyond. The effect was like looking into a mirror with mirrors behind him. He was dying to rush in after Madgwick.

Thud! Jeff leapt into the air with fright. "Man, Rhed!" Jeff yelled.

Rhed had dropped the bag at Jeff's feet. It was the bag that he had been carrying when he arrived.

Rhed just grinned at his friend. "Matt is out there. We don't know where and they," he pointed in the direction of where Rig and Madgwick had disappeared, "don't know either! So are we just going to sit here and tell our folks that Matt is gone but not to worry, the magic sandman is on top of it! Or are we going to find him?" He grinned, thumbing at the doorway. "They can't stop us now."

Jeff stepped forward then stopped. He wanted to go. He did not know what was on the other side, he did not want to lead his friend into danger, but the thought of little Matt, in a strange place, all alone ... He had no choice. What kind of brother would he be if he did not even try?

"Rhed, they weren't telling the truth when I asked why Matt was taken. I don't know what is going on and somehow I don't think any

72

of this is any good. We could get into a lot of trouble. But I can't just stay here. I have to do something."

Rhed nodded, hoisting his bag over his shoulder. "Let's go."

Jeff took the bag from Rhed and tossed it over his shoulder. "What the heck have you got in here?" He grunted with the weight as the bag landed on his back. Then he turned towards the doorway.

The door was starting to get brighter again.

"It's closing," yelled Jeff, and jumped through the doorway with Rhed right after him. They ran through the empty room and the door slammed behind them, but they kept moving through to the next room, which was the same, each room identical to the last.

The boys ran to the next door. As they ran through the rooms, so the light in each became brighter and brighter. They had to move and move fast.

Jeff and Rhed exploded through the next door, and just kept running, going from room to room, the doors slamming behind them. They were getting through the doors with mere seconds to spare. They could feel the brightness heating up their necks and they did not dare look back, they did not dare stop to catch their breath. They were committed now. There was no going back.

Somehow Jeff knew that if they were caught in these rooms they would not get out easily. After what seemed like ten doors, ten rooms and running like their lives depended on it, Jeff and Rhed rushed through the last door and found themselves in a green, dark forest.

The door behind them slammed and they skidded to a stop, bumping into each other trying to stop their momentum. They turned around in time to see the doorway become hazy before disappearing.

The silence was deafening. They blinked several times as their eyes adjusted from the brightness to the darkness.

Jeff and Rhed flopped onto the soft forest floor, exhausted and yet exhilarated.

"Man, what the heck was that?" Rhed panted.

Jeff was silent. Rhed looked at his friend's eyes. They were fixed, staring into the forest.

Rhed followed Jeff's gaze into the dark forest, drew in a breath and whispered, "Uh oh."

Peering from the darkness was a set of red shining eyes. As the boys watched in apprehension, more and more red eyes were lighting up until they were surrounded.

10

Matt knew he was going somewhere, but he did not know where. The light around him was very bright but also warm. Not hot, just warm, like when he put his sweater on after a cool breeze.

Although he was trying to stay brave, he was scared. He wished that Jeff were here with him.

The light was dimming and Matt screwed his eyes to try to see where he was. His feet touched a cold floor and suddenly the light was gone leaving Matt blinking, trying to adjust to the sudden change in light. There was a thick, dark mist that felt very cold and moist.

Again Matt longed for his older brother. He would know what to do. Jeff was always the captain and Matt would follow the orders. He even knew how to salute properly. Jeff and Rhed had taught him one easy salute, but one day his mother saw him saluting the fleet commander and they all got into serious trouble. For some reason Jeff and Rhed howled with laughter around the back while their mother interrogated Matt. He had a hard time explaining. Afterwards Jeff said they would use that hand greeting when serious attitude was necessary and, of course, when Mom was not near.

Matt smiled at the memory, but shivered as the mist engulfed him. There were thin orange bolts streaking through the mist like lightning across a stormy sky. Slowly the mist lifted and then it was daylight, as if a light had been switched on.

Matt looked around, his jaw dropping. This place was great!

He turned in a circle, standing on a grey cobblestone path in the middle of a beautiful square garden. He was surrounded by flowers of all colours, pink, blue, red, yellow. So many that he could not count. The flowers were different shapes and sizes: some looked like cups and saucers and one looked like a kettle. They smelt wonderful, just like his mother's garden smelled in summer.

Matt gasped when he looked up and saw a turret. He was in a castle garden. He knew what a castle was because he had seen them in pictures from his books back home. And here he was, in a big one. There was even a wall with the staggered blocks to the side, a real castle wall.

Matt ran to the wall and looked out over the edge. Wow. He was high up. The view stretched towards forever. He could see rolling hills, trees, even a blue lake in the distance, and it was twilight so the sky was fading from orange to golden yellow, moving towards the pink and purple of the oncoming night.

Looking down was scary as he could not see further than a few paces before it became too dark to see.

A short "uhm uhm" behind him whipped Matt around. An old grey man was standing watching him intensely. Matt stood quietly, not sure what he should say.

The old man was staring at Matt, as if he were trying to look inside him. There was a look of longing on his face. Under the old man's stare Matt started to shuffle his feet. The man looked like a typical grandpa, half bald, with the remaining hair pure white. He had a round face and his cheeks were full. It was a face that could be friendly and warm, if he wanted to be.

Matt thought the old man's deep green eyes looked just like his mother's. The man stood up straight with his hands linked in front of his chest. He had a green cloak that hung to the floor, moving gently in the evening breeze.

Hoping that the old man was friendly and would help him, he spoke tentatively. "I would like to go home. Can you help me?"

The old man started at the sound of Matt's voice. His face hardened and he lifted his arm pointing to the right. "Come this way if you will," the old man said.

The old man raised his white eyebrows and Matt headed towards the large wooden doors laced with iron. His heart lurched as he walked through the doors to find himself in a long and vast room with white pillars on either side. The walls were covered in heavy curtains and tapestries, and the colours were rich with plenty of gold. The ceiling was high with arched windows that seemed to stretch into the distance. Matt could not even tell where the ceiling stopped and the blue sky from the windows started. He glanced behind him. The old man was a few steps behind him and he nodded towards Matt, urging him forward.

Matt stepped forward, his feet shuffling on the stone floor. Right at the end of the room was a slightly raised platform with a huge golden chair. On it sat a figure dressed in black, patiently waiting for him to cross the room towards him.

The walk down to the end of the room seemed like an eternity. Matt was slow and he kept glancing behind him, checking to see if the old man was still there. He was very scared.

Finally Matt reached the end and looked at the man, thinking he must be a king or something. He was old, like as old as his father, but not as old as the grandpa-looking man behind him.

The man had a black goatee splashed with gray, which matched his thick eyebrows. His eyes were dark and Matt could not tell if they were brown or black. But he could see they were not friendly. There were no wrinkles on the corners of his eyes. Matt knew about those. His mother told him that they were laugh lines. This man had no laugh lines in his face.

It was not an ugly face, and there was a smile on the lips, but that smile did not reach his eyes. He had a large, sparkling gold crown on his head.

Matt shivered under the gaze of the king.

"Matt." The man's voice was low and powerful. "I am pleased to meet you. I hope you enjoyed the moonbeam journey. Welcome to my castle and welcome to Drakmere. My name is King Grzegorz, ruler of the Kingdom of Drakmere."

While he was making his introduction he rose from his chair and his arms swept in a grand gesture of welcome.

Because his mother would frown on his manners if he did not respond, Matt answered with, "Nice to meet you King Grrrre ..."

He broke off, not knowing how to pronounce the name. "Please, can you take me home?"

The king stared at Matt like he had just grown horns, his jaw working up and down like he was chewing gum. Eventually he sank back into his chair, dropping his hand on the armrest with a great slap, making Matt jump with fright.

The king glared over to the old man and snapped. "Okay, Thirza, I did not get any of that!"

The old man, Thirza, bowed his head and responded respectfully. "The boy speaks with a lisp, your highness. He said that it was nice to meet you and asked if he could go home."

The king smiled at the old man, turning back to Matt.

"Such good manners, young man, how pleasing. We are not sure how you got here, but we will find a way for you to go home soon, Matt."

King Grzegorz gave the old man a side glance and smiled slyly as if lying to a child was very enjoyable and so very easy.

"While we are sorting things out, do you think that you can stay here for a bit? I have a big castle and you can explore and do things." He stuttered to a stop.

"Do you need anything?" he asked Matt who was standing staring at him. The king fingered his crown irritably. Then, with a smile, he asked, "Do you like my crown, Matt?"

Matt shrugged his shoulders, and replied, "It's cool. It looks like marbles."

Grzegorz slowly turned his head to Thirza, narrowed his eyes as if he was sure the old man was hiding a smile, and glared at him until he hurriedly gave the obviously required translation.

"He thinks it's cool, your highness, and he thinks the gems look like marbles."

Matt stared at the king's face. His eyes bulged out of his head, and on his temple Matt saw a vein throbbing furiously.

11

The king ground his teeth, trying to relax his face before he turned back to Matt. It was vital for this child to be in a happy place in his mind. Screaming into his face that his crown jewels were not marbles was not going to help.

He clapped his hands once and a young lady appeared through the curtains. When she came to a stop in front of him, she bowed low. She kept her eyes on the floor, never looking directly at the king.

"Matt, this is Holka. She will be taking care of you while you are here."

He looked from Matt to Holka and then swept his hand across the room.

"Holka, please take Matt to his chamber. Make sure that he is fed and is resting comfortably."

His voice dropped low and although he kept it pleasant, he sneered as he finished with, "You know your duty."

"Go with Holka, my boy. Oh, and ... Matt?"

Matt turned back to the king.

"Sweet dreams." The king made sure to say the words with a big smile.

Matt glanced at Holka and then back at the king, who had a funny looking grin on his face.

Holka was very pretty with a long golden plait the colour of maize running down her back. She was about as tall as Jeff. Her eyes were the strangest colour: pale pink. Her cheeks had a dash of rosiness and her lips were red. And she smiled shyly as if she did not want her teeth to show.

She wore an orange tunic that looked like a long shirt with yellow ribbon that laced up the front. Her pale yellow leggings went up to her knees.

Matt's heart skipped a beat when he thought about going home tomorrow. He hoped his mother would not be too mad at him for staying out all night.

The girl with the golden hair stood to the side, waiting for Matt to fall in next to her. She led him away from the room, ducking through the blood-red curtain, leading him through another hallway lined with golden statues and bright colourful tapestries hanging from the endless ceilings.

Holka did not say anything to him as she led the way, and Matt was way too shy to say anything. Besides, he was so busy looking at everything, his head going from left to right, taking in all the colour and richness of the castle.

Endless carpets ran along the long corridors. The arch windows were lined with thick draped curtains that changed colour, glowing brighter as darkness overcame twilight. There were many corridors that led off the one Matt walked down, some with large wooden doors that were so big that Matt would have needed a ladder to reach the handles.

Some doors were so small they came to his knees.

Matt sniffed the air. It smelt like fresh doughnuts, choc-chip cookies and bubblegum. It made his mouth water.

Then he walked past a corridor that made him gulp. It was grey, black, and cold, nothing like the rest of the castle. It was scary.

Matt went back to the start of the corridor he had just passed, heart thumping. He took a deep breath as he peeked around the corner. He exhaled as the corridor turned out to be awash in colour like everywhere else. His eyes must have been playing tricks on him. Matt turned back to Holka. She had a little smile on her face and beckoned him to follow her.

They reached the end of the hall and went up a flight of stairs. The staircase was so wide that Matt was sure his whole house would be able to fit right in the middle of it. At the top they again turned right and headed up a smaller staircase which seemed to be getting narrower as they went up.

By now Matt was lost and his eyes were drooping. Eventually he realised they were going up another staircase in a spiral, going round and round. They reached a wooden door that swung open with an echoing creak when Holka whistled a tune.

Inside the circular room was a large bed, a sofa and a fireplace. To the side was a large arch window. A table with fruit, cheese and bread was next to the window but Matt could not see past the bed.

He managed to get to the bed, flopped down, and was practically asleep when he thought he heard Jeff whisper to him.

"G'night, Jeff," he mumbled in return, his voice muffled into the pillow as sleep took him. He did not feel his shoes slipping off his feet, or the blanket that gently covered him. He did not hear the door close or the soft whistle that locked it.

12

Madgwick and Rig were moving silently through the forest, leaping over roots and ducking under branches, trying to put as much distance as possible between themselves and the evil shimmers that were waiting in ambush at the doorway.

Just before they stepped through the doorway, Rig tossed a pinch of silver dust over Madgwick and himself. Now they were invisible even to the shimmers that Rig was convinced were waiting for them.

As they stepped through, the shimmers drifted impatiently, their red glowing eyes scrutinising the open door. There was a gust of wind as Rig and Madgwick moved rapidly past them.

The warriors could not stay invisible for long, so they had get past the shimmers and deeper into the forest. Madgwick shook his head. Had it not been for Rig he would have already been in trouble. And how did the shimmers know where to wait? Rig was shrewd and anticipated the ambush. Once they were past the surrounding shimmers, they shook off the invisibility and moved deeper into the forest.

They were moving at a good pace when a loud scream behind them made both of them stumble. They grabbed branches and shrubs to balance themselves as they stopped.

The scream was either Jeff or Rhed who must have followed them through the doorway and walked straight into the still-waiting shimmers. A second scream pierced the forest air and the branch in Rig's hand broke in two with a loud snap.

"Tell me they didn't," Rig growled, his eyebrows almost touching.

Madgwick blew out his cheeks. "Why? Why would they do this? I told them. No. We have to go back. We need to go back!"

"You think?" Rig's hands were balled into fists, but he had already spun around and was heading back in the direction they had just come from, back to the doorway.

If they had been moving quickly before then they had to move like lighting now if they had any hope of saving Jeff and Rhed. Judging by the yells and screams, the boys were in terrible danger.

They did not bother to keep their race back through the forest quiet. The racket ahead was enough to drown out their rapid approach.

* * *

Jeff leapt to his feet, turned in a crouch, trying to see a way out, a direction to run, but everywhere he looked were red eyes.

He could not see more than just the eyes, and not knowing what was attached to the eyes was terrifying. He grabbed Rhed by the arm, yelling, "Get up! We have to move!"

Rhed scrambled to his feet, his eyes darting. They were standing back to back, holding each other up, giving each other support. Jeff tried to make out what they were but still they just looked like a black mist with piercing red eyes.

'What is it?" Rhed whispered to Jeff.

Jeff shook his head. It was a bit late for the hushed toned. These things, whatever they were, were advancing, taking their time as if they knew that these two boys had no chance against them. Jeff had his back to where the doorway was, but he had to try anyway.

"Rhed!" He did not bother to keep his voice down. "Check to see if the door is open! Maybe we can get back through the door-way."

"It's long gone." Rhed was still turning in a slow circle, keeping his back tight against Jeff's, but he had pulled his backpack off Jeff's back and started rummaging through it, looking for a weapon, any weapon, anything at all would do right now.

"Rhed!" Jeff's voice rose as the dark shapes were coming in closer. "What are you doing, man? If you have a plan, now would be a good time to tell me."

Rhed grabbed two cans and shoved one into Jeff's hand behind him.

"No plan, but this may stop them. We spray and then run." He kept his eyes pinned to the dark mist approaching.

The eyes started to advance, moving in slowly at first but pur-posely from both sides. In a gasping speed, the balls of mist rushed at them. Both Rhed and Jeff yelled and brought the spray up, aiming for the only distinguishable features, the eyes.

Jeff's spray hit the red eyes full on and they blinked in apparent pain. The black mist still ploughed into Jeff, separating him from Rhed who was spraying his can at whatever he could reach.

The force hit Jeff hard, whooshing the air out of him. He dropped the can as he was sent into a tumble away from Rhed. The mist was on him then with the blood-red eyes inches away from his face.

Jeff flailed his arms and bunched his fists but he was not making any serious impact. It was like hitting jelly. He could not connect with anything solid. The pain was like a thousand razor-sharp teeth clamped onto the length of his arm. He screamed in agony, trying to pull his arm away from the mist and the invisible teeth.

The mist was brutally strong as it picked Jeff up and shook him like a rag doll, the pain excruciating. Jeff saw stars as the sensation threatened to overwhelm him.

The mist shook him again and then dropped him, probably to come at him from another angle. Jeff, still in shock, landed on the ground with a huff, blinked and shook his head.

Immediately he started to crawl away from the mist. He saw Rhed engulfed in the blackness with only his face showing, screaming in terror and pain.

Jeff felt the can against his hand as he tried to scramble along the ground, clutched it and sprayed wildly around him. The spray hit the mist behind him and it recoiled. Jeff sprayed full force again, pushing it back further, slowing the mist but not stopping it.

Jeff whirled and sprayed at Rhed and the mass moved away as it got a full load of the spray. Rhed was panting, his eyes round and his mouth open in a silent scream, like he could get no more sound out. There was nothing left.

Jeff pulled his friend close. If these things were going to attack them again they would face it together. Jeff glanced around wildly for Rhed's can, but it was out of reach. Only two black fog-like monsters had attacked them, and there were at least four more that he could see.

Shaking and trembling, Jeff pulled Rhed back, his legs jerking against the ground as he forced them back away from the next attack. With their backs against a tree, Rhed started to whimper as the dark mist advanced.

Jeff and Rhed shrunk against the tree behind them. They were finished. There was no saving them now. Rhed had his eyes screwed shut, as if he did not want to see what was coming. Jeff had his eyes open in terror and this is when he saw a rapid movement from the forest behind the shimmers.

Jeff's eyes opened wide as Madgwick and Rig leapt over the shimmers with their arms spread wide on either side, palms facing down, both in the exact same leap pose.

Like a practised dance move, they landed lightly in front of the boys and sank into in a deep crouch. Their heads bowed as if they were taking a moment.

Jeff blinked and tugged at Rhed. "Madg ... Madgwick," he whispered. He could not get more than that out. His body was still in the aftermath of the pain inflicted by the red-eyed mists.

Rhed, clutching at Jeff, opened his eyes. They widened at the sight of the two warriors in front of them.

13

As one, Rig and Madgwick's heads snapped up. Their purple eyes glowed brightly. Madgwick's eyes met Jeff's. They narrowed as he witnessed the pain and fear on the boy's face. Rig was staring just as hard at Rhed, his body stiffened in anger.

"Hello boys. Stay where you are." Rig spoke softly but there was no way either of them was going anywhere. Besides the fact that they could not move even if they wanted to, the look in Rig's eyes was deadly. Jeff nodded numbly.

In a single movement both Madgwick and Rig pushed up from their crouch and whirled to face the shimmers. Both had fistfuls of silver dust, their arms hanging loosely at their sides. They looked very calm and in control of the situation.

"Ah, my favourite toys. Some fun at last," Rig said, smiling grimly at the mist that had started to advance towards them.

The shimmers rushed the two warriors but they whirled out of the way nimbly, their cloaks billowing around them. The dust dropped from their hands but did not fall to the ground as normal dust would. It hovered and sparkled as if it was alive and connected to each warrior.

The dust looked liquid as it flowed, rippled and glittered. Madgwick made an elaborate movement and stuck his hand out, palm facing out, letting the silver dust shoot out like an arrow. It stretched ahead as it speared the shimmer, slicing the darkness in two.

The shimmer shrieked and tumbled back away from the dust. Madgwick retracted his hand and the dust neatly rushed back to him, curling into his hand. The fight had begun.

The shimmers were advancing. Rig had a mean grin on his face as he spun on the spot, his hands moving faster than the eye could track. He stretched his hand out and the dust shot off in strands, encasing the shimmer in the silver net.

Rig twirled his hand and the net contracted, squeezing the shimmer into itself. The screeching shimmer imploded and the net collapsed, merging with the other strands. The dust bounced back to Rig, who was again twirling his hands towards the next shimmer.

Madgwick was holding his own fight. Out of the corner of his eye he saw the shimmer implode in the net. Two shimmers rushed towards him. He divided the dust into between his hands and opened his palms, the silver dust swirling like two miniature thunderclouds in his palms with lightning splitting the air in wickedly jagged edges. With a flick of the wrist he sent the clouds and their lightning bolts to each shimmer, racing in two directions.

The dust swelled, engulfing the shimmers so that the silver and the darkness became an intricate cloud. Bolts of lighting were sparking furiously until the silver slowly started to win out and the engulf the darkness.

With a loud screech the shimmers were suddenly gone and dust leapt back into Madgwick's hand, once again in the form of miniature silver lightening storms.

Madgwick did not stand still. He leapt into the air as a shimmer rushed beneath him. Coming down with his back to it, he immediately dropped into a low crouch as Rig sent a silver dustball over Madgwick's head and straight into the shimmer. The ball of dust hit the shimmer hard like a cannon ball. The shimmer flew into different directions and evaporated with a pop.

Rig faced the last two shimmers, but they were rapidly retreating, melting back into the shadows of the forest.

Madgwick and Rig took a few steps after the shimmers but they were gone.

The two warriors looked at each other.

"They will be back," muttered Rig, "and they will come with more."

"More than we can easily handle," finished Madgwick.

Rig turned to Madgwick with a scowl. "Huh, we can manage a lot more than that! I was just warming up. Nice lightning," he complimented Madgwick. They turned back to face Jeff and Rhed.

The boys clutched at each other, their eyes wide and mouths hanging open.

Rig stood with his back to them, staring at the forest just in case the shimmers were sneaking back for another attack. He stood with arms hanging loosely at his side. His dust bounced in his hands as if eager to be sent into battle.

Despite the fight, there was not a hair out of place and his ponytail hung over his shoulder.

Madgwick rushed to the boys who were still huddled together against the tree.

"Jeff, Rhed, it's okay now," murmured Madgwick as he crouched down next to Jeff and lifted his arm, which was bleeding. Madgwick pulled open his bag and took out some bottles of different sizes. He pulled at Jeff's sweater so that he could treat the wounds. Gently he cleaned Jeff's arm, glancing at the boy's face.

Jeff's eyes were screwed shut as Madgwick dabbed and cleaned. Jeff was babbling, wanting to know what these things were. Madgwick hushed him. Now was not the time for conversation. Once the blood was cleaned up, he dropped some blue liquid over Jeff's arm. The bleeding stopped instantly and the bite marks healed.

The next bottle had green potion in it.

"You have to drink some of this. It tastes disgusting but it will get you on your feet." He glanced around. "We can't stay here."

He lifted the bottle to Jeff's lips. Jeff took a gulp. Shivers went down his back and he felt his face pull as the awful taste registered. Madgwick was smearing gooey white stuff all over his arm. The pain went away instantly. Jeff stretched his arm, staring at the skin. He could still see the bite marks but they only looked bruised and red.

He opened his mouth to ask Madgwick what he had done but he had already moved to Rhed. Madgwick's face become serious and he frowned as he examined Rhed.

Madgwick's heart contracted. Rhed was hurt badly. He must have been completely caught in the shimmer. It had not bitten him like the one that had grabbed Jeff. It was like he was bruised all over. Every inch of his body, except for his face, was blue. His glasses were hanging off one ear.

Madgwick lifted Rhed's face and gazed into his eyes. "Rhed, relax. It will be fine." Rhed, who had not said a word since the shimmer grabbed him, just nodded weakly.

Without turning around, Rig whispered, "We ready to move?"

"In a few minutes," Madgwick answered.

Rig dropped into a fighting stance, crouched low. "We don't have minutes. Make it sooner Madgwick, make it seconds."

Madgwick rummaged through his bag, holding his breath as he looked for a potion. He had packed it as an afterthought, one of those I-may-not-need-it-but-you-never-know things. His hand found the bottle and he pulled it out with relief. He shook it, uncorked it, and held it to Rhed's lips.

"It's going to taste terrible but it will help ease the pain and start to heal you from the inside."

Rhed's lips were white. He opened his mouth as if he did not care how bad the stuff tasted. As he swallowed it looked like he wanted to gag, but he found the movement too painful, so he swallowed and swallowed until he kept the stuff down.

Rig appeared next to them and spoke in a low voice.

"There are four shimmers about fifty metres away but they are gathering. We will be able to fight them. But we will not be able to fight them and still protect the boys."

Madgwick turned and anxiously surveyed the forest. Turning back to Rig, he said, "Rhed is not ready to walk, never mind run."

"Well, we have no choice. We have to make a break for it." Rig turned to Jeff. "We need to get out of here. How is your arm, can you move?"

Jeff nodded.

"Good, you carry that." Jeff barely caught the bag that Rig tossed at him. It was Rhed's bag.

Jeff quickly gathered the two cans lying nearby on the ground. He tossed them into the bag before swinging it onto his back. He stretched his arm. His sleeve was torn to shreds and bloodstained but all the bite marks had faded. It was a bit stiff but otherwise the arm was good.

Rig took off his cloak, handed it to Madgwick and told him to wrap Rhed up tight.

"We have run out of time. It's either leave now or prepare for another fight."

"I am not leaving without Rhed," Jeff muttered to Madgwick.

Rig stared coldly at Jeff before bending down to Rhed. He sprinkled a tinge of dust into Rhed's face and within seconds Rhed's eyes closed as he went to sleep. Rig carefully lifted and draped him over his shoulder. He got up and held Rhed in place with one arm. Rig stood up with such ease, it seemed to Jeff that Rhed did not weigh anything at all.

Then Rig turned back to Jeff and said, "I am not leaving him either." His eyes glowed.

14

Madgwick led the way, plunging into the forest. Jeff followed with Rig carrying Rhed following closely behind. They were moving fast, trying to put distance between them and the shimmers.

Rig grimaced. This was the second time he was rushing through the forest trying to outrun the shimmers in the last hour. Every now and then Madgwick indicated to Jeff to keep going while he doubled back to toss silver dust into the air before taking his place in the lead again.

Jeff was dying to ask. He had so many questions but he was so busy trying to keep pace that he did not have enough air in his lungs to talk as well as run. After what seemed like forever, Rig stopped and waited for Madgwick who had doubled back to toss the dust.

Jeff watched Rig who still had the sleeping Rhed over his shoulder. He did not even look tired or show any sign that Rhed was heavy.

"What is Madgwick doing?" asked Jeff, also scanning the forest now.

"Covering our trail, making it harder for the shimmers to track us. They will still find us but it will take a bit longer. Of course," he continued, "it would not be necessary if you had stayed behind like we told you to. What were you thinking? That we were going on a hike?"

Rig was staring directly at Jeff as if he was waiting for an explanation.

Jeff bristled. "It's my brother who is missing, and I thought we could help."

Rig snorted. "Help? And exactly how were you going to help? By bleeding all over the shimmers until they could not move? Or, oh wait, I see, you were the decoy, yes that would work. While they were eating you, we could get to Matt and back without any interference. A walk in the park. Now why didn't I think of that?"

"There is no need to be nasty, it was not like we expected that, whatever that was!" retorted Jeff.

"Exactly!" said Madgwick from behind them, pushing through the branches and making Jeff jump. "You did not know and still do not know what to expect. This is serious and dangerous."

When Jeff opened his mouth to argue, Madgwick raised his eyebrows and looked pointedly at Rhed, still draped over Rig's shoulders.

This was by far the biggest trouble that he and Rhed had ever gotten into. And if Rig and Madgwick had not come back for them they would have been elaborate toothpicks by now. Jeff shivered as he remembered those teeth.

Jeff looked at Rhed and he swallowed loudly. "You are right, I'm sorry, we're sorry, we should have listened. Is he ..." Jeff hesitated as his throat closed up. The events of the night with Matt being kidnapped and the attack in the forest were just too much. "Is he going to be okay, Madgwick?"

Madgwick smiled and he patted Jeff on the arm, "Yes, he is going to be fine. We thought it would be easier for him to travel while sleeping and give his body time to heal, but he will be awake later on. The shimmers are following us but the dust is confusing them. Nevertheless they will catch up sooner or later, we have to keep going. Which way do you think, Rig?"

Rig turned in a circle, his eyes closed. He stopped, facing a huge oak tree. "We go this way. There is a lake not far from here, we can lose them there."

Rig chose the way with his eyes closed.

Jeff thought he was the strangest thing. He had just seen Rig fight better than any ninja or marine in any combat movie. He was as strong as anything, he has been carrying Rhed while making a run through dense forest and he was not even breathing hard. In fact, it did not even look like he noticed that Rhed was on his shoulder. He was not the friendliest, but he was a fierce warrior. Jeff was glad he was on Team Rig.

They started in the direction that Rig pointed out. The older warrior was quiet as usual, but Madgwick seemed more approachable. However, after seeing the fierce warrior fight with deadly precision just a short while ago, he was wary of talking out of turn.

Jeff had badly underestimated them. They were not just some silly fairytale sandmen. They were still going fast but not in a mad rush like earlier. Jeff thought he could ask Madgwick a few questions, hopefully without making him angry.

"Um, Madgwick," he ventured, "What exactly were those things in the forest? You called them shims?"

Madgwick answered without turning or slowing down. "Shimmers, they are called shimmers. They are the works of an evil witch called Wiedzma. Her little pets." He snorted in disgust. "Their sole aim is to force themselves into children's dreams. That's where we come in. It's our job to stop them."

"What do you mean, force themselves?"

"They arrive as invisible mist but they infiltrate dreams. They turn them into nightmares. Quite horrid."

"And you fight them? But how do they get into dreams?"

"They search for a crack and sneak through from Drakmere into your world. They are invisible and create misery. Do you ever have shivers that run down your back for no reason?"

"Shimmers?" Jeff asked with wide eyes, his eyebrows high in his forehead.

"Shimmers," confirmed Madgwick, "They settle on a child at night and their misery and terror flows into the child's subconscious and feeds the nightmares they pass into the child, understand?"

"So do you infiltrate the dreams to get them out?"

Rig snorted with laughter behind Jeff. Jeff did not even realise he was listening. He glanced behind him. Rig was grinning at Jeff's questions, which he obviously thought were quite silly.

It was Rig who answered. "We don't infiltrate the dreams. We have ways of forcing them out and then we finish them off. They have no chance against our warriors. In fact, many don't make it into the dream state in the first place."

Jeff stumbled to a halt as a horrible thought hit him. He stopped so suddenly that Rig skidded and almost dropped the still sleeping Rhed.

"Madgwick! Rig! Matt! Is he with...are the shimmers...?"

He was so horrified at the thought of Matt being at the mercy of shimmers that he could not get his words out.

Madgwick turned back to him, and put his hand on Jeff's shoulder.

"Matt is nowhere near the shimmers." Making eye contact with Jeff's wide eyes, he continued. "I promise, he has not encountered shimmers. He is at Drakmere castle. They will not have shimmers anywhere near him, and he is safe, for now."

Rig came to stand next to him. "Do you think we would be taking it easy with you, taking the long way to Drakmere if a child was in danger of a waking shimmer attack? One of us would have reached him already." He turned away. "But we had to save your bacon so now we are completely off course."

Madgwick nodded at Jeff, then turned and resumed the pace. Jeff, relieved, followed. *This is taking it easy?*

"What was in those cans anyway?" Madgwick asked.

"Don't know. Rhed did the packing. He gave them to me. Didn't really have time to read the label, if you know what I mean."

"Too busy screaming?" Rig asked innocently from behind.

"Well yeah, I suppose, if you had a monster with red eyes and a huge mouth with a thousand teeth ripping you apart, I think you would be screaming too," retorted Jeff.

"A thousand teeth? That's what you saw and felt?" Madgwick's voice was slightly raised.

"It felt like a thousand teeth. I thought I saw a monster but it really just looked like mist and eyes. What did you see?"

Rig answered, "We saw shimmers. Black mist. No teeth."

Madgwick added, "The shimmers take on your fears. It won't be the same as what Rhed saw or what any other child would see in their dreams. Each person and their monster is different, just as each nightmare is different, understand?"

"What do you see then?" asked Jeff.

"Us? We just saw black mist. They would have been easier to kill if they had a true form when we got to them but we just saw the red eyes and black mist. Our minds are different, protected. We were born into a race that fights this evil."

"Lily air freshener," a thin voice croaked from behind them.

Madgwick and Jeff turned. Rhed was waking up.

Rig put him gently on the ground. Jeff and Madgwick rushed to Rhed. Madgwick was digging in his bag again.

"Rhed!" Jeff exclaimed, "Are you okay?" Jeff was trying to re-assure Rhed but did not really know where to touch him. He looked so fragile.

"Stop that," muttered Rhed. "All hovering and batting with your hands, you look like a girl."

Jeff sat back on his haunches. "Welcome back," Jeff smiled at the wisecrack, too relieved to be insulted.

Madgwick asked Rhed to drink some liquid again. This time it was green and gooey.

"Do I have to? I don't think I can get that stuff down again."

Madgwick laughed. "This is different stuff, really!"

He held the bottle to Rhed's lips. Rhed took a gulp, his eyes widening as the liquid hit his throat, but he had no choice as it was already half down.

"Yuck! That was gross!"

The effect was instant. Rhed's eyebrows shot up and his hair rose as if he had been electrified. He looked wide-eyed as if his whole body had come alive. His pain and sleepiness were gone and he tried to smile but his lips ended up in a grimace as the awful taste lingered in his mouth.

"What on earth is that? It tasted as bad as the white stuff."

Madgwick smiled and packed it back into his bag. "That, dear boy was frog vomit. Excellent stuff that."

"Frog vomit!" Rhed's nose wrinkled and he started scraping his tongue with his nails, then he dragged his sleeve over his tongue, but it was too late, the stuff was down.

Jeff started gagging and had tears in his eyes from laughter. "Wait till Matt hears you drank frog vomit."

He punched Jeff on the arm for that but by then he had joined in on the laughter.

Rhed got to his feet and stretched gingerly, testing his arms and legs. He still looked bruised and battered but the pain seemed gone and he looked energised.

"What was that? Because I feel great."

Madgwick said, "Really. It was frog vomit. It's hard to get and it works like a charm. The snail snot gave your body the essence it needs to heal and the frog vomit gave you a boost to get you back on your feet. Of course the potions have enchantments in them too."

Rhed gasped and could hardly get the words out. "The white stuff was snail snot? Who keeps this stuff?"

Jeff stared at Madgwick with an odd look. "If that was really frog vomit and snail snot, what did I have earlier?"

Madgwick smiled and turned back to Rig, over his shoulder he said, "Mixture of cockroach saliva and maggot poop."

Jeff sat down heavily while Rhed huffed with laughter. Once Rhed got his laughing under control, Jeff brought Rhed up to speed on what happened while he was out.

15

Madgwick and Rig glanced into the forest every few moments. They were talking furiously. Rig was muttering and gesturing with his hands, and it seemed like they were having an argument.

Rhed took a step closer to them. Yes, Rig and Madgwick were arguing. But they stopped when they realised that the boys were edging closer. "We will continue this discussion later," Rig muttered.

"There is nothing to discuss. This is the only way," Madgwick stated, picking up his bag.

He had a half smile on his face, maybe trying to reassure them that all was okay with Rig. "Good to go? We need to make it to the lake before twilight. It's a bit of a walk but the sooner we get there the better. Shall we go?"

"Twilight?" Jeff asked, his forehead rumpled. He looked towards the sun, which was very low on the horizon. Back home it was dark, the moon had already risen.

Madgwick attempted a smile. "I know. It can get confusing here in Drakmere. Day, night … time flows differently in this place."

"Time in Drakmere isn't the same as the way you understand it at home," Rig snapped. "We do not have time," he rolled his eyes at himself, "to philosophise about it now. Let's just say that time is an illusion. And each part of the kingdom is different. By now, it's anyone's guess as to how many days and nights have passed in the castle."

Jeff and Rhed stood up, ready. Jeff had Rhed's backpack. "So what were those cans that we used to spray?" He was trying to keep the tone light, trying to prevent himself from thinking about Matt in the castle, and the fact that by now he might have more than just one lonely, nightmare-filled night behind him.

"Lily air freshener," replied Rhed.

Jeff stared at him with a blank expression. "You expected that we may need to use two cans of air freshener?"

"Well," said Rhed, "I didn't really have much time to pack so I just grabbed a few things."

They started through the forest. It was slow going because although Rhed was awake and feeling good, he was a little slow. Rig doubled back every now and then to confuse the shimmers.

The second time he came back, he muttered, "They are gaining on us. We need to go faster."

"Can we speed up, boys? Less talking more walking," he grumbled to Rhed and Jeff.

"Going as fast as I can," complained Rhed, looking at Jeff with big eyes as if he were asking, who is this guy?

Jeff was giving Rig dirty looks while Rhed tried to go faster.

Madgwick stepped between them when Rig opened his mouth to give a smart retort. "Not helping, Rig!"

Madgwick pointed through the trees. "See that shimmer in the distance?"

Rhed and Jeff winced at his choice of words. The word shimmer had a different meaning to them now. They looked in the direction Madgwick was pointing.

"What it that?"

"That is a lake. What's it called Rig, do you know?"

"Therror, Lake Therror," Rig answered.

"The shimmers are gaining on us and there are more than the six we were fighting before. If we make it to the lake before the sun sets then we have a chance to stay ahead of them. They won't know which way we have gone."

Glancing at Rig, he continued softly, "If we don't we will fight but it will not be pretty."

Rhed and Jeff looked at each other. "Let's go, we can do this," Rhed muttered. Jeff nodded. They gave each other a fist bump, stopped talking and started to walk faster.

They made a good distance. The sweat was running down their backs but they did not stop. The lake was getting closer until finally they broke through the trees and found themselves on a grassy slope that stretched all the way to the stony shore. The lake was an impossible blue. The orange glow of the setting sun glistened on the water, which made it sparkle like diamonds. Both boys looked longingly at the water.

Judging by the way Rig and Madgwick kept turning around, there was no time for swimming unless they wanted to get a mouthful from Rig or, even worse, a disapproving look from Madgwick.

The boys exchanged looks and kept their mouths shut. It was obvious that Rig and Madgwick were worried about the shimmers.

The warriors made their way to the shore line, arguing again. Rig had his hands on his hips, his face like stone. "No!"

Madgwick smiled and lifted his hands with his palms facing down. "It's the only way to get the boys to safety. One of us has to make a stand and keep them fighting here until the boat is far enough that the shimmers cannot follow. There is no other way. There are too many for us to fight and still protect the boys."

"I disagree," growled Rig. "I know what it was like to lose someone in this place and I promised to never lose another. We stick together."

Jeff gasped as he realised what they were arguing about. Madgwick wanted one of them to stay behind on the shore to fight the shimmers.

"Rig, please, you are a warrior. Think about it. Our mission is to rescue Matt. One of us has to get to Drakmere, one of us *must* do that and bring Matt back or we fail our mission. We swore an oath when we became warriors, to keep children safe. That includes those two boys," Madgwick pointed in their direction.

Both boys cringed. Their impulsive decision to go through the doorway was having disastrous consequences. "Please, no," both Jeff and Rhed whispered to no one in particular.

Rig dropped his head. Madgwick had won this fight.

Jeff and Rhed could not hear what they were saying. It looked like Madgwick had won his argument. Rig's head was dipped as if he were submitting. Was Rig staying behind? They did not like Rig much but he was fierce and strong. What a blow.

"Fine, you win," whispered Rig, "but then it must be me."

Madgwick whispered back. "It can't be you, Rig. You are the best chance all these kids have in getting out of here and back home alive. You are the most experienced warrior. There is not a trick you don't know. You have been here before, you know what to do, where to go, what to expect. You are the best warrior."

"They don't like me," Rig replied.

"They don't have to like you. They just have to do what you tell them to do, but if you're nice about it they won't argue." Then, with a smile, he added, "If they give you a hard time, there is always frog vomit."

Rig moved towards the shore. He closed his eyes and stretched his hands out. The dust in his hands bubbled and dropped to the floor, and within moments a silver, glittery row boat was bobbing in the water.

The boat was see-through. They could see the water beneath the boat and lapping on the sides.

Rig threw his bag in and addressed the boys. "Get in! Get in!" He rolled his eyes at their hesitation and got into the boat, grabbing the oars to steady it.

Still they hesitated until Rig yelled, "Stop wasting time, get in now!"

Jeff and Rhed clambered into the rocking boat, holding onto the sides. The boat felt solid, but it was weird that it was see-through.

Jeff was looking from Rig to Madgwick. As the understanding hit, his eyes went wide.

Jeff stuttered as Madgwick pushed the boat out, but Madgwick smiled at him.

"Listen to Rig. Promise me that you will listen to him." Both Jeff and Rhed nodded glumly.

Rig settled the oars in the water then looked at Madgwick. "You have fighting skills, you are cunning and brave. Use that. Survive and get back."

He started to row away. He raised his voice to ensure that Madgwick could hear him. "Because if you don't, I'm coming back for you!"

Rig's muscles bulged as he pulled harder and the boat started to move rapidly away from Madgwick who was standing knee high in the water staring after them. He nodded and gave a short wave before turning and wading back to the shore.

16

Madgwick stood with his back to the water. Angie's warning that they do not like water made complete sense now, although he had no idea how she would have known. Shimmers did not like water and would do anything to avoid it.

They would go out but not too far so he was pretty sure his back was safe from an attack. He could feel that the shimmers were just a few moments away. In a rush, he saw the dust he had tossed in the forest streaking through the trees to join him. He felt better with all his magic in place.

He took a handful of this silver dust, moved his bag to his back and dropped the particles to the ground. He dipped his head before nimbly side-stepping a shimmer that was rushing him from the front. Then he flicked his wrist and the dust rose in a glittering flash, wrapping around the shimmer like a whip.

With another flick Madgwick tossed the shimmer into another, causing them both to disintegrate. Their shrieks of pain brought a smile to his face.

Standing still was a death sentence so Madgwick did not count how many there were. He knew he was outnumbered and kept on the move so that the shimmers could not touch him. He was so fast with his dust, using it a sword, a whip, a net, daggers, a boomerang.

It moved and flowed with precision, forming many weapons at once. Madgwick tumbled, crouched down, rolled and tried to stay one step ahead, and yet the shimmers kept coming.

* * *

By now Madgwick was receding in the distance. Rig watched him with narrow eyes, his lips pressed together and his face like stone.

It took every ounce of discipline to keep rowing away from the fight. There were so many shimmers that it would soon be one-sided.

The sounds of the shimmers shrieking in pain and anger drifted over the water. Madgwick was a blur and his silver dust was moving so fast and in so many directions that it looked like silver drops were raining around him.

Jeff moved from one side of the boat to the other, trying not to lose sight of Madgwick. He pushed his head forward and strained to see the battle in the creeping darkness.

His movements rocked the boat and after a few minutes Rhed snapped, "Jeff, you know that we are in a boat, right? You're going to make us tip and I don't swim well!"

"Oh please, it's hardly rocking. Get a grip."

"I'll give you a grip just now!" muttered Rhed.

"Sit down. Keep quiet!" ordered Rig.

Jeff sat down and the boys sat hushed, not taking their eyes off the fight that was moving further and further away into the distance

But even though Madgwick was a brilliant warrior, he was still out numbered and the darkness was starting to overtake their view of Madgwick. Twilight was over and they could no longer see the shoreline. Even the shrieking was fading as they move further away.

* * *

Madgwick could tell he was losing. A number of shimmers had touched him and had gotten in a few good bites, although they did not portray themselves as monsters like they had with Jeff and Rhed. They still bit quite painfully, except it was just black mist with red eyes. There was nothing to really see or avoid.

Even with so many around him, Madgwick kept going. He could not use his left arm anymore as it had been bitten too many times and was now hanging limp. Without him seeing it, a shimmer landed on his back and buried its teeth into his flesh. Madgwick dropped to his knees. This was the end.

A whoosh of wind ripped through the shimmers, shoving them away from Madgwick. The wind doubled back and Madgwick found himself surrounded by it. It was like standing in the funnel of a tornado. With a growl he stood up and sliced the shimmer off his back using his dust as a guillotine. Madgwick, tired and bleeding, turned around, not quite understanding what the swirling wind was or who was behind it. Was this another evil messenger from Wiedzma?

Most of the shimmers were rushing away, probably heading around the lake to chase after Rig and the boys, but it would take days to catch up by taking that route.

There were still about eighteen shimmers hovering a few steps away from Madgwick, just waiting for the wind to die down so that they could attack anew.

Then from out of nowhere, a figure appeared, moving closer. And plop, plop, plop … There were eighteen toads hopping around left and right, bumping into each other as if they were very confused.

Madgwick turned around, his mouth hanging open at the sight of all the toads. He was too tired and too hurt to jump for joy, but he did manage a little laugh as he realised who his rescuer was.

"Angie," he whispered.

"Madgwick, I'm late! I tried to hurry but I got caught at the garden gate by an elder. I told him I had to go but he wouldn't listen. My oh my, Madgwick, you really are a good warrior, but allowing a shimmer to grab you from the back ... Not clever. Not clever at all."

Madgwick smiled at her and dropped down at her feet. The toads hopped frantically out of the way as he hit the stony beach hard.

17

The king was tapping his hand on the armrest of his chair, his face not as handsome now as he sneered at the old man.

"Well, Thirza, does the enchantment hold? Does the boy believe that he is in a beautiful castle, a beautiful land, some fantasy adventure?"

Thirza nodded. "The enchantment is in place and the boy will see only what the spell will allow him to see."

"Marvellous. I could skip for joy." The king rolled his eyes as he spoke. He stood up and began pacing. Then he stopped and turned around as if he had just thought of something. "Thirza! Where are the rest of my council, why are you here alone?"

Thirza was very careful as he prepared his answer. The king was not one to trifle with and he often let his displeasure show on those around him.

"Your Highness," he bowed his head held low. "They displeased you, thus they are either in the dungeon or have been killed."

He did not dare mention that Wiedzma was to blame.

"Take that to be a lesson to never displease me. I hope this child learns the lesson quickly or he will be spending more time in the dungeon than out." The king threw his head back as he gave an evil laugh.

The side door opened and the powerful witch Wiedzma entered. Her scent floated through the room like a butterfly on a summer's day. She headed straight for the king, smiling as she passed Thirza but ignored his presence.

Her hair was as black as the night and hung straight and long down her back. Her deep green eyes sparkled with malice. Her face was smooth and flawless and her skin was chalk white with a hint of a blush on her cheeks. On her left cheek was a dark mole. Her face was friendly but that was just part of the ruse, as she was as dangerous as she was beautiful.

Nodding at Wiedzma, the king asked, "How long before his dreams are mine? As you well know, I have been planning his arrival for a long time. I don't want to waste a single moment more."

Thirza folded his hands into his cloak sleeves and waited patiently for the witch to answer.

"It may take some time for the illusion spell to take hold. It will start only once the child starts to forget about his family. The boy must be encouraged to play, have fun, run around and laugh. While he does that the spell will start to wean him away from his memories. Once that has happened, then the spell will seal and his dreams will be ours to manipulate."

King Grzegorz sat with an evil smile on his face. Thirza understood what his expression meant: once Wiedzma's spell had taken hold of Matt, the king would finally have access to a child's dreams. And by using his dreams and a mareweaver spell Wiedzma was sure to cast next, Grzegorz and Wiedzma would be able to cause havoc all over the world.

The king all but jumped out of his seat.

"All the children's dreams will be mine to terrorise. It is going to be fabulous!"

Now Wiedzma's shimmers, which she and the king had managed to sneak into the world over time, would enter in full force as nightmares.

"Ahhh, I cannot wait," the king sighed.

He stopped as if a horrible thought had just hit him. "Wait a minute, does this mean that we are going to have to entertain a happy child for a while? Lovely! Can't you speed up the process, Wiedzma?"

Wiedzma laughed and clapped her hands in delight. "I wish I could. That would have been so much fun."

The king laughed with her, tucked her arm into the crook of his and turned for the door.

"Your Highness," began Thirza. "There is another matter, if you have a moment to spare."

What Thirza was about to say could be met with either anger or indifference, depending on the king's frame of mind. He had to try and obtain some idea of what their plans were and what protection they were planning with the castle.

Thirza spoke quickly. "If my knowledge of the Sandustians is correct, then they will be setting out to rescue the child as we speak. It will be good to increase the number of guards around the kingdom and especially around the castle."

The king's smile dropped. "Those Sandustians. Ugly bunch of nitwits waving their foolish little dust all over the place. Yes, let them come. They destroyed my plans last time but not this time. This time I am prepared, is that not so my beauty?" He smiled at Wiedzma.

"No need to increase security. Wiedzma has unleashed her shimmers to intercept them. They will not survive that, and don't forget that they cannot get into the castle while the enchantment is in place," he replied over his shoulder.

With that he swept out of the room with Wiedzma at his side, the muttering and laughter between them disappearing down the corridor.

Thirza remained where he was. He frowned as if deep in thought.

What were they planning and how was he going to save Matt? He dared not reveal his desire to help the boy, as the witch would read the child's mind in a heartbeat.

The child's mind was too innocent and unlike Thirza or most other adults, he had no natural barriers against a powerful witch such as Wiedzma. No, he was going to have to be subtle about this, and quick.

Thirza knew he was playing a very dangerous game, and smiled a hard smile. He was not worried about himself. He had a secret. The witch could not touch him with her magic. Oh, she had tried to hurt him with her spells over time, but he had a protective barrier that could not be penetrated by Wiedzma or any other witch.

That she could not touch him was driving her crazy, but she dared not tell the king about her failure to control Thirza. She could not afford to let the king think she was losing her power, so Thirza's barrier-secret was safe.

But Matt was a different story. If Matt became happy, the spell would take his memories and would complete the magic process, and there was no telling was that evil hag would do to Matt then.

Thirza had remained in the king's service all those years because he knew some day another child would be taken. And this time he was going to stop it for good. Or die trying! Now he had three jobs to do. One, as hard and as cruel as it was, he had to keep the child miserable so that the spell could not seal. Second, he had to find out how to break the castle spell so that the warriors could enter. And third, he had to save Holka. Nodding to himself, Thirza left the room.

18

Wiedzma twirled her hair between her fingers. She watched Thirza through the magic mirror she had placed in the throne room. It was important to know what and who was visiting the king. That way, she could manipulate him more easily.

She watched Thirza stand there with a frown on his face and then smile before leaving. Wiedzma gripped her hair. It frustrated her that she had no magic hold over Thirza. How? How could that be? No one could deny her. Her magic was the ultimate power. All minds were open to her, except Thirza. She could forge a magical link by touch, forcing memories and thoughts to flow into her, but not with Thirza. With him she could see nothing. It was as if he had no memories or thoughts to share.

Wiedzma sighed and stared into the empty mirror, lost in thought over the king. He was such a powerful and evil man, and that was refreshing. And she could only become queen and ruler if she married him. But the king was not about to give his kingdom away by marriage to a witch. He was always so polite and gracious with her, but if she lost her usefulness he would drop her in a heartbeat.

Thanks to her cunning interferences, all of his advisors were already imprisoned in the dungeon or killed except for that tiresome Thirza.

Wiedzma turned away from the mirror. She had preparations to complete should there be a rescue attempt.

* * *

Matt woke up and stretched out, the fragrance of waffles drifting past him. With a smile on his face he opened his eyes.

Holka looked up and smiled at Matt.

"Hey sleepyhead. I was wondering when you would be saying hello." Her voice had a soft hushed tone that made him think of drizzled honey. Her smile was so sweet and friendly that he could not help but smile back at her.

"Are you hungry? Because you went to bed last night without eating anything." She seemed a bit concerned. Matt nodded shyly and stretched again.

"Well," she said, getting to her feet, "wash up in that room there." She pointed to a door that Matt had not even seen last night. "You will find clean clothes in there too. Then meet me here for some breakfast."

Matt went into the side room. It was huge: the biggest bathroom he had ever seen. The bath was the size of the bed he had just slept in and the shower was like a room on its own. Matt hopped in the shower and gasped. There was a rainbow in there!

Matt sat down at the table laid with fruit, pancakes, sausages and eggs. Holka dished a plate for him and nodded that he should begin.

"We have a full day ahead of us," she said as she watched Matt dig into his breakfast.

He sat on the chair, swinging his legs as he studied the room. He looked up and smiled at the sky blue ceiling dotted with clouds. Miniature hot air balloons with little wicker baskets were floating around and little aeroplanes darted in between the balloons.

Matt looked at Holka. He was anxious to go home but it was not as if he could pick up a phone and ask his mother to fetch him.

"Holka, can't I phone?"

Holka laughed. "No, Matt I am sorry. No phones here."

"Geez, no phones." He looked around. "No TVs either. This is no holiday camp."

Holka smiled. "My job is to make sure that you are happy and have lots of fun while you are here." Her smile faltered while she said this, and she frowned as if she could not quite understand something, but in the next instant her smile was back.

She stood up hands on her hips. "Come on," she said, holding out her hand, "There is a lot of castle to explore. Where do you want to start first, the dungeons?" she asked wiggling her eyebrows at Matt.

Matt laughed and clapped his hands. "Oooh the dungeons!"

And so Matt and Holka explored the castle, running from room to room. Matt gaped at some of the strange rooms they stumbled into. One room was completely upside down. He dropped his head back and stared at the ceiling. The bed, tables, chairs and even the wardrobe were in perfect place but on the ceiling.

"Holka, how?" he started, but Holka had already started pulling him away.

Around lunchtime, they entered a room with a lovely balcony. There was a picnic basket waiting for them on a table with a bright red table cloth. They had lunch, watching the trees sway in the distance.

Lunch was a delight: sandwiches with thick blobs of caramel and sliced banana. There was custard and jelly, and cupcakes that exploded chocolate and fudge into your mouth. Matt asked questions about the castle and Drakmere. Holka did her best to answer what she knew, which did not seem to be a lot.

Every morning it was the same thing, breakfast and then exploring the castle and the grounds. Sometimes when Matt glanced in a room, it first appeared grey and dull, but after blinking a few times, the rooms were back to normal.

Every now and then the old man called Thirza would appear and shout at them for something or the other, like walking in front of a mirror.

Matt was convinced that Thirza did not like him and that he was determined to make his day as unpleasant as possible. Thirza's eyebrows were bunched up and his mouth in a straight line as he stalked Matt and Holka, trying to catch Matt doing something wrong, or right or simply doing nothing at all.

But Holka was always there to hug him and make him smile again. She even yelled at Thirza a few times.

Eventually their explorations took them down to the dungeons, and to Matt they were the best of all: dark and spooky. There were lots of doors, the air smelt musty and dirty, and there was moss on the walls. Some corridors became smaller and smaller until he had to crawl.

Matt and Holka spent a lot of time down there. Of course there were lots of locked doors, so they could not go everywhere they wanted. It was fun and creepy to explore the vast tunnel system that led away from the dungeons.

Now and then Matt thought he heard sobbing and begging for help but when he listened carefully the sounds were gone. Holka did not know if anyone was down there. She was very quiet. Her pink eyes gleamed when she said this. Matt, not wanting to upset her did not ask any further.

One day they ventured out into the fields beyond the gardens, hopped over a stream, dashed under a waterfall and wandered until they stopped for lunch under a tree.

Matt sat silently, chewing on a chocolate squashed inside a bread roll. He stared so blankly at the grass that Holka just had to ask what he was thinking about.

Matt sighed. "I was wondering if this tree could be the one my mom tells me about. You know, the one at the entrance to dreamland." He swallowed and then continued. "When my mom tucks me in at night, she tells me to wait at the big tree at the entrance of dreamland. Then we can go in together, hand in hand. I miss my mom, and my dad and I miss Jeff and ..." Matt frowned. He could not remember Jeff's friend's name, or the names of his friends at school, or even his teacher's name. Matt sniffed, his bottom lip trembling. "I want to go home Holka ... I'm forgetting things. I'm scared!"

Holka gazed adoringly at Matt but had no answer to give him. It was her duty to keep Matt happy. She stared at him and bit her lip as if she was convinced that Matt was the link to her past that she could not remember. It was impossible to explain. She could not remember anything about her life other than being here.

Her eyes filled with tears but she blinked them away. If she started to cry now then Matt was sure to follow and that would get them into trouble. Except with Thirza, of course. He did everything he could to make the child miserable. He had always taken care of her but since Matt arrived he had become a mean and bad-tempered old man.

Holka cleared her throat, "No, Matt, this is not that tree, that tree is much bigger." Matt looked over at her.

"How do you know Holka, climbed it lately?"

She nodded. "And I will race you to the top of this one."

They leapt to their feet and started to climb, going from branch to branch. Holka laughed with Matt while they were swinging upside down on the lower branch. While they swung, Holka became silent and her eyes narrowed as if she strained to remember that tree in Dreamland, that particular tree Matt was talking about.

19

Matt was sleeping badly. Every night in his dreams he heard whispering but he could not make out what was being said or who was saying it. Yet the voice had a sense of urgency.

He knew it was important to listen, important like learning your ABCs when there was a test coming up. But when Matt woke up, he could not remember.

Tearful and miserable, all he wanted was to go home. He had lost count of how long he had been at the castle. A few days already, maybe a week or two, he just did not know anymore.

And it was becoming harder to hold onto his memories. Even his dreams were becoming hazy. Matt sat looking out of his window with Holka with him. And as hard as she tried, she could not make him laugh or go out to play.

Eventually a messenger came with a note. The king wanted to see him.

* * *

King Grzegorz turned away from the window, his dark eyebrows drawn in and his mouth pulled back in a scowl. "What is going wrong? The brat has had free rein around the whole castle. I have had to endure," he slammed his hand on the table to make his point,

121

"his laughing and giggling, and now he is crying, sobbing, ugh."

There was a pause. "Why has the enchantment not taken hold yet?" he demanded, glaring at both Thirza and Wiedzma.

Thirza stood with his eyes on the floor. He dared not look up. He was hardly daring to breathe.

Matt was unhappy, and as long as he was unhappy then the enchantment could not take its final hold. The sealing of the enchantment was close and the loop was almost complete. Another day or two and Matt would be under the spell, lost. The boy was already starting to lose his memories. Just today he could not remember his father's name.

"Why?" screamed the king, spit shooting from his mouth. "Why is he unhappy!"

Wiedzma, who was standing in front of a mirror admiring her reflection, smoothed down her pale peach gown and pinched her cheeks for colour. It was tiresome when he was in a mood like this, but he did have a point.

"The child should be under the spell already. It is a powerful spell, and its hold over Matt should have been complete by now. I have been watching his days exploring the castle with the girl. There was a lot of laughing and fun and all he had to do was to have fun. No school, and no chores, just fun."

Wiedzma frowned as if the thought of her spell being tampered with crossed her mind. She shook her head and clicked her tongue. No one had her power. If there were other magic here then she would have sensed it.

* * *

Believing that he was finally going home, Matt was happy, skipping alongside Holka who held his hand as they made their way to the king.

The castle seemed brighter, the sun shone through the windows and the flowers inside the castle were blooming with splashes of colour. Castle staff whistled tunes to themselves as they polished. They looked up and gave him a small wave or a wink as he passed. There was laughter in another room but when Matt strained back to see who was laughing the door slowly swung shut, dulling the sound. The castle was so cheery, full of laughter, colour and music that Matt could not help but smile at everyone he passed.

When they reached the doorway, Holka hung back. "I'm not allowed in there," she whispered. "But I will be here when you come out."

Matt opened the door and peeped inside. His mouth went very dry at the sight of the king. He was standing at a tall window, talking, waving his hands in the air with that lady called Wiedzma. Matt had only ever seen her standing on a balcony or at the end of the corridor watching him.

As he came in, Wiedzma turned her head and gave him a smile of welcome. "Matt," she said in her high singing voice.

Matt stared at her. Her hair was coiled high on her head and she had a mole on her left cheek. Matt blinked and stared. The mole was creeping upwards very slowly. He could hardly drag his eyes away from the crawling mole.

The king was dressed in black, again, just like the last time. His smile looked strained, he seemed irritated and was a little more to the point.

"I hear you are not too happy, Matt? What is the problem?" he asked in a level voice.

Matt was scared. Their faces looked friendly, but they were not.

"I want to go home."

"But Matt, darling, you *are* home," said Wiedzma coming to stand behind Matt and curling his hair in the nape of his neck between her fingers. She glanced at the king who was staring directly at the wall behind Matt, probably trying to rein in his temper.

"No," said Matt, pulling away from Wiedzma so that she was not touching him. "I want my mom and Jeff and …"

Tears filled his eyes. He could not remember who else was at home but he knew there was more than Jeff and his mother.

The king came over to Matt, putting his hand on his small shoulder, his face in a grimace as he tried to sound friendly. "But Matt," he said in a soothing voice, "your home is here now, with us. Don't we make you happy? Have we not been nice?"

Matt nodded. "You have been very nice but this is not my home and my mom told me I'm allowed to say no when I don't want to do something. I don't want to stay here. I want to go home."

His voice was wobbling again. Matt kept in his tears. *What would, would, would uhhh …* Matt could not get the name he was searching for. *What would … ummm. Jeff think.*

The sound of the tears in Matt's voice was just too much for King Grzegorz. He turned away and nodded to Wiedzma. It was time for tough measures.

"Matt, you can't go home. Your mother has forgotten about you. I did not want to tell you but I can see now that I must tell you the truth. Your mother is out having parties. You are no longer wanted at home. Even your brother is gone."

Matt gasped. "That's not true! No way!"

The king smiled slyly. "Come and see for yourself." He pointed at a large glass ball in Wiedzma's hand.

Matt came closer, eyes glued to the ball. He could make out images. It looked like his mother who was staring into the distance, her vacant green eyes flooded with unshed tears.

ee, she is at a party!" The king leaned over Wiedzma's shoulder
gazing into the ball.

Matt squinted into the ball again. He gasped, not knowing what
to say. Behind his mother were flashing blue and red lights.

"That's not a party," whispered Matt.

Wiedzma and the king shared a little smile only to have their
faces drop at Matt's next words.

Matt stepped back a few steps, bumping into a table. "That is not
a party, that's the police. They're looking for me!"

Wiedzma swirled around, her face red and angry. "Maybe it's
that maid, Holka, and maybe we must get rid of her. Maybe she is
making you unhappy."

"No," gasped Matt, "Holka is my friend."

Taking Wiedzma's lead the king spoke. "Well, I think we must
make new friends. Guards!" he yelled. "Bring Holka in here."

The next moment, Holka was dragged in, her feet hardly
touching the floor between the two large grim-looking men, their
faces like stone. Their eyes had a blank stare to them, like they were
in a trance. They were dressed in the guards' uniform of a black
tunic. The bright red sash looked like a streak of blood draped over
their shoulders. Long swords dangled from their belts.

JEFF MADISON AND THE SHIMMERS OF DRAKMERE

Holka's face displayed shock. Her mouth hung open, her eyes darting frantically between Wiedzma and the king.

It was just too much for Matt. The tears started to pour down his face, but more than just unhappy tears, they were angry tears. He constantly wanted to cry, and this not was normal for him.

Holka blinked and stumbled back when her feet touched the ground. What were they doing, why was the child in such a state?

She did not know where this anger was coming from but her jaw clamped so tightly the veins on her neck stood out. The next moment she was yelling at both the king and at Wiedzma.

"Leave him alone! Why are you making him cry? What is wrong with you?"

Both the king and Wiedzma stopped, their eyes wide, clearly shocked at being spoken to like this.

The king turned slowly, his mouth in a cruel sneer. "Perhaps a lesson in manners and obedience," he whispered in his fury. "Take her away to the dungeon. Make it hurt."

Holka and Matt both screamed and cried out for each other. Matt sputtered but his words wouldn't form as Holka was dragged out kicking and screaming.

His tears had dried up and he dropped his head. All he could hear softly in the back of his head was his mother's voice.

Although he had just seen her face in the ball, he could not recall his mother's features. Everything was hazy, but he could remember her voice.

A rhyme ran through his head. He whispered part of it, the only part he could remember right now.

"But … but if I'm late and you become afraid, mischief runs amok."

Matt screwed his eyes shut as he tried to remember the rest of the poem. He was not sure why these words had come to him. His mother used to whisper it to him before he went to sleep every night. He just knew that now he had to finish it.

This was the whispering he heard in his dreams. This is what was so important to remember although he had no idea why.

The last line came to him. *Raise your voice, stamp your feet and shout smok, smok, smok.*

Without thinking about it, without knowing what he was about to do or what was going to happen, Matt whispered the word: "Smok."

Wiedzma whipped her head towards Matt, her eyes wide. "What?" she asked. "What did you say?" By now she was screeching, her red face no longer so beautiful.

Angrily, Matt spoke up.

"Smok!" And then louder still, "Smok!" He kept repeating it until he was screaming the word over and over.

Wiedzma clapped her hands to her mouth, her eyes wild with fury. She moved to grab the child and force him to stop.

King Grzegorz was staring from Wiedzma to Matt, not sure what was happening, or what the brat was screaming. What did it mean?

Thirza was staring at Matt. How did he know that word? Who taught it to him? This could not have worked any better if he planned it himself.

There was a loud crack, so loud that everyone felt the shock-wave of the violent noise.

Everyone in the room fell over and rolled on the floor, some trying to grab chair legs, crying with fear from the immense force. The shockwave moved swiftly through the castle, sweeping people along like a broom. The wave moved out through all the windows and onto the lands beyond causing chaos as it swept out in all directions.

The beautiful colours of the room faded to grey. The colourful walls that had been dressed with vibrant tapestries were now bare, grey stones that oozed coldness. Matt was swept across the carpetless floors, coming to rest against the wall. He felt the hard cold floor beneath him as he passed out.

CRACK ... The deafening sound rolled like thunder over the land. The force of the shockwave swelled like a river rushing in all directions.

Once the wave passed there was nothing, just quiet. Then life in the forest, the plains and the hills carried on as normal. Villagers ran after their scattered farm animals, fixing their straw roofs, collecting the washing that had flown around and talked excitedly among themselves. Many looked towards Drakmere castle.

Far away, the shockwave reached a cliff face, a vast wall of rock that stretched up towards the heavens. The wave hit the stone wall with a massive bang, so hard that the loose stones were rattled and tumbled down the cliff.

High up was a gaping hole, where the darkness sucked in the wave like a hungry beast. The animals that lived on the forest floor beneath existed in peace and harmony but they also knew not to enter that cavern. Not that they could get that high up, but there were ancient stories that passed through generations. There was something dangerous in that vast cavern.

A thunderous roar now came out of the cavern. All the creatures in the surrounding area stopped and looked up. The roar was pure power, loud, fearsome and angry. Birds exploded from the trees, small animals scattered in all directions and hurried into their burrows and shelters.

If any had dared to stop and look up they would have seen a steady stream of smoke flowing from the cavern.

He was awake and he was angry.

A dark shadow moved to the edge of the cavern mouth, looked around at the blue sky, lifted his monstrous head and roared with all his power, allowing the anger to flow out in a single stream of fire. With a shove, he dropped into nothingness.

The dark creature must have dropped about fifty metres before huge wings stretched out from either side of his massive body and pumped him into flight. The powerful wings pushed up and down, propelling him to a good height before they spread out wide and he started to glide through the air.

He rolled his head from side to side. As he circled a few times he surveyed the land. Below him were forests, stretching out in all directions. Pockets of fields with tall swaying grass like green carpets were interspersed with the forest, making the landscape look like green boxes. Tiny specks of flowers dotted the fields.

To the north, as far as the eye could see, was a long row of snow-capped mountains, so high that the peaks disappeared into the deep blue.

A sapphire lake sparkled in the distance. The creature was so high up that he would not look like a massive dragon to anyone scanning the skies: you might have mistaken him for a large bird.

The dragon cut out of his lazy circle and glided through a white waterfall that rushed down the mountainside just to the left of where his cavern entrance was. Feeling refreshed he turned and headed west.

He had to be quick now. He had heard the call. Well sort of. The call was not exactly right but it was enough to touch his awareness, enough to wake him. And the call had come from Drakmere, so to Drakmere he had to go, and fast.

* * *

Ella Madison did not know where her boys were. The police had taken statements and the search party had been organised to search the forest. Ella knew, she did not know how, but she knew they were not in the forest.

She could sense that her boys were much further away than that, and they were in trouble.

Quietly she sat next to Rhed's mother who was sobbing into her tissue. She was thinking hard. There was someone who could help, but she could not remember who it was. Every time she tried to recall a name, mist clouded her thoughts and she ended up thinking of fudge, of all things.

It was very frustrating. Who on earth would think of fudge when their children were missing? She slapped her hands on the side of the couch trying to force the memories to come back. She walked up and down, gnawing at her knuckles as she pushed at her memories.

She wanted to go and search for the children too but the police said she should stay home in case they contacted her on the phone.

Ella shook her head. She did not know where they were but … she would eat her fudge if there were phones wherever they were.

22

The occupants in the boat were quiet as Rig rowed, dipping the oars in and out of the black water. They were more than halfway and they could not hear or see anything on the shore they had just left behind, where they had parted with Madgwick.

Jeff looked at Rig's face. The glittering dust that swirled around them illuminated them in a silver glow. Rig's forehead was drawn into a deep frown and his mouth was in a straight line. He was concentrating on keeping the magic boat in place and rowing.

As he watched Rig, Jeff noticed he still had not taken his eyes off the shore where he had left Madgwick to fight alone.

They were almost on the other side and Rig started to pull the boat towards the shore, feeling the gravel underneath. He gave the boys a nod, motioned for them to stand. As they stood up in the boat the dust dissolved around them, letting them sink into the water up to their ankles. Neither Jeff nor Rhed could find anything to say. The loss of Madgwick cut deep. He had sacrificed himself to save them.

Rig watched the darkness of the opposite shore. The silver dust that had just been the boat flowed effortlessly back into his hands.

Slowly he shook his head. How could this happen again? How could he lose another warrior here in Drakmere? As skilful as

Madgwick was, there were too many shimmers to fight. Rig would have made himself invisible and then fought them but Madgwick, being younger, did not posses that power yet. There had been no time to teach him those valuable skills as they had been on the run since entering through the doorway.

Rig's lips were clenched but he was careful not to show his anger. In the boat there had been complete silence with just the odd sniff. No, he had to keep it together now. As Madgwick would say, they were just kids.

A sharp purple light flashed in the distant darkness. It was so quick you could almost believe your eyes were playing tricks on you. Rig stared intensely, not even blinking, his eyes narrowing in concentration as he leaned forward. Flash. Yes! There it was again. It was a little purple flash, very far away but he definitely saw it.

There was no way the flash had come from Madgwick and no way that the shimmers produced that bright light. They were all about darkness. There was only one person who could summon a flash that purple. Rig bit his lip. How could she have made her way through the doorway?

Jeff and Rhed were standing next to him, also squinting and leaning forward.

"What are you looking at?" Rhed whispered to Jeff.

"No idea," whispered Jeff in return. "But Rig saw something."

Jeff kept his voice low. "What do you see, Rig?" Despite himself, the whispered banter and their comical poses lifted Rig's spirits and he grinned reluctantly.

"I am hoping a lot of toads, but I cannot be sure," he whispered back.

Jeff and Rhed turned their heads to look at Rig, but they could not tell whether he was joking. Rig turned away from the shore.

"Come on, boys. Let's find a place to sleep." Rig moved into the bush.

Jeff and Rhed followed, not wanting to be left behind outside Rig's silver glow. He was like a dimly glowing walking torch.

Rig waded a good way into the forest before he found a large tree with huge roots tangled in knots above the ground. This would give them cover. He told them to get comfortable but not to move away. He would not go far.

A few minutes later he returned with fruit, berries and nuts. Rhed pulled out some cookies and chips from his bag and added them to the pile that Rig produced. Soon they were all nibbling and enjoying the fruit and berries, some of which were different from anything they had ever had but they were good and filling.

Rig had them take off their wet sneakers and socks and covered them in a silver dust blanket.

"They will be dry in no time," he said.

Then Jeff asked the dreaded question. "Rig ... will Madgwick?" He could not finish the sentence, could not get the words out, as if saying it out loud would make their worst fears would come true.

Rig sighed heavily and stared into the night, as if he were lost in thought about Madgwick. He did not want to raise the boy's hopes. Besides, they would all know soon enough if his hunch was right.

Rig kept his answer simple. "I am not sure. There were a lot of shimmers to fight."

"Why?" asked Rhed in a small voice, as if he did not want to upset Rig, but Rig seemed to know what he was asking.

"I wanted to fight in place of Madgwick. Madgwick is a good warrior but his magic is limited and young. It still needs to grow. He would not have been able to take you all the way across the lake in the magic dust boat like I just did. We had to get you to safety. That was our first concern."

"I suppose there is no harm in telling you now. They have Matt right now but you, Jeff, would serve their purposes to infiltrate the dreams of children just as well. They took Matt because he is younger and it's easier to manipulate him. It would have been harder with you, but they would have done it in the end, with disastrous consequences to your mind. That is why we wanted you to stay behind, but you are here." He paused. "So we will do what we have to do to protect you and get Matt back."

Jeff was surprised. "Me? What about Rhed?"

"You and Matt come from a line of dream catchers. In a nutshell, you can catch dreams and influence them."

"Wow, I can?"

Rig sighed. "You don't know yet how to catch dreams but with training and some practice you could do it. But on the downside, with the right spell or enchantment, your dreams could also be manipulated and used for evil."

"So Matt and I are dream catchers, but what about my mom and dad?"

"Your mother is a dream catcher."

"I think by now you have realised this is a dangerous place, not just a great adventure. I can't get you back to the doorway, and I can't leave you here. I am stuck with you and you are stuck with me. My mission is to rescue Matt and since you are here with me perhaps you could start to listening to me while I try and figure a way of finding Matt and getting everyone back home in one piece."

Jeff and Rhed were quiet.

Then Jeff asked, "Do you think the shimmers will still come over the water?"

"They will not stop until they have fulfilled their mission, which is to stop us, although by now they may have another order for your capture as well. They are coming but they will have to come around the lake. They cannot go too far over water before the moisture makes them evaporate. This lake is very wide. They will have to go around so it will take a few days for them to catch up with us."

"Rig, how?" began Jeff.

Rig put his hands up. "Enough questions for now. We need to go at a good pace tomorrow so we need some sleep. There will be time to answer more questions tomorrow."

They were on their way as the sun rose in the morning. Jeff was still upset about Madgwick and pulled his lips tight to put on a brave face. Rig was taking no nonsense either. He gave them each a large root to chew on.

"It will help with your bruises, aches and pains, and give you some energy."

Jeff looked at the root with trepidation, wondering whose snot or vomit they were about to chew on. The root looked like a potato but it was a deep pink with bright yellow spots.

"It's a tree root, really," Rig sighed and walked away, laughing under his breath.

Jeff nibbled on the root and raised his eyebrows.

"Watermelon," he informed Rhed.

"Oh, cool." Rhed took a bite.

The boys were keeping up, chewing on their roots as they walked through the forest.

The trees were so old that the trunks had deep grooves and the forest floor was carpeted with bright green moss covering the roots that protruded like spaghetti.

The sun filtered down in between the branches and leaves. He heard birds and other animals but could not see them. They were too high up.

"Do not touch anything. Not a flower, not a leaf, nothing in this forest is as it seems," Rig warned.

"What do you mean? This place is stunning, weird but stunning." Jeff grimaced as he sidestepped a huge pink flower that was oozing red juice looking suspiciously like blood.

"This is the land of Drakmere, where nightmares originate. The closer we get to the castle, the more its enchantment will work to entice you. Nothing you see is real."

Jeff pushed his hair out of his eyes and looked up. Silly as it was, he could not shake the idea that the trees were watching them. He heard the rustle of the leaves far above him.

"Uh, Rig," he started. He did not want to sound foolish, so he worded his sentence carefully.

"I think someone is watching us."

"Probably the trees," answered Rig, not breaking his stride.

"Okaaaay," said Jeff. He grinned as Rhed, who was so busy watching the trees, tripped over a root.

Rhed scrambled to his feet, pushing his glasses back up his nose and shoving his thick ropes of black hair back over his shoulder.

"The trees are watching us, really?"

"The trees," called Rig over his shoulder. "This forest is enchanted just like the forest surrounding Little Falls, but this one is not as friendly."

Rig stopped and looked up, taking in the gigantic trees. He turned around and saw that both boys had stopped and were staring at him with their mouths open.

"Our forest, the forest back home is enchanted?"

"Of course it is. Who do think got rid of that maremist that attacked you in the forest?" Rig carried on, but not hearing any sound of movement behind him made him stop and turn back. He threw his hands in the air in frustration and his purple eyes flashed. "Now what?"

Both boys were still staring at him. Rhed found his voice and words first.

"The forest attacked the mare ... thingy?"

"Maremist," said Rig. "It caught Matt and planted a spell, the forest fought it off, and gave you time to get away."

"Matt was in a spell? So he was not sick? Is he sick?" Jeff asked.

Rig headed back to where Jeff was standing. It was obvious that Jeff could not walk and talk at the same time. If he did not sort this out they would be camping right here tonight. About half a day from their camp last night!

Rig took in a jagged breath and had a look of irritation on his face. "They're just kids, they're just kids," he muttered.

"Matt was attacked by the maremist. He was never sick. He was just in a spell. The spell was completed by a full moonbeam that touched Matt that night. It put him into a moontrance."

Rig stopped for breath. "Our spell weavers were working on a spell to wake him but it could only be woven during a full moon, which was going to be last night. But then he got snatched by the moonglow first. The trance lifted when he entered the moonglow. When you saw Matt in the glow, he was awake and normal, true?"

Jeff, remembering Matt's eyes, full of excitement, nodded.

"The maremist was sent by the evil witch Wiedzma and Drakmere's King Grzegorz to catch Matt. Which it did. Had we known what she was planning, we would have never let it get close to Matt. Anyway the forest reacted to the attack. And your friend Rhed here," Rig nodded in Rhed's direction, "by knocking your brother out of the mist so quickly, helped to prevent the spell from being completed." Rig grinned crookedly. "Which means there is a very good chance that Wiedzma, not knowing this, may find it harder to enchant Matt with her spell than she thinks. It gives us a chance to get to Matt."

Rig pointed in the direction they were walking and swung his arms. "Can we try walking *and* talking? We've got quite a way to go."

Jeff got going again. They were wasting time. Matt was waiting for them, he was awake and normal, and if he was normal then he was probably driving everyone crazy.

Rhed followed closely. He was walking straighter and puffed his chest out as if he was feeling quite chuffed with himself. His quick tackle may have helped Matt. He began a detailed account of how he exactly tackled Matt out of the mist.

Rig watched them pass him. He bit his lip as if he felt bad for being so abrupt. For the longest time, well since Gwyndion was lost in Drakmere, he had not allowed himself to be sidetracked by anything or anyone.

For all these years, he had carefully kept his emotions locked behind a wall. These kids were not so bad. Rig shook himself and followed the boys down the path.

Madgwick woke up with a start. It was morning and the newness of the day was a breath of fresh air. For a moment he did not know where he was, then it all came flooding back to him.

The kids were in the silver dust boat edging away into the darkness, Rig pulling at the glittering oars, his face fierce in concentration. Then there were the shimmers pouring over the shoreline, the intense fight and the flashes of light blinding him, the hopping toads and Angie wailing in the background.

Madgwick pushed to his knees. He stretched and smiled. He felt good. He checked for bite marks but found nothing. Angie must have done some magic on him. He looked around for her, wondering how she got there and how she knew when to arrive.

She had saved him! Then Madgwick stiffened. Angie was still wailing in the background, and the sound was coming from the trees. He jumped to his feet alarmed and made his way as quickly as he could in the direction of the squealing.

"Angie!" he shouted as he ran.

He found Angie sitting with crossed legs on a green patch of grass. Bright red mushrooms with white polka-dots were popping up around her. She was smiling and clapping her hands. She was not squealing, she was singing!

Madgwick winced as she missed the note completely. It sounded like she was screeching in a soprano voice. He stopped, not sure he wanted to get any closer. Perhaps he should go back to the shore where he could not hear her as well.

Don't be mean, he told himself, *if it hadn't been for Angie I would not even be here to hear her screeching, squealing, wailing ... uh, singing.* He continued slowly, calling a little more quietly so that she would not get a fright and turn him into something smelly.

The wailing stopped. "You're awake," exclaimed Angie. "I was just about to sing another a spell. This one's for you, do you want to hear?"

Madgwick stood next to the tree, not sure what to say. He had always liked Angie very much, but she was usually the crankiest person ever. He had never seen her so full of smiles. He was unsure of how to handle this Angie.

"Ummm, sure," Madgwick said, not really sure what spell she was singing, wondering if he could ask her to sing under her breath. Deciding that the combination of green and warts would not suit him at all, Madgwick sat on a tree root and prepared for the onslaught.

Angie started. As the song progressed the mushrooms were popping up, pop, pop, pop. Probably in fear, mused Madgwick. And Angie sang. She belted it out as loud as she could, her voice wobbling in her effort to reach the notes and failing miserably, but that did not stop her. Her hands were moving faster than the eye could see as she was weaving the intricate spell. It was impossible to follow. Just when Madgwick's ears were burning from the pain and he thought he really had to make an excuse and leave for a bit, she stopped.

Dead quiet, Angie sat watching the spell hover in the air in front of her before it whooshed away, disappearing into thin air. She looked up at Madgwick. "There, all done."

"What spell was that, Angie?"

"That spell, my dear boy, will help you in your time of need. When you think all is lost, this spell will activate."

"But what does ..."

"Don't bother me with silly questions, Madgwick. It will come when you need it. Do you need it now? No, you don't! So it won't come, will it?" barked Angie.

Madgwick sighed. She was back to her cranky self.

"Angie," Madgwick began. "Thank you so much for arriving when you did. I was almost a goner ..."

Angie waved her hands, cutting him off.

"I arrived too late. They got you a few times, boy. You are a brave warrior, but not so smart. Why did you not go for the invisible man look?"

"I don't have enough power for that kind of magic yet. I'm only due for a magic enhancement session in a few months."

Angie looked at him, opened and closed her mouth as if she wanted to say something but kept changing her mind. She shook her head and then said it anyway.

"What utter rubbish! You have that power! Madgwick, it's there and it is strong. The only difference between you and Rig is that you are friendlier, a little shorter, perhaps. Your hair is messier, your toes are longer, your nose is smaller. I think your one arm is longer than the other, your teeth are whiter ... You have that thingie ..."

"Uh, Angie?" It was apparent that she could go on for hours.

She stopped mid-sentence and stared at him as if she had forgotten he was there. Then she continued. "Aaaannd more experience than you, but that is it really. You have to apply yourself, Madgwick. Focus. Anything is possible if you focus. Try it, try it now! Take your dust, and when the dust comes down, *be* invisible. Go, go, go, do it now!"

There was no arguing with her. Resigned to trying, Madgwick took a pinch of dust. He tossed it in the air and as it rained down over him. He applied his mind, concentrating hard and was delighted to see he was invisible up to his knees.

Wow, okay, with just some practice he could actually do it. Feeling elated, Madgwick sat down on the trunk of a tree, eager to try again.

But Angie was having none of that. "Practice, Madgwick, but not right now. We have to get going. I think that you are well enough to travel, not?"

Not waiting for his nod, she healed him with magic. After all, she was one of the best.

"We have to go. You have to catch up with Rig and I have a few things to do myself, so I will travel a bit with you but we will go separate ways before long."

Madgwick got up. "You're not coming with us?" He had assumed that Angie was joining them, giving them the edge they would need over the feared Grzegorz and the evil Wiedzma.

"I am not going that way." Seeing Madgwick's face, she added, "That does not mean you will not see me again during your time here, but I have urgent things to do too."

Madgwick nodded. You did not question a witch. She would be where she thought she was needed. After all, she had just saved him.

She came when he needed help the most, so it was best to just trust her and let it go at that.

Angie packed her bag and slung it over her back. She grabbed a handful of purple dust and let it drizzle out of her hands. It took form as a witch's broom but with a small seat. Madgwick's mouth hung open.

Angie glanced at him. "You don't expect me to walk, do you? I rather like the idea of a witch on a traditional witch broom. Whizzing through the air." Angie giggled, obviously highly entertained at her witch-on-a-broom vision.

Madgwick was not as amused. How was he going to keep up with her whizzing through the air?

Angie hopped on her broom and took off. Cackling loudly, she circled twice before landing again. She walked up to Madgwick, glaring into his face, looking cranky once more.

"Don't tell me you can't! Just don't tell me."

Madgwick did not know what to say. He had never performed that kind of magic before, which is why Rig had to take the boys across the lake. Besides, he'd rather walk than fly a broom.

"I haven't …" Madgwick started.

Angie interrupted. "Magic enhancement blah blah blah you said. Ugh."

She stopped in front of Madgwick. Holding her own magical purple dust she clapped her hands millimetres from Madgwick's face, then reached back and whacked him hard on the forehead. So hard that the purple dust stuck to his face like glitter.

Madgwick stiffened in shock and stumbled back from the force. The dust swirled around him, glitter everywhere.

"Owww!" Madgwick howled. "What was that for?"

Angie grinned. "There! Consider yourself enhanced, fast-tracked! You may need to practice, but you're good to go." She hopped back onto her broom and took off. "So let's go," she yelled, whooshing past.

Madgwick stared after her. He grabbed some silver dust and with concentration tossed it in the air. In front of him a form was taking shape. He grinned as he jumped on his scrambler. He revved the engine and adjusted the noise level.

Within a few minutes he was racing after Angie on his silent off-road bike, the wind streaming through his hair.

This was wonderful. He was really good at this. He ducked under branches and jumped over roots, swerving here and there. He was enjoying himself so much that he did not hear Angie.

At first, he did not understand. There was this screeching noise behind him, no next to him, oh no wait, above him. Madgwick looked around, and up. It was Angie, she was screaming. She was trying to keep up with him but was screaming in fear, her broom was flying low, then high, zigging and zagging, trying to copy the motorbike's moves, trying to race the bike.

Angie's hands were gripping the handle, trying to hold on. Her hair was flying behind her. At times her screams were interrupted as she got slapped in the face by leaves and branches, spluttering as she spat out an insect or two.

"Madgwiiiick, stop! Why a bike? A flying horse, take a horse! Madgwiiiick!"

25

Rhed and Jeff entertained Rig with tales of school, gave detailed descriptions of their secret hideout in the forest and spoke about Matt.

It was easy to walk and listen. At times the laughter bubbled over. They made good time and had come far since the morning's camp. Jeff asked about the plan to rescue Matt, but did not notice when Rig skirted around the question.

They saw a few farmers and travellers during the day but Rig made them wait in the forest out of sight. He explained that not everyone in the land was evil. There were very good folk that lived here, but the problem was that they were ruled by the cruel King Grzegorz and the evil witch Wiedzma, the two who had sent the maremist to capture Matt.

Everyone tried to stay away from Drakmere castle. It was rumoured that once you entered the dreaded Drakmere you never left and few entered of their own free will. Many people had entered never to be seen again.

Rhed lagged behind. They had already walked quite far, so Rig let them stop at a small blue pool for some water. He would not let them swim or linger on the bank, because the water looked dangerous to him.

Jeff watched a ripple start from the middle of the pool, growing towards the bank. He shivered and backed away from the ominous ripple.

Rig was relentless. He had the energy of a super-charged battery. It was hard to keep up. Rhed leaned against a tree and looked up at it. It was a stunning tree, the trunk was so broad you could not hug it properly.

"Get a move on," yelled Rig.

Rhed sighed and pulled away only to be dragged back against the tree, looking at his hand in surprise and then horror. His hand had disappeared into the tree. He yanked his arm, trying to pull it loose but it was like his hand had grown into the trunk.

"Rig! Rig! Riiiiiiig!" he yelled. "Help, I'm stuck."

Jeff grabbed Rhed's arm and pulled, but it was no good, the hand was imbedded in the tree.

Rig tossed dust at the tree. It swirled around, making the tree look like a glittering rope light.

"What did you do?" he demanded.

"Nothing. I was just standing here and then I lost my hand."

Rig was quiet for a moment then asked, "What were you thinking?"

"Well, nothing, except that it's so large that I could not hug it even if I wanted to."

"You wanted to hug a tree? We're in a race to reach Matt and you wanted to hug a tree? For real, Rhed?" Jeff said hotly, his voice rising.

"Well, it's a huge tree." Rhed's scowl matched Jeff's as they glared at each other.

Rig dropped his head and was quiet for a brief moment and then he started chanting in a swaying sing-song voice.

"What's he doing?" whispered Rhed, still straining at the tree.

"Not sure. Maybe he's talking to the tree," muttered Jeff.

The tree started to sway in time to the chanting.

Rig nodded once at it.

He smiled pleasantly at Jeff and Rhed and said very matter of factly. "Okay, so, the thing is, Rhed, that tree likes you, and has, as it happens, decided to keep you. It is quite an honour to be adopted by a tree."

"Whaaaaat?" gasped Rhed.

"Nothing I can do about that. What is done is done. He has decided to call you Twigwig, so, well, good luck and we'll see you around."

Jeff's jaw dropped.

Rhed spluttered. "But Rig, uhh ..."

Rig grabbed Jeff's arm and dragged him away from the tree. Jeff was too stunned to put up a fight. Rhed stared at Rig with big brown eyes, magnified by his lenses. Rig stopped and smacked his forehead as if he had forgotten something. Then he turned around.

He gave the stunned Rhed, or Twigwig, a sheepish smile and said, "Forgot to give you your root, you know." Rig paused and emphasised the words "The *pongsap* root that you love so much."

The tree shook and released Rhed's hand, pulling away from him as if he were smelly.

"I think that now is a good time for Twigwig to *run*," yelled Rig.

Rhed did not need an invitation. He raced away down the path with Jeff behind him and Rig following on his heels. There was huffing and puffing and only after a while did they realise that Jeff could not run anymore, he was laughing too much.

"You were going to leave me," Rhed accused Rig.

"The tree had to release his Twigwig on his own accord," he grinned. "It worked!"

They carried on through the forest, both boys careful not to touch any trees or leaves. Jeff was still hiccupping and Rig had a rare grin on his face. Rhed did not feel like laughing much, ignored them and marched on, muttering about being called Twigwig. Everything that had seemed to matter or worried them at home did not seem so important now, not school, teachers or even Jessica.

Rig glanced over his shoulder every few minutes, watching for the shimmers. He had a wistful look on his face as if he was hoping that Madgwick would magically appear over the horizon.

"Are they catching up?" asked Jeff when Rig was surveying the countryside again.

"I don't see them," answered Rig. "They can travel fast so I am not sure how long it will take for them to catch up." He gave a grimace. "But they will, that's for sure."

Rig made camp. They could not risk a fire but that did not matter. It was not cold at all. They ate fruit and berries again, talking about the day.

"So what exactly is pongsap root?" asked Rhed.

Rig grinned, "It's a root, just a normal root." But neither Jeff nor Rhed believed him. Not really.

Jeff was scratching his chin, his lips pursed as he thought about being a dream catcher. "Rig, how exactly does the dream catching thing work?"

"It runs in your family, so it should come easy to you. Let's see, the best way to explain. Imagine a large filing cabinet with thousands of files in each drawer. Now imagine that each file is a dream that a child somewhere is busy dreaming at the moment. You can access those files and use them."

"Access them? How?"

"Close your eyes, think of a darkened room, go to the drawer, open a file and see the dream, use what you need from that dream." Rig waited for the information to hit home. "If you think of the item, it be taken from whichever dream it's currently in. It takes a bit of practice. You just have to try and keep trying."

Jeff sat quietly for the rest of the evening, concentrating on a dark room. So far he could not see the filing cabinet that Rig was talking about.

* * *

Angie and Madgwick were camping in a meadow. Angie was grumpy again and her hair was full of twigs and leaves and a fair amount of insects that had been caught in her flying mane.

"Just what is wrong with a graceful trotting horse, Madgwick?" she asked. "I have never been so frightened in all my life!"

Madgwick was sceptical. "Angie, in all your life, that was the scariest? For me the thought of losing Matt to Drakmere takes the cake, or the thought of Grzegorz or even worse than Grzegorz, Wiedzma!" Madgwick shivered.

"Bah," said Angie. "Grzegorz is easy to handle. He is as vain as he is evil. Use that to your advantage. Wiedzma, well, yes she is powerful but not *the* most powerful. Not that she knows that! That will be her downfall. You will have to be quick and cunning with her, Madgwick. Don't let her ensnare you or you will be lost like the other warrior."

"No one talks about the lost warrior. How was she ensnared? Trapped by Wiedzma?"

Angie stopped combing her hair. "No, not ensnared by Wiedzma. She just vanished. She sacrificed her own life for the last child that was taken by the moonglow, the ultimate sign of bravery, very much like you did on the shoreline. I was too late to help her. She was never heard from again."

Angie sniffed, and then continued. "She was Rig's true love, you know. It nearly broke him when she did not return."

Madgwick was gobsmacked.

"True to their plan, Rig escaped with the child. They got separated and Gwyndion did not make it back to the doorway. Rig searched for many years for her. He has never given up on her. Poor lad. Sometimes I wish I could speak with Azghar. He may know what happened to her, but no one has seen him for ages."

"Who is Azghar, Angie?"

"Hope you never find out, Madgwick, because the day you do, you will probably be dinner!" Angie cackled. "Azghar is Azghar. He is the most powerful magical creature in existence."

Angie became serious again. "Tell me what you said to Matt just before he vanished. The trees told me about it, but they could not hear what you were saying."

Madgwick looked down at his hands. "I did not know what to say to him, except I did not want him to be afraid and I wanted him to know I would come for him. I also recited a small part of the Warrior oath."

Keeper of dreams, I fight with all means,

Keeping dreams pure, mares will not endure,

A warrior am I

Angie nodded. She would not say anything more except to moan about Madgwick's motorbike and scold her broom about its sudden desire to act like a bike. The bristles at the back of the broom kept shaking every few moments as if it was trying to rev its engine.

The next morning Angie announced that she would be heading in the other direction. Madgwick was sorry to see her go. He thought they would have a much better chance of saving all three children if she was with them.

He looked into the distance. Somewhere Rig was running with the boys and between him and Rig were a lot of shimmers. He had to reach them before the shimmers did.

Angie slung her bag over her shoulder, winked at Madgwick and took off on her broom. She promptly started screaming again as the broom decided it liked the bike idea. The tail of the broom quivered as it raced away at full speed, darting around trees, under roots, over branches. It was going so fast that Angie's screams soon faded into the distance.

Madgwick climbed onto his scrambler again and took off as fast as it could go. His face was full of determination and his eyes glowed behind his silver dust goggles.

26

Matt woke up on his bed. Not his bed back home, but the one in the castle.

As he lay there, the thoughts raced through his mind. He realised he was thinking clearly. He could remember his mother, his father, Jeff and even Rhed. It was like a cloud had been lifted from his memory. He remembered Holka!

Sitting up, he whipped his head towards where she normally sat and with a pang saw she was not there. The room was also changed: that warm, colourful room was gone. Now it was just place with stone walls, bare furniture, cold and impersonal.

The hot air balloons lay deflated on the floor and the aeroplanes that once darted in and out of the clouds were in little heaps on the stone floor. The bedspread was black and the once bright red curtains were grey.

Matt wandered around the castle, going from room to room. He was startled to see how much it had changed. All the colour and vibrance was gone, curtains faded or missing, tapestries gone. As he walked his shoes echoed on the stone floor as the carpets were gone too. Matt sniffed the air. The smell of bubblegum and choc-chip cookies was gone, replaced with emptiness. There was not even the fragrance of the flowers left.

Matt could not remember the way down to the dungeons and every passage he tried took him anywhere but towards the dungeon. And it was not like he could ask for directions. So he ended up cross and lonely and bored.

He found a sword so huge that he needed two hands to lift it. While trying to balance it, he accidently sliced some curtains in half. He stood for a few moments, waiting for someone to yell at him but when no one came he shrugged and went on.

He was playing with marbles he had collected in one of the rooms, when one of the guards came past and slipped on one. With legs sprawled he hit the floor with a mighty crash and his helmet went flying.

Matt, who was sitting on the floor, winced as the guard landed in front of him. The man towered over Matt, pulling his uniform back into place as he retied his sash. His red moustache quivered as he yelled at Matt to go back to his room, but Matt kicked him as hard as he could on the shin and ran off in the opposite direction. Hobbling and cursing, the guard followed.

Matt quickly lost him by running down many different flights of stairs and long winding corridors. By this point Matt felt a little lost himself. Then, at the bottom of a long corridor, was a large wooden door.

Matt looked over his shoulder but he was alone. He creaked the door open and crept inside. This room was huge. Two wingback chairs flanked a fireplace so large Matt could stand inside it without stooping.

When he glanced behind a half-open door, Matt saw another room with a white four-poster bed with thick lace netting that draped to the floor. The side table had a matching lace table cloth.

There was a silence to the room that was broken by the rhythmic tick-tock, tick-tock of a clock on the mantelpiece. Matt stared at the clock. There were no hour hands, minutes or numbers, just a black clock face with two eerie-looking eyes that followed his movements.

The smell of moth balls hung in the air. Dark beams lined the walls and ran across the ceiling. The stone floor was covered by a carpet that looked like the slimy green stuff they had found in the pond back home. Matt wrinkled his nose at the carpet and walked around it. He was about to go back to the corridor when a counter caught his attention. It was covered with interesting bottles and things.

Matt hopped onto a chair and looked at the little bottles all in a row.

Some were filled with liquid, others looked like stars trapped in a bottle. Some contained colourful sand and some had a sparkling glitter. Matt picked up a bottle and held it closer to his face. It was silver and sparkled like diamonds, and whatever it was moved around inside the bottle like a breeze. He loved that one. Another bottle caught his eye: a shiny blue liquid that looked like someone had bottled a piece of sky. Matt looked around and then slipped both bottles into his pocket.

Matt remembered how his mother had taught him to paint so he looked for paper and found some that had some funny writing on the one side. He nodded in approval. He would paint on the other side.

Next he opened a few bottles, dipped a stick into a bottle and made a circle, then coloured it in with bright red paint. The two colours started to steam when mixed. It was wonderful and cool.

Matt mixed different colours, drawing trees and houses and then he painted a castle. Some of the colours went "poof!" and some had a thin stream of smoke trailing up, others made smoke balls in exciting colours that raced around in circles. Matt laughed with delight and used more of those.

He tried all the bottles to see what would happen, but some really stank. Ooh, lovely, he thought. He pocketed one of these. Every little bottle he opened, eager to see the effect of mixing colours, poured them out, or just letting them drift into the air.

A laugh came from the corridor and Matt nearly dropped a bottle in fright. Suddenly he had the feeling that he was not meant to be there. He turned around, frantically searching for a place to hide.

On the balcony was a large flower pot. Matt raced to it and dived in just as the door opened behind him. It was Wiedzma, chuckling at something when the sound caught in her throat. She gasped and rushed over towards the table. She screeched in horror. Matt pushed deeper into the flower pot as her screeches filled the room.

The shouts went out all over the castle. Everyone was racing around trying to find the source of the ear-splitting screams while Matt, hidden from view by some plants, sneaked a look over the edge of the flower pot.

Guards and officials streamed into the room to find Wiedzma bent over and wheezing, her face red with anger. No one was paying any attention to the balcony ... yet.

The witch was so angry that smoke streamed into the room, appearing out of thin air, swirling, twirling around like a silent tornado. It was terrifying. A guard got caught in the torrent of the dark funnel and promptly disappeared. After that people scattered from the path of the deadly swirling darkness. It moved around Wiedzma as if dancing in tune with her anger.

Matt lay low, listening to the yelling and screaming in the room. Again he lifted his head to see and looked straight into Thirza's green eyes.

The old man was standing by the door. His eyes narrowed and very slowly he moved his head from side to side. Matt understood Thirza's message instantly. Even though he did not like the old man, he appreciated that he had chosen not to point out Matt's hiding place.

He lay quietly for what seemed like forever. The shouts moved out of the room and headed down the corridor. The room sounded empty. Matt lifted his head only to gasp as he was pulled out of the flower pot by his collar.

Thirza grabbed Matt by the collar and lifted the small frame up out of the flower pot. The kid looked scared and so he should be. If he were caught here there would be no stopping the witch in her anger.

He had to get Matt away immediately. He was lucky he had noticed the crumpled flowers. Thank goodness Matt had had the good sense to just lie as quiet as a mouse. Then Thirza's eyes fell to Matt's shirt and lingered on the potion stains, evidence of Matt's recent painting session. His mouth twitched. Oh, what a sight. This was priceless.

Thirza held Matt behind him as he glanced out of the door. The corridor was empty so he slipped out and marched Matt down the hall, never letting go of his collar. The old man did not say a word to Matt the whole way back to his room. A few times the boy opened his mouth but then seemed to lose his courage.

Thirza took a different route back to Matt's room so they did not meet anyone.

He looked down at the boy's face, which looked as if he was expecting to be punished. But once they reached his room, Thirza pushed Matt gently inside.

"I think you should change. Grzegorz will be calling for you soon, and it would not be good if you still had the evidence all over you." He stared at Matt, then nodded and closed the door.

Matt sat down on his bed with a heavy sigh. With horror he realised he still had some bottles of potion in his hands. In a hurry he stored the bottles behind the large cabinet. He washed his hands and changed into clean clothes. The moment he finished the door was flung open and Thirza stood there looking as grim as ever. This time he had a guard with him.

"You are wanted in the king's room, boy." His tone was calm.

Matt pushed his hair around so that it was spiky and silently followed Thirza out of the room. They entered the hallway where Matt had been playing earlier. Thirza stopped at the slashed curtains; he turned towards Matt with a single raised eyebrow.

Matt stared at his shoelaces. "There were pirates hiding behind them," he mumbled.

"Indeed."

They reached the king's throne room. The doors swung open and Matt entered behind Thirza.

Grzegorz was sitting on his golden throne, his head resting on the palm of his hand. He had a very bored look on his face. His black hair was pulled back and looked sleek and wet. His thin lips were pulled in a sneer as he watched Matt walk across the room. Wiedzma was standing behind him, her normally pale face still blotched with vivid red marks.

27

Rig and the boys were up before the sun. Rig was nervous about the shimmers. So they did not talk much but walked, and rather fast.

Jeff was in front. He still could not see the filing cabinet in the darkened room but the more he thought about being there, the more he *felt* something was there, just out of his reach.

By late afternoon they moved out of the forest and into a large green meadow, carpeted with yellow and white daisies. There was not much hiding space, which made Rig twitchy.

Every now and then Jeff would swat his ear, looking around for the bug that had stung him. After about the eighth time, his ears were throbbing and red from all his slapping and swatting. Rhed could not keep his laughter in.

"What are you laughing at?" asked Jeff.

Rig walked innocently behind him, and every few minutes he would send a pinhead of dust in Jeff's direction, zapping him on the ear.

"Stop that!" yelled Jeff.

Rhed and Rig could not walk from laughing at Jeff's red ears.

The boys loved the magic dust and were disappointed that it would only work for a true Sandustian warrior. During the walk,

Rig entertained them by moulding the dust into different shapes and antics. He had them in gales of laughter, with the result that they covered quite a distance without even noticing it.

Rig rubbed his neck as if he felt a prickling sensation. When he checked behind them, his heart lurched abruptly. The shimmers had caught up. They had just left the tree line and were racing into the meadow, coming fast.

"They're here, run, make for the water!" yelled Rig.

The three of them tore across the meadow. There was a stream directly in front of them but when they got there, they saw it was not wide enough to stop the shimmers. They sloshed through the stream to the other side. Rig stopped. They were not going to be able to outrun them. He had better make a stand and use his energy to fight.

"Stay close," he ordered the boys.

Rhed fumbled with his bag and pulled out their air freshener. Both Jeff and Rhed lined up next to Rig, ready to spray. Jeff had his heart in his stomach. Rhed's white lips were clenched together.

"Don't you have anything else in that bag than air freshener?" yelled Jeff in a panic.

"Why don't you take something from *your* bag, oh, wait, you didn't pack one!" yelled Rhed.

He dived back into his bag and brought out a flare gun from his father's boat.

"Cool! Now we're talking."

Rig made an elaborate hand movement before releasing the dust in to the air. The dust moved at the speed of light towards the shimmers, exploding into them like fireworks. But they kept coming.

"Try water!" yelled Rhed.

Rig, his eyes narrowed, moved his hands, his dust forming the shape of a huge toilet. A giant silver, glittering toilet with gushing, brimming water formed, the dust swirling until the first five shimmers were in the middle of what looked like a toilet bowl.

Rig dipped his finger towards the silver-dust toilet and flushed, washing the shimmers away into nothingness while Jeff and Rhed were whooping and fist-bumping.

"That was brilliant," gasped Rhed.

Rig was quiet. Five were gone in one shot but there were so many more, more than he could count. "Looks like they have reinforcements," he said grimly.

"Flush them again, Rig!" yelled Rhed.

Rig had his hands raised but he was squinting into the distance. Jeff and Rhed were struck quiet. What on earth was that?

It looked like a sand storm. It was white, silver and glittered: a wall of sand about fifteen metres high and as wide as the meadow.

"What is that?" asked Rhed, getting hysterical and waving the flare gun around over his head.

"A mother of a shimmer," answered Jeff yelling.

"Or a shimmer's mother," groaned Rhed.

They glanced at Rig, waiting for him to conjure up another toilet, or create a tornado like Madgwick did, or at the very least tell them to run, but incredibly, he was smiling a tight grimace of a smile.

"Toads boys, it was definitely toads!" Jeff and Rhed looked at each other. This was not a good time for Rig to lose his mind.

The shimmers were closing in. The dust wall was rushing behind them. Rig was very calm. He dipped his head.

"Huddle down," he said to the boys. "This is going to be rough."

Rig tossed his dust into the air and a solid wall formed in front of them. They watched in horror as the dust storm overtook the shimmers, swallowing them, tossing them around as if they were in a washing machine. The dust wall hit Rig's wall with a bang and the dust showered around them. Shielding their eyes, they could make out a figure coming out of the storm, riding a motorbike, wielding a long sword, slashing at the shimmers that had managed to escape the storm.

Rig gave a war cry and leapt over the wall. In his one hand was a sword and in the other was a whip.

"It's Madgwick!" Jeff punched Rhed on the shoulder. "It's Madgwick!"

Within minutes the remaining shimmers were gone and the dust storm flowed back to Madgwick, who was grinning while getting off his bike. Rig walked through the stream towards Madgwick, and promptly pulled him into a bear hug.

"I made it," panted Madgwick.

Rig did not have any words, but Madgwick nodded as if he understood.

The boys raced over, yelling Madgwick's name.

He staggered back as the boys grabbed him, and then they were all laughing.

"Did you see the toilet? Rig flushed them down a toilet!" gushed Rhed. The storm took second place as far as he was concerned. If it had not been for Rig, he would still be Twigwig in the forest. Everyone was talking at once.

"Let's go, guys," yelled Rig.

After making sure there were no shimmers close by, they made camp and shared fruit, berries and a packet of chips from Rhed's bag. Jeff explained his progress at being a dream catcher, which was … none.

Madgwick had them enthralled as he told them about the fight and Angie's arrival. He left out the part about her lack of singing talent. Spreading that little fact would not be wise.

The boys gave Madgwick a detailed account of the tree that had decided to keep Rhed and call him Twigwig.

Madgwick's head snapped towards Rig. "Tree root … uh, Rig?"

Rig grinned broadly and nodded. "Pongsap root."

Madgwick's eyebrows shot up. "Pongsap?"

Jeff and Rhed were watching this exchange with growing unease, both of them asking what it was, but it was no use. By this time Madgwick had tears in his eyes and was slumped over with laughter. Rig was slapping him on his back, his chest huffing with laughter.

28

The next morning Rig and Madgwick walked to the edge of the forest while the boys were getting ready at the brook.

"So, Angie said we may see her again but she had some urgent things to do? Like what is more important than this?" Rig asked, annoyed.

Madgwick shrugged. He had given up trying to understand her a long time ago.

The boys joined them and they were ready to set off.

"What were you riding yesterday?" Jeff asked Madgwick.

"A scrambler, you know, an off-road bike."

He took a handful of dust and it flowed into the form of a bike.

"So cool," breathed Jeff.

Rig's gaze moved along the bike and then he raised an eyebrow at Madgwick but he was smiling. Finally the young warrior could look after himself.

"Angie fast-tracked me," Madgwick explained sheepishly.

Rig did not answer except to drop his own dust to the ground to form an identical bike.

"Let's go then."

Jeff and Rhed whooped and gave each high fives. Turning back to the bikes they found that both Rig and Madgwick were holding full-face helmets out to them.

"Awww," groaned Jeff, "Do we have to? We won't fall!"

"Helmet or walk, your choice." Rig was stern.

By late afternoon they had reached a very deep ravine. Everyone's butt was a little sore from biking all day.

Jeff was complaining to Madgwick. "Next time we go by bike, can I have a cushion on top of my seat?"

The ravine was steep and they had to be very careful of loose rocks that could plunge them over the side. Some places went straight down and it was a long long way to go.

"It's going to be a long climb down. I suggest we go with ladders or we harness the boys and send them down one at a time," suggested Madgwick.

Rig snorted. "It will take us about a week to get down. Great! A week to get over this ravine, then to Drakmere. At this rate it will be two weeks to get everyone home. We don't even know what state the child will be in. We will probably have to carry him, never mind the force that Wiedzma will be sending after us. Jeepers, Madgwick!"

"I know," said Madgwick. "Do you have a better idea?"

Rig sighed. "You are right, I don't like that you are, but you are right. Bah!"

They made their way back to the boys. Jeff was standing on the rocky outcrop looking across the ravine.

Something was not right. Both Rig and Madgwick felt it. They turned around looking at the trees, looking at the sky. They did not know what was spooking them but both felt something big was coming and coming fast.

Madgwick looked back at Jeff and Rhed. Jeff was standing too close to the edge. He yelled in alarm. "Jeff, get back from the edge!"

Jeff turned around at the panic in Madgwick's voice. He had barely taken a step when a thunderous crack made them grab their ears and bend over and then they were hit by a force that slammed everyone to the ground. The trees were bending so far that they seemed about to snap. It felt like the wind had a fury of its own as it swept over everything in its path.

While flying through the air and smacking into the ground, Madgwick's eyes were glued to Jeff's startled face. The wind took Jeff straight off the edge, hurling him over and into the ravine below.

Madgwick and Rig leapt to their feet, silver dust sword already in Rig's hands, ready to fight. Madgwick did not bother with a sword. His only thought was Jeff. Madgwick did not break his stride as he threw himself over the edge where Jeff had just disappeared.

Rig's eyes widened as Madgwick went over. He raced to Rhed who was lying on the ground. He was okay. Rig rushed to the edge and looked down.

Madgwick hurtled down after Jeff. He could see the boy in front of him. Madgwick focused with his entire mind. He had a pinch of dust in his one hand. He released it, the dust spinning away from him. Madgwick focused harder. He needed to catch Jeff. He could not go faster so he needed to slow the boy down. The dust shot out as a bungee cord and wrapped around Jeff's ankles.

Madgwick, still plummeting, opened his other hand and immediately the dust wove itself around his body and trailed up above him, opening in to a beautiful parachute. Madgwick's body jerked as the chute slowed his fall. He checked on Jeff, who was swinging by his ankles, bouncing.

Jeff screamed in exhilaration, whooping and shouting, "Yeaaah! Whooooooo!"

Madgwick pulled the bungee cord in until he could reach Jeff's arms to pull him and clench him in his arms. The dust recoiled, securing him to Madgwick. Madgwick pulled his strings left and right, negotiating the wind in the channel between the two ravine walls. Eventually Madgwick's feet touched the ground and they were on the other side of the ravine.

As the cords fell away and the dust flowed back to his hands, Madgwick waved to Rig. "I found a faster way across," he yelled.

"Are you nuts?" yelled back Rig, but he was grinning and already pulling a reluctant Rhed to the edge.

With Rhed tied to his front, Rig jumped over the edge and opened his chute. He was a lot more graceful in negotiating the wind and floated easily across.

Rhed's mouth was opened wide as he screamed in terror, his dreadlocks flying in all directions.

Rig shook his head.

29

"Matt, Matt, Matt." The king sighed loudly.

Wiedzma, too angry to allow Grzegorz to continue with his infuriating approach, pushed in front of Matt and screamed into his face.

"I know you were in my room! My chambers are carefully hidden away by spells and enchantments! How did you get in there?"

The smoke tornado was still bellowing darkly behind her, moving and pulsating, like it was alive.

"Don't know," muttered Matt and shoved his hands into his pockets. His eyebrows pulled inwards as he stared at the witch's mole, which had left her cheek and moved to her forehead. Her hair was plaited and intertwined like snakes on the top of her head and her bright yellow dress looked out of place against the dullness of the room.

"Don't know what? Explain how all my bottles of potions were dumped on the table and these, these stupid drawings were all over the place," screamed Wiedzma, her mouth pulled back in a rictus and her eyes never leaving Matt as she threw the pages covered in his paintings up in the air. In her anger, her magic made the paper fly around the room, flapping around in circles. Some of it flapped into the smoke and rushed around in a wild frenzy before tiny little pieces flew out of the smoke and floated down to the floor like little snow flakes.

Matt's gaze darted left and right as he tracked the bits of paper raining down all over him.

"I was only playing and … and you can't tell me what to do. You're not my mother," said Matt crossly.

He glanced up at Wiedzma's face and he swallowed as Wiedzma's complexion reddened again. She lunged for him but the king moved in front of her and put a hand on her arm. At the same time Thirza moved forward so that he was right behind Matt.

"Now, now, Wiedzma," soothed Grzegorz. "He is just a child after all. Annoying as it is, we can replace all your potions. And he has not burnt the place down, which I suppose we can be grateful for."

Matt backed up some more to put distance between Wiedzma and himself and, not realising Thirza was so close, bumped into the old man. He pressed back into him, finding it comforting, even though he knew Thirza did not like him.

"You don't scare me and you're ugly!" yelled Matt, but he was scared, very scared.

Grzegorz turned back to Wiedzma and tried to shout over Matt's yelling. "How long before that damn potion is ready?"

"It *was* ready but now I have to start again, thanks to my potions being mixed and destroyed! I don't even know what is still left. I am amazed that the child did not lose his hands!" she yelled, whirling towards Matt.

Grzegorz snapped his fingers. A guard whipped Matt up over his shoulder and marched out of the room.

"What do you mean you have to start again?"

Wiedzma faced Grzegorz. "My dear king," she said scathingly, "that is the whole point. I cannot just *get* more potions. Some take years to create. I will have to travel hundreds of kilometres to replace ingredients. If I can even get them again. And who is going to protect your precious castle then?"

Grzegorz's mouth snapped closed. This was a disaster. Wiedzma was a powerful and feared witch but even she needed potions, and she was needed here. Grzegorz knew a rescue attempt would be made for the child, of course. But if the rescue party got here after the enchantment spell was completed, it would not matter how they tried or what they did, they would not be able to break the spell. With the spell sealed, they would never be able to take the child away. He would be theirs forever, and willingly.

With Matt's mind open to him, he would be able to manipulate the child's dreams. But Grzegorz was not just interested in just *Matt's* dreams. They would open up the doorway to the dreams of all the children in the world. Oh, what chaos, fear and misery Grzegorz would cause! The misery and fear would feed his army of nightmares, and soon he would be able to conquer all realms, including Sandustian.

Wiedzma also had her own plans for the dreams of all the children. Her wish was to implant an evil dream snatcher into the minds of all human children. Sleep deprivation was a powerful tool in causing despair and anguish in the world.

Grzegorz slowly turned away from the door through which Matt had just disappeared to stare at Thirza, his black eyes narrowed and his cruel lips pouted.

"And just where were you?" he demanded. "You were supposed to know everything. You were supposed to know the child's whereabouts at all times. How did that brat find Wiedzma's room and who helped him?"

Thirza inhaled deeply. He had to be careful now or he would end up in the dungeons like everyone else that had served Grzegorz and given him a wrong answer or not the answer he was expecting. Ending up in the dungeon would not help Matt.

He had to buy some time. He was convinced that the call had been heard. That crack was loud enough to travel through time and space. It was inconceivable that it might not have been heard. And if it had been heard then it wouldn't be long before he got here. Perhaps he was already on his way.

Thirza had slowed the spell down in the beginning by keeping Matt unhappy, and thanks to Matt's painting episode the spell was ruined for now. However, it was never wise to underestimate Wiedzma.

Thirza cleared his throat and smoothed down his grey hair around his ears. "My Lord, it may be that Matt was not actually looking for Wiedzma's room in particular, thus the disguise spell would not stop him from entering what would be, in theory, just any room to him."

Wiedzma straightened suddenly. She had not thought of that. What a stupid loophole. She looked down at the king.

"I don't care. I want to punish him anyway."

Grzegorz laughed. "Yes that would be splendid. I am all for squealing, screaming children but I need that potion to work. I need that little brat to be happy, even if we have to force it."

He turned back to Thirza. "From now on you keep that boy away from Wiedzma's room or you will pay for his mistakes."

Thirza bowed his head, turned and left the room.

30

Grzegorz stared out of the window. "How long before the child's mind is mine? I need this to happen faster. I can't stand the boy around me anymore." he muttered angrily.

Wiedzma pouted. "My potions are ruined." She paused, weighing up her options. "I can try another potion that was not in my room when the brat went into artist mode. It's a bit drastic but I did not anticipate how horrible a six-year-old could be." Wiedzma breathed hard. "This is the ultimate potion, made from the rarest flower as well as blood from a witch. Mine, of course." She laughed as if the thought of another witch's blood as powerful as hers was ridiculous.

"Once I use this potion, the child will be asleep for the rest of his life. He will never age and never awake again. He will be asleep but his dreams will be accessible to us at all times." She laughed. "Like a dream donor."

Grzegorz clapped his hands. "I love it! Why on Drakmere did you not tell me about this before, really Wiedzma! This a much better plan. We should have done this from the start."

Wiedzma shrugged. "It is very powerful magic and irreversible. It's also forbidden, but since I am the most powerful witch over all the lands, I don't really care and I doubt anyone will have the power to stop me."

Wiedzma's eyes glistened; she rubbed her hands. "I will prepare the potion and administer it at twilight. It must be given while the sky is fading from pink to purple or the magic will not work. Besides," she sighed, "the child uttered smo… that unmentionable word, so I don't want to delay any longer."

"When are you going to tell me what that was all about? What do you mean, what is sm… that word?" demanded Grzegorz.

"Legend has it that it's a word forgotten in time, an ancient call for help. The one who calls this word awakens a mythical magical being, more powerful than anything else in existence. I don't believe in this mumbo jumbo fairytale nonsense. Quite honestly, who could be more powerful than me? Tsk!"

Wiedzma rolled her eyes as if the whole idea was ludicrous.

"Anyway, I don't want to delay any longer, because something has interfered with my spell. Maybe the maremist did not complete the spell in the forest. I don't know."

* * *

The dungeon was dark and smelt musty. The floor was cold with large slabs covered with moss. The slimly walls had frightening grooves, scored by prisoners counting the days and years of their endless captivity.

Each cell had a stone door with black bars that dropped down the middle providing a little light from the torches that lined the walls. It was easy to get lost in the maze of tunnels; some passages were forgotten or caved in. Some led to a mysterious underwater lake or all the way to the forest.

The entrances and exits had been blocked by the magic of the castle. The cells were filled with men, women and children, from servants who worked in the castle or in the grounds to farmers who happened to have the wrong hair colour. All memories of their past life had faded away, leaving only the present.

The crack of the breaking enchantment had swept through the castle, penetrating walls and floors. It punched into the dungeons far below the castle where Holka was curled into a ball, alone in her misery.

The walls trembled, loose earth from between the cold stones scattered onto the prisoners who were huddled together and crying out in fear. The silence lasted a while before it was broken by the voice of a small child echoing through the tunnels, a child crying out for its mother.

Alerted, Holka strained to hear the child, wanting to soothe his or her fear. Then she grabbed her head as hazy memories started flashing through her mind, almost like a dream of another life that could not possibly be hers.

Bewildered, she leaned against the bars of the door and listened to people calling out. They were calling out for daughters, fathers, mothers. The flashes were fast and bright and Holka could hardly stand at the onslaught as she started to remember who she was.

* * *

In another part of the castle, Thirza grimaced as he closed the door to Wiedzma's room and hurried down the corridor as fast as he could. He had been watching them in the spy mirror that she had placed so conveniently for her own devious use. Wiedzma was not the only one who knew secrets. But Thirza was worried. He had to come up with a plan, and quickly.

He could try to free Holka but her memories were not restored yet. Although the crack had broken her enchantment too, she was so long under the spell that it was going to take some time for her memories to return in full. No, the safest place for Holka right now was in the dungeon, where Grzegorz and Wiedzma would not think about her. If they knew that they had a Sandustian warrior in their dungeon, they would be doing cartwheels down the corridors and laughing like mad at the evil they could perform with her in their power. Holka would never survive that. And Thirza had so carefully kept her identity hidden all these years.

To wait for the rescue would be too late for Matt. The doorway was opened, but the warriors were still far away and Wiedzma and Grzegorz had already sent menacing shimmers to intercept the rescue party. There was no way to say if they had even survived the attack.

He could not take the chance that Azghar would arrive in time and even if he did, there was no guarantee that he would protect Matt. The chance that Azghar would just eat them all was also pretty good.

Thirza was keeping an eye on where Matt was. He somehow had to get him out of the castle before twilight, but Grzegorz had guards stationed around the boy, out of sight but there all the same.

Watching the child play, Thirza idly wondered where he had actually found marbles to play with. Then he blinked and blinked again. Could those be … Oh, this was not going to go down well.

In the short time Matt had been in the castle, without meaning to, he had caused absolute chaos, from tying together the shoelaces of unsuspecting guards to painting with potions, destroying the decor in his imaginative games, and now the marbles.

On Wiedzma's orders, the guards tried to frog march Matt back to his room. He lifted his legs and the guards grunted as they were forced to carry his full weight down the corridors and up the staircases.

31

Matt sat miserably at the window and stared longingly at the forest in the distance. After a while, the door opened, and Thirza came in. He was alone and he closed the door.

"We are going on a secret trip," the old man said. He held his hands up when Matt opened his mouth to ask questions. "No questions! I don't have the time!" he barked. "Be ready to go when I come back, and don't tell anyone." As an afterthought, he turned back and added, "Wear a jacket."

Matt grinned and clapped his hands together. This was better than staying in the room, doing nothing. He put on a jacket he had found in the wardrobe. It was large and had lots of pockets, which he promptly filled with his treasures such as the bottles of cool glitter stuff and other potions. He then sat by the window to wait, staring at the forest again. Maybe he was going home.

The door opened again. Thirza stood at the doorway. He beckoned to Matt, holding his fingers to his lips. They walked in silence, not meeting anyone. Thirza had reassigned guard shifts so there was a brief moment when the corridors would be empty. The change in shift was so subtle that no one would even notice or get suspicious.

Matt kept quiet, skipping now and then to keep up.

Thirza increased the pace. They were almost there. Just around the next corner and they would reach a doorway that would lead them into the forest.

But as they turned the corner, Thirza's heart sank. Wiedzma was leaning against the wall with a row of guards behind her. She had a huge contented smile on her face.

Wiedzma lazily pushed away from the wall, not looking up. She was inspecting her nails.

"Now, why would you believe you could get that child away from me? I worked for months to bring him here. Do you really think I would allow anyone to just walk away with him?"

The guards stepped up to either side of Thirza, neither of them looking at him as if they did not want to meet his eyes.

Next Thirza and Matt were herded down the corridor, no doubt to see Grzegorz. Matt was stumbling next to Wiedzma. She held his jacket tightly and hauled him along, not caring that his little legs could not keep up.

Thirza berated himself mentally. Why had he waited so long? He felt the despair descend on him, thinking that he was nothing but an old fool.

When they entered his throne room, Grzegorz's face was purple and his black eyes flashed. It was not like he trusted anyone anyway, but of everyone he had least suspected that Thirza would betray him. Wiedzma was a snake in disguise but she needed access to the child's dreams and she wanted his kingdom, which she could not get without him, alive. This kept her by his side, right where he could watch her. But Thirza had free reign over his castle; he had been there for a long time.

"Why?" he demanded of Thirza. "It's not like you have any attachment to this child, why would you risk eternity in the dungeon for this boy?"

Thirza lifted his head and stared at Grzegorz. He was not afraid for himself, he was afraid for the child. He had seen Grzegorz perform the most evil deeds during his reign and *that* was even before Wiedzma had come knocking at the gate. Together, they wreaked havoc, caused pain and suffering. And they laughed like children about their deeds.

"Your plan with this child is evil and all the children you will damage in the process, it cannot happen. It will not be allowed."

The words were strong but they sounded empty and looking at the smirks on Wiedzma and Grzegorz's faces, he knew they sounded weak to them too.

Thirza was devastated. He slumped over, held up by the two guards on either side. He had failed.

"We have limited time, Grzegorz," Wiedzma muttered, pulling a small blue bottle out of her pocket. She walked over to Matt very casually. Like she didn't have a care in the world, she spoke. "Matt, my darling."

Matt's eyes grew large. She was never nice to him. Now she was all cuddly. Eeeuuw.

"Matt, darling, I have something you need to drink, something that will, umm ..." Her eyes went from left to right as she searched for the right words. "Help you see your mother," she finished.

She pushed the bottle of potion into his hands. It looked just like the blue bottle he had hidden in his pocket.

"Drink up!" She smiled brightly, flashing her white teeth.

Grzegorz was looking at the guards. They stared oddly at him then quickly looked away when their eyes met. What were they staring at? Peering at them, his eyes narrowed. He lifted his crown off his head and turned it around in his hands. His mouth dropped open at the same time his stomach dropped to the floor.

The gems, his precious gems were gone. Blank empty holes stared at him where sparkling gems used to dazzle. He closed his eyes, opened them, and yes, they were still gone.

In a hoarse voice he whispered, "Where are my gems?"

No one answered. Everyone looked at each other and then stared resolutely at the floor, not daring to even breathe loudly in case they got noticed.

Grzegorz was battling to swallow, this crown was his symbol, his sign of power, it was all about him. He asked a little louder, almost pleasantly, "Where are my gems?"

He stopped in front of Matt who was staring, totally absorbed, at the bottle in his hands, holding it up to his eyes as he peered in, trying to see his mother.

"Where are my gems, Matt?" The king's voice was dangerously soft.

Matt shifted his gaze from the bottle to meet Grzegorz's eyes. "You mean the marbles? I played with them in the courtyard," he said with a dimpled smile. He did not register the dangerous mood Grzegorz was in. He was excited that he was going to see his mother!

Grzegorz's eyes widened before turning to slits. His precious diamonds, emeralds, sapphires, rubies just rolling in the sand. His fury bubbled over as he leaned down into Matt's face. His screaming was so intense that his spit sprayed into Matt startled face. "I do not want you to play with my marbles."

He straightened and gasped. "Gems," he hollered. "I mean gems."

As Matt flinched at Grzegorz screaming directly in his face the bottle of potion slipped from his hands.

Matt watched in horror as the bottle tumbled to the floor. It was like it was falling in slow motion. He gasped as it hit the floor, expecting a splash of blue stuff. Somehow the bottle did not break, it just plopped onto the floor and rolled half under the velvet curtain against the wall.

"Oops." Matt's head shot up as he glanced at Wiedzma. She had not noticed the bottle rolling away. A quick glance around confirmed that no one else had noticed the bottle dropping either. Everyone was staring at Grzegorz, some with their mouths open.

Matt stuffed his hands in his pockets. He was not sure if he should rush and pick it up or tell Wiedzma about the bottle. Grzegorz was still shouting about the marbles.

"Now now, Grzegorz," soothed Wiedzma. There was an obvious laugh in her voice. "He is just a child after all. Now stop wasting time about gems, or should I rather say, marbles." She was taking great delight in throwing his words back into his face. She whirled back to Matt, making him jump.

"Drink your potion, Matt," she barked. "Oh just give it here!"

Matt was so rattled that in a panic he grabbed the bottle of potion he had been touching in his pocket and pulled it out handing it over without even looking at it. He was so relieved when he saw that he had pulled out the blue bottle. But would she notice that it was not the same bottle?

"Nooo," wailed Thirza, still standing imprisoned between the two guards. "Don't drink it Matt, throw it down! Break the bottle Matt, don't drink it!"

Wiedzma grabbed the potion from his trembling hands, pulled the cork and shoved it to Matt's lips. "Drink," she ordered.

Wiedzma grabbed Matt's face, lifted his chin and tilted the bottle so that he had no choice but to drink.

She clicked her fingers and ordered that the sobbing Thirza be taken to the dungeon. The guards hauled the old man away. His feet dragged on the floor behind him, his head was hung low as the sound of his sobbing faded down the hall.

Grzegorz was still grinding his teeth together and muttering that he wanted his gems back before Matt went to sleep.

M att felt butterflies flying around in his tummy. He sank to his knees. He felt like everything was going hazy around him.

A shadow fell over the castle, like the sun went behind a cloud. There was an earth-shattering roar, a thunderous noise that made even the air shake and wobble.

The castle foundations and walls sagged as a tremendous weight landed just outside in the courtyard.

Grzegorz came to stand next to Wiedzma, facing the doors. "What in Drakmere is that?"

Wiedzma did not reply. Perhaps she did not know, but whatever it was she looked confident that she could and would deal with it.

Suddenly the doors flew open, off their hinges, landing with a crash against the walls on either side. There was another mighty roar that had everyone's hair blowing back from the force of the wind. Curtains waved like flags, some of them tearing away. The guards cringed in fear as a huge dragon stood at the entrance.

The dragon was massive, with midnight blue scales that glistened and shimmered as he moved. His powerful body easily crumbled the walls at the broken door frames as he forced his way into the room. He roared; his gaping jaw was laced with massive white teeth row upon row. His muscular body was lined with pure white spikes running along the top of his back and down his magnificent tail, which was whipping back and forth, clearing anything in its path with mighty crashes.

There were two sharp spikes on the edge of the tail, and he was using them to gouge through the castle floor, dragging up stones and debris in rows. A thin line of blue fire blew from his nostrils in a steady stream, like a blow torch. His eyes were a steely blue that glared down at the people before him. No one escaped his gaze.

His name was Azghar, and he was extremely angry.

Matt was still kneeling on the floor when Azghar forced his way into the room. In his still hazy state he looked up in utter fear and awe. He had seen pictures of dragons and dinosaurs before, but none of them were as huge and fearsome as this one, or as alive!

If Matt had not been feeling so fuzzy he would have run away screaming but for some reason his legs would not move.

In a thunderous voice, Azghar asked, "What evil magic are you weaving here?"

Wiedzma started as if she had been caught out doing something she should not be doing.

"I am Wiedzma." She pulled herself up to her full height and her eyes flashed. "No one dares to question me. Announce your name or face my wrath."

Azghar's body heaved up and down. It sounded like an earthquake.

"Your wrath?" he thundered "I think you should be worrying about *my* wrath!"

His head moved from side to side as his eyes roamed around the room. "Now who uttered the word 'smok?'"

Grzegorz turned to Wiedzma, the vein on his neck bulging. "You said it was nothing, some old long forgotten fairytale! What is going on? Either tell him to leave or kill him!"

Wiedzma's face was flushed. She started with her elaborated hand movements, shaping the air between her fingers and moulding the space to form powerful magic. The energy started to pulse and rotate. Her magic was almost ready to be released in a thrust towards the dragon. A killing blow.

Azghar snapped his head towards Wiedzma. His eyes widened as if he was surprised she was going to try magic on him.

With a blink of his eyes, the dragon froze her hands and started towards her, watching her struggle to release her hands from his own brand of magic. The look of horror on her face would have been very amusing if the energy she had so foolishly entrapped in an air pocket was not going to explode, about to kill everyone in the room. He opened his mouth and in a single gulp swallowed the energy enclosed in the air pocket. Somewhere in his huge frame there was an explosion, but to the dragon it was nothing more than an insect bite.

Azghar snorted at Wiedzma and her stricken face. A lava-red flame shot out of his nostrils, setting Grzegorz's chair alight. The king shouted out and stumbled back against the wall. In his hasty retreat he stood on the bottle of blue potion that Matt had accidentally dropped. It was partially hidden under the curtain. The potion splashed up and soaked the king's foot as he crushed it with his weight.

Azghar searched the room until his eyes settled on Matt, still on his knees. The boy's mouth was hanging open as he stared at Azghar in awe. Mentally he reached out to Matt's consciousness very gently. He did not want to bruise the child's mind as he probed his thoughts. It was very scrambled but the words "Giganotosaurus" and "cool," were in the forefront. Searching gently, Azghar found the trace he was looking for. This was the one who had called him, this was the child who had called "smok".

Azghar reached out to Matt and gently lifted him up in his massive talons, careful to not hurt the little thing.

"Time to come with me, boy," he said as gently as he could, yet it came through as a deep thunderous roaring voice.

Matt's eyes were large. "Am I a dragon rider?"

Azghar had no idea what this kid was going on about.

"Stop!" yelled Wiedzma. She stepped forward as if she had just realised she was about to lose Matt just after he had taken the potion. "He stays here, he belongs to me, just who do you think you are?"

Azghar waddled off to the doorway with a talkative Matt dangling in his clutches. Matt was talking about flying over a desert and doing tricks. Azghar was so busy listening to the boy that he almost missed what the witch was saying

Once he cleared the broken doorway, Azghar spread his wings. Azghar turned his head back to Wiedzma who was storming forward, having regained some of her confidence.

"You are not the most powerful, Wiedzma. I am." A blue flame shot of his nostrils. "I am Azghar. I am the ancient protector of Smok."

The dragon looked left and right, surveying the castle and grounds. Then with a mighty thrust of his wings he shot up into the sky, below him he heard Wiedzma gasp, "Azghar?"

Wiedzma, shocked to her core, rushed outside. It cannot be, Azghar was not alive, no one had heard from him for decades! She watched the dragon until he was just a blue speck in the sky.

33

Matt was flying underneath a huge dragon, holding onto the white talons with both hands. Jeff would never believe that he was flying with a dragon. Matt frowned and shook his head as if he could silence the faint whispering which was growing louder until it was a rumbling hum. He was telling the dragon all about his dinosaur book at home. So far the dragon had not talked except for a couple of humphs here and there, both times accompanied with a stunning flame from his nostrils. Matt was so enthralled by the plumes of flame that shot out of his nostrils that every now and then he asked any question to see the flame thrower in action.

Azghar was taken with this child. Why Wiedzma wanted him was becoming obvious. His dreams would have been an open book to every dream of every child in existence. He was innocent, ready to give all trust and imagination he had to give. Azghar seethed in fury that Wiedzma thought she could get away with this, or that she would even try! Azghar felt his blood boiling and willed for inner quiet, Azghar had no intention of scaring this child.

While the child chattered, Azghar scanned Matt for enchantments and magic potions. He was appalled at how much had been thrown at this boy. What Azghar could not understand was how most of the enchantments had failed to lock Matt into anything.

The most worrying, however, was the potion that Matt had drunk. Azghar could smell it as he flew, but could not place the scent. He would have to land to examine the damage, and to see what he could repair.

Azghar could sense an enormous amount of tears had been spent from this little boy. Oh, he was so going to make Wiedzma pay dearly for that alone. He was itching to roar and shoot his blue fire in anger.

The dragon landed in a green meadow that had bright yellow daisies bobbing in the breeze. Just as gently he put Matt on his feet and lowered his head to gaze into Matt's face. Matt was a little off balance and tottered back a step or two. The dragon pushed his face up against Matt's and stared so intensely that Matt started to clean his face with his sleeve as if he had spaghetti sauce on his chin, warily watching the dragon.

Azghar huffed and reared back. How on earth did the child manage to get hold of and drink Potion Amispekus? It was a powerful potion, very rare and took years to make. Oh, surely Wiedzma had not given him this particular potion to drink? He was looking forward to hearing the whole story.

Matt's eye widened as if he was surprised that the humming in his head had stopped. He looked up at the fearsome dragon and gulped. "Are you going to eat me now?"

Azghar laughed. "No, child."

Matt responded with a smile. "Okay. But I'm very tasty. I'm Matt."

"Indeed you must be … Matt."

The dragon settled down on the grass, squashing the yellow daisies under his massive body.

"Tell me how you got here."

It took a long time for Azghar to get the story out, and even then there were a lot of holes. The child could not remember everything in sequence either.

Matt was all over the place. Azghar was so interested and entertained he did not even notice that Matt was climbing all over him like a jungle gym the whole while he was telling him all he had done at the castle.

My old friend Thirza is at the castle ... Why? Azghar mused. *And Holka? She does not sound familiar but I think I should investigate that further.*

Matt was happily swinging upside down. His legs hooked over Azghar's talons. He went into detail about his painting works, showing Azghar his treasures. He also showed his fine collection of marbles. At this Azghar snorted with laughter, roasting the nearby daisies by accident.

Matt stopped in front of Azghar's face and asked, "How come you can talk? My mom and dad have read many books about dragons to me and none of them could talk."

Azghar smiled when he answered. "I am Azghar the dragon and Azghar am I. I have always been able to talk, but you can hear me because of that blue potion you drank at the castle. How come are you not afraid of me?" he asked in return.

Matt smiled. "Everyone likes me and I can do addition and subtraction already."

Azghar sent a toothy smile back at Matt, enjoying how the boy's grin got even bigger at the sight of his teeth. Most people would be screaming in fear if they saw so many teeth just a short space from their faces.

He knew by Matt's magic footprint that he was the one who had uttered the word smok. It was also clear why it came through so hazy. Matt had a lisp, so what he had in fact said was closer to "thmok". Azghar regarded the boy. He was little and it was doubtful he knew what the word "smok" would unleash.

"How do you know this word, 'smok'?" Azghar asked.

Matt screwed up his face as if he was trying to remember. "I don't know. My mom tells me a poem every night before I go to sleep. 'Stamp my foot and shout smok, smok, smok.'"

"Humph," replied Azghar. He knew this poem. It was a little old rhyme surely forgotten in time. How did Matt's mother know it?

Azghar dropped his head so that his massive blue eye, the same size as Matt's head, was level to the boy's face.

"I need to do more magic on you. This will make all the other nasty magic go away."

Azghar pondered the situation. *My magic won't take away the effects of the Amispekus. That is permanent, but we can work around that.*

"Will it hurt?" asked Matt.

"You won't feel a thing. Then, afterwards, I am going to see if we can get you home."

Matt clapped his hands. "Yeeees! Can you come with me? You can share my room."

Azghar laughed then stared into Matt's eyes. For a dragon as powerful as him, it was not hard to undo the threads of magic tied to Matt, but there was a lot to undo.

Quickly the dragon put Matt in a mild trance to keep him still, which was best, as Matt had already proved to be a busy bee. After a short time the magic threads were untied and Matt was free.

After Azghar released him from the trance, Matt blinked and immediately picked up a small stone to toss it across the meadow.

Azghar was satisfied that the child would be fine, despite the Amispekus potion, which was already deeply threaded into Matt.

Azghar got up. "Come Matt, let's go."

Matt watched as Azghar stretched his wings. There was a loud fffprrrruppph. Matt looked around. Fffprrrruppph, it came again.

Matt looked at Azghar. "Was that you?" His eyes were large.

Matt giggled. "Did you just fart? 'Cos it was not me. That was some fart!"

Azghar looked at Matt like the child had just lost his mind. Did he really just tell him that he had farted? Him? Azghar the Dragon?

"I did not fart," he answered.

Fffprrrruppph, there it was again. Matt was grinning broadly, his eyebrows shooting up and down.

"That is not a fart, Matt. It's the wind chambers under my wings, and it helps to propel me into flight. That's the noise you hear. Wind." To prove the point, he spread his wings and a loud fffpwwrrrruppph came out.

Matt fell into a fit of giggles. "It sounds just like a fart," he hiccupped in between the giggles.

Azghar glared at Matt. "It was not a fart. I, Azghar do not 'fart.'" He pushed his wings up and down, frrrruppptt frruppptt.

It was just too much for Matt, who laughed till tears were rolling down his cheeks.

"Well! Come on then," said Azghar with his bottom lip jutting out. He wondered if he should have left Matt in the trance. He flapped his wings to create momentum, fphrrruruuurrrp, fphrrrruuurrppp. He had to move closer to Matt, as Matt could not move, his head hanging down loosely on his shoulders, helpless with laughter. Although he was thoroughly annoyed by now, Azghar picked Matt up with his talons and gently folded him close to his body. Matt was still laughing, his little body shaking. After a few moments in flight, Matt's giggles subsided into hiccups.

Azghar felt his lips twitching. It was the first time someone had actually asked him if he had farted, laughed at him and *lived*. It was also the first time someone had made Azghar smile in a long, long time.

34

Wiedzma was frowning and shaking her head as she walked around the room.

"Just what was that?" yelled Grzegorz, who was still standing at the window, holding onto the curtain. He motioned for one of the guards to bring him another chair. Guards were running around the room, some trying to put out the flames of his beloved throne. Not that it mattered. The dragon's flames were so hot that the chair was still lava red and molten into a golden blob.

"Just look at my throne!" shouted Grzegorz. "And tell me the brat left my marbles behind." He motioned frantically for guards to search on hands and knees for his precious gems.

Wiedzma stopped in front of him. "Stop your snivelling. We have bigger problems than your marbles or your blobby chair."

"Who was that?" demanded Grzegorz. "Explain how he managed to take our child away, why did you not stop him!"

Wiedzma was seemingly too deep in thought to be annoyed by Grzegorz's tone.

"That was Azghar, and I can't explain who he is. He is Azghar and Azghar is him! He was supposed to be gone. No one had heard from him in a very long time. I never knew he was the keeper of

Smok. The brat cried 'smok' yesterday, and then the crack happened and then *he* arrived."

Wiedzma flicked her hair over her shoulder while the king glared at her.

"It must have called him from wherever he was. I should have seen it yesterday but who knew that the kid would, or could, call the dragon!" She was still walking up and down as she made sense of the events that had just passed.

"He must have been quite far away, because he only came today." She turned back to Grzegorz. "Which means sooner or later he will come back."

"Why?" asked Grzegorz.

"We kidnapped a child to steal his dreams, why do you think!" she snapped back at Grzegorz. Then she smiled. "But I will deal with him when he arrives. A lot has happened while he has been away and I was caught unawares today."

She smiled slowly, the corner of her mouth lifting. "He will find the child quite useless. He drank the potion, after all. I saw him swallow it myself. Even the all-powerful Azghar would not be able to unweave that enchantment. He will be carrying a comatose child with him, like a bag of potatoes! With a clever spell, I will still be able to access the child's dreams. All is not lost." She turned to smile at Grzegorz. "I have work to do."

"What about the rescue party? Have your shimmers taken care of them yet?" demanded Grzegorz.

"The shimmers ran into a bit of difficulty and have not come back to me yet, but I have sent reinforcements." She looked thoughtfully out of the window in the direction of where Azghar disappeared.

"I tried to summon them in my ball the other morning but all I got was a lot of croaks and splashing, and," she paused as if she were reluctant to admit, "and one said 'ribbit ribbit'. It's very confusing. Now I can't reach any of them." She scratched her chin, looking frustrated.

Grzegorz tried to stand but found that his foot was asleep, totally numb. In fact, it was sleeping so deeply that it was snoring slightly. Grzegorz tried to shake it awake but to no avail. It was the foot that had accidently stepped into that small bottle half hidden under the curtain. He stood on it when that dratted dragon sent a flame to his chair and he had to vacate it rather urgently. He dragged his foot across the floor with Wiedzma staring at him.

"What is wrong with your foot?" she asked.

"I don't know. It has just gone to sleep. I stood in something."

Wiedzma's smile was replaced by an ugly grimace as if she just had a horrible thought. She strode over to the curtain and hitched it up to reveal the broken shards with traces of blue liquid still in small puddles. Wiedzma bent down and sniffed the liquid.

She gasped. She jumped up, turned to the window and shrieked "Noooooo!"

Her black tornado was suddenly all around her in her fury. "I saw him drink the potion, I gave it to him! How did he swap it?"

Her black hair flew from side to side as she looked from Grzegorz's snoring foot to the potion on the floor.

"Nooooooo," she screamed again. Matt was not going to sleep, she would not be able infiltrate his dreams. Her plans were shattered. She was so angry with Grzegorz and his foot that the tornado started pelting the king with vases, wooden splinters from the broken door, ornaments, anything that could move. He ducked and dived behind his guards who were staring at her, horrified, trying to block the debris with their shields.

"Stop it, you witch! You gave him the potion, not me! Stop messing around and fix my foot!"

Wiedzma breathed evenly until her tornado became a mere gale-force wind. If the brat did not take her potion, then what *did* he drink and how did he get it? He had been in her room. He could have taken some potions with him. Perhaps they were not all ruined but still standing in his room. If she knew what potion he had taken, then perhaps she could enchant him in another way.

Wiedzma swirled around and stormed out of the room, leaving the chaos and the still shouting Grzegorz behind her.

Fuming, wanting to kick anything in her path and frustrated that no one was crossing her way, she stormed off to Matt's room. She reached the wooden door and whistled for it to open, but nothing happened. She tried a different tune: still nothing. Frowning, she whistled tune after tune after tune until she eventually kicked the door in anger. Ugh! She would have to find that slave girl Holka to get the correct tune. Muttering under her breath, she marched off to the dungeon.

35

Elder Galagedra sat in front of the orb which was pulsating and glowing brightly. He felt like he had aged years since Matt was taken. His silver hair was hanging down his back in a neat twist. His normally twinkling eyes were weary and tired and he drummed his fingers in time with the pulse of the orb.

The cushions reacted to the tense atmosphere in the chamber. They were flying across the room like shooting stars. The light bounced off the walls and caused an eerie glow on Galagedra's drawn face, making the lines on his cheeks seem more severe.

"What news?" the elders asked.

They popped in as often as their other duties would allow. Sometimes one at a time, sometimes they came in threes and fours. Galagedra kept everyone updated as much as he could. There was not much they could see or assist with in Drakmere. It was all so terribly frustrating and frightening.

Galagedra sighed. "No news since the children went into Drakmere."

One of the elders shook his head. "It was very irresponsible of Madgwick and Rig to take them in with them."

Galagedra lifted his hand to stay the rising murmurs. "We have already discussed that. The warriors had no idea that the two boys

were following them through the doorway. However, we know that
Madgwick and Rig went back for them. The boys will be safe as long
as they stay with the warriors."

"Does anyone know what made Angie rush into the forest. Has
anyone seen her since?"

The elders present all shook their heads.

Galagedra continued. "There is evidence that she is in Drakmere. I see her face in the orb every now and then."

The elders gasped at the news.

"She must have seen something and decided she was needed, or
at least I hope so. Her magic and temper will be most helpful to our
rescue team."

Although Angie chose to live in their realm and amongst the
Sandustians, she was not a Sandustian. Angie was a witch with her
own powerful and peculiar brand of magic. She was last seen in her
garden when she shrieked and rushed into her home. A few minutes
later she was racing towards the forest. One of the elders met her at
the forest gate and wanted to discuss the magical use of something
called arila sand, but she had no time. The elder was annoyed that
she would not listen and made the grave error of blocking her exit.
He was later found hopping into town. The spell that had turned
the elder into a toad was so strong that the spell weavers were still
trying to undo it. The poor toad-man would have to wait for her
return to untie the knots of the spell.

* * *

Thirza sat silently by the wall in the corner of the cell he shared with
Holka. The castle magic had been broken by the crack that
resounded through the kingdom and by now the prisoners were
starting to remember wives, children, and husbands.

But Thirza had never been affected by the castle magic in the first place. He was as immune to the castle magic as he was to Wiedzma's magic. And all these years he had stayed to protect Holka and because sooner or later, he knew, Grzegorz would find another way to take a child. And he was determined to stop him.

Holka sat quietly, her orange tunic smeared with dirt and moss. Her yellow stockings had holes from her legs brushing against the roughness of the walls. Her golden hair was plaited and gleamed dimly in the faint torchlight while her pink eyes were large in her pale face. The memories had started to flood back.

Unlike all the others, Holka was not gasping and weeping, because she was a warrior, a Sandustian warrior. Her eyes started to shine when she remembered that her true name was Gwyndion.

She was not going to waste time on what she could not change. She was trying to remember as much as she could. Her training would help her get out of this situation and back to Matt upstairs. Now she understood her urge to protect the boy. It was her natural instinct.

She glared at Thirza every now and then. He was shuddering, wallowing in misery, probably because he was down there with the rest of them, she thought bitterly.

"Your plan failed, did it? Your 'friends' betrayed you," she said.

Thirza looked up. Gwyndion's mouth dropped open when she saw how old he suddenly looked.

"Yes," he sobbed. "I failed. I could not save Matt."

"You never intended to save him, you were horrible from the start," Gwyndion fumed.

"I had to keep him unhappy. It was the only way to ensure the enchantment would not work. I was trying to sneak him out of the castle tonight but I was too late. It's too late."

Gwyndion frowned. She could see that Thirza was distraught. Could it be that he was telling the truth? Over the years he had been the only one she could talk to and rely on but since Matt had arrived, he had changed. He went from being a sweet old soul to a horrible grumpy old man who was very much like Grzegorz.

"What do you mean about the enchantment? Why would Matt need to be unhappy?"

Gwyndion gasped as she understood the spell that was used. She slapped her hand on her knee.

"No! That evil, wicked witch! They needed him happy, and I fell for it! I was helping to entrap his mind. You were keeping the spell from binding."

Gwyndion was beside herself. She stood up and walked over to Thirza.

"What do you mean it's too late?"

"Wiedzma forced him to drink a potion that would make him fall into a coma. It's irreversible. That poor child."

Thirza's shoulders were bunched up. He looked like a broken man. Gwyndion shook her head.

"Are you sure you saw it, maybe ..."

"I saw it. The little boy drank it all."

Gwyndion sank back down to the floor, a frown wrinkling her forehead.

"We have to get out of here. Perhaps the elders' magic would help Matt."

There was also someone else that could help, someone called Allie or Angel or something, but Gwyndion could not remember her name.

Sleeping or not, she was not leaving Matt here. She did not know where the moonglow doorway was, but if she could get to the enchanted trees in the forest, they might spread word of her desperate plight. She was positive that help would come if they knew she was there.

"Hang on …" Gwyndion clicked her fingers as if she had a thought. "Do you think they know that the magic of the castle has been broken?"

Thirza frowned. "I am not sure. I don't think so. They are so confident about the spell woven into the castle. Why?"

"Listen …" Thirza put his head to one side. All he heard was sounds of anguish. He looked at Gwyndion blankly.

Impatiently Gwyndion explained.

"They are all remembering. You said yourself the castle magic has been broken. Could it be that the exits are broken too? Perhaps you can get out through the tunnels. You can save all of these people here. Their memories of their families are starting to return. Once the castle enchantment is restored, their memories will be wiped clean again. We have to save them now while we can, while they remember who they are and why they need to flee."

Thirza stood up. "We could! But why are you only saying *you*?" He frowned at Gwyndion. "What are you going to do?"

Gwyndion stood up as well. "I am going to fetch that child. He is not staying here even if there is nothing I can do to wake him. I will keep searching until I find a spell or someone that can undo that spell."

"But," started Thirza.

"But nothing. You get these people out!" Gwyndion snapped.

Then she turned to him and asked, "You have been here since I can remember and since my memories are not all back yet, how long I have been here? Who are you really?" Gwyndion pushed. She wanted some answers.

"I got here when Grzegorz took the last child. I swore it would never happen to another." Thirza had his head bowed as if he could not go on.

"When they first captured you, Gwyndion, some years ago, you were almost broken. I kept you down here until the castle magic had taken hold. I am sorry I did that. Once it was safe and your memories were blocked, you were introduced as the slave girl Holka. No one knew you were a Sandustian warrior. It was just in time too, because then the witch arrived. Had she known, she would have tortured you. But it never occurred to her to scan your memories. To her you were just a servant girl and not important."

A noise came from outside the door. Both Thirza and Gwyndion gasped as they looked into the grinning face of Wiedzma, who had heard everything.

"Well, well, well," whispered Wiedzma. She stared at Gwyndion as if she could not believe her eyes. Here, in the castle, a Sandustian warrior. She snapped her fingers.

Two guards came down to unlock the doors. One grabbed Gwyndion by the upper arm and dragged her out, and the other had a tight grip under her armpit. She immediately struggled and made it difficult for them to hold her, but her strength was not fully returned and she had no dust either. She was helpless.

Thirza yelled at Wiedzma to let her go, but within minutes he was alone, Wiedzma's laugher receded down the corridor until there was just silence.

After the sound of footsteps disappeared, Thirza tested the door to his chamber. There was an orange spark but the door swung open easily. It was not locked as he had anticipated. Thirza quickly pushed the other doors open and slowly the prisoners started to come out. He explained briefly what was happening. "We do not have a lot of time. The magic will try to repair the damage or Wiedzma will realise the problem and fix it with a wave of her hand. We have to leave now and quickly."

Thirza sent men down the different corridors to open doors and to make sure that they did not leave anyone behind. His heart sank when he realised how many people were down there.

He barely remembered the way as he led the cold, dirty, hungry people away from the dungeon. The lit torches were their only light. The tunnels crawled in circles, intercepting with other tunnels.

The shuffling crowd followed Thirza along the tunnels until all sense of direction was gone. The passages started off wide with high ceilings and then became so narrow people had to shuffle one behind the other.

Nobody spoke. There was no whispering, everyone was quiet. Everyone understood the urgency and blindly followed Thirza into the darkness.

36

Madgwick stopped and leaned against a huge tree, staring at the castle ahead of him. They had made it! This was Drakmere castle, and Matt was inside.

The building was grey, dull and huge with high walls and turrets. Dark thunderclouds, almost black, hung over the castle, looking ready to burst. A cold wind gusted around the castle walls, lifting leaves before slapping them against the stone. Every now and then an orange spark jumped randomly along the castle walls and windows.

Rig came up beside Madgwick. "What's with the sparks?" he asked.

"No idea," answered Madgwick.

Rig looked at the castle with distaste, not liking the sparks at all. "Something is off here," he muttered.

Jeff and Rhed finally caught up with them.

"That's it?" breathed Jeff. "Whoa, it's amazing. It looks like some kind of a fairytale castle."

Madgwick turned away, facing Jeff and Rhed. "That is not what it really looks like. You are not seeing the real thing. Remember what we told you. Nothing is as it seems in Drakmere and the closer to the castle you get the more enticing everything around you becomes. You are seeing the fantasy, not the reality. As warriors, our minds are protected so we see the real thing, thunderclouds and all."

"Let's sit. We need to talk," Madgwick began. Then he put on his most serious face. "You cannot come into the castle with us."

Jeff opened his mouth to complain but Rig silenced him with a finger and a severe look, then motioned for Madgwick to continue.

"Rig and I intend to go into that castle to rescue Matt. We don't know what condition he will be in but we do know we will have to fight our way in *and* out. We cannot do that and survive if we have to watch your backs as well. We know the risks and are aware that either one of us may not come out of that castle. That is what we signed up for. You *have* to stay here."

Jeff muttered, "This sucks!"

"So uncool," added Rhed.

Rig had to be firm. "Boys, this is our one shot, our only shot at rescuing Matt."

Rhed nodded in agreement. "But is there anything we can do to help? From here," he hurriedly added on seeing Rig's face cloud over.

Rig answered, "Stay inside the tree line, stay out of sight. Be ready to move and move fast when we get back. If we are not back by sunset, climb the trees. The shimmers will not look for you there. They can't go too high or they will float away."

Madgwick looked at Rig when he said this but Rig ignored him.

Rhed was appalled with the idea of climbing a tree. "Are you nuts? The last tree tried to adopt me."

"First of all, these trees on the edge of the forest are not as magical as the trees deeper in the forest. There is no way any of these are even awake enough to take a liking to you. Besides, you are already adopted. A tree adoption is forever, so these trees will recognise you as kin but won't try and keep you. Secondly," Rig reached into his bag and took out two pongsap roots. "Carry this with you. No self-respecting tree will touch you with that in your hand."

Jeff nodded solemnly and looked at his root with a wrinkled nose and then up at the trees, mentally picking which tree they would climb.

Madgwick and Rig looked around. Rig slapped the kids on the back, Madgwick ruffled their hair and they were off. They moved silently through the trees and stopped just before they reached the edge of the forest.

"Rig? What was all that about the boys climbing the trees to escape the shimmers, and shimmers floating away?"

Rig snorted. "Well, they won't wander off if they think that there may be shimmers around, and we must be able to find them when we get back. It will be best if they climb a tree and stay nice and quiet. I have scouted; the shimmers are quite far off."

Madgwick shook his head, "Cruel. Rig, that's just cruel." After a brief pause Madgwick spoke again. "Okay, what's the plan?" he muttered while he was counting the guards he could see.

"Don't have one. You? I count six on the north side ..."

"Three guards on this side. We can get past them easily. No plan? Well, how about this. We get in, try and stay undetected for as long as possible, find the child and get out, silently or violently, their choice," said Madgwick.

Rig nodded. "Sounds good to me."

They sprinkled dust and became invisible. It would not last long but it was enough to get them to the castle walls and out of sight from the guards patrolling the walls. They made for the tunnel entrance that Rig knew about. He had tried to gain access there many years ago when he was searching for Gwyndion. The tunnels were locked back then and he was on his own. Now he had Madgwick and together they could try to force the tunnel open.

It was a lousy plan but better than knocking on the front gate. They reached the narrow tunnel, half hidden behind a glossy green creeper. The entrance did not have a gate or bars but it did have an orange spark flitting across every few minutes. Rig tentatively pushed his hand past the entrance, wincing in preparation for the electrical shock he was expecting. But nothing: he felt nothing at all as his hand passed the barrier.

Rig whispered, "I don't know what is going on, but the entrance is open. Something is happening here."

"It could be a trap. But we have no choice, so let's go."

Rig nodded. Without hesitation he disappeared deeper into the tunnel. Madgwick took a long look at the bright sunshine before turning and going in after Rig.

They walked in the darkness, only daring to spare a little light, just enough for their path. After a while, they entered a cavern with walls so high that the light did not reach all the way to the ceiling or to the sides. They heard shuffling and quickly pushed against a wall, dropping the light so that they were in darkness.

A light was flickering in the distance. It seemed to be coming down one of the tunnels, and then the shuffling grew louder. It was creepy. The circle of light grew bigger and bigger, bobbing up and down.

To Madgwick and Rig's surprise, it was a horde of people dragging their feet and huddled close to each other as if they were cold. In the dim light their faces looked haggard. No one was talking. Everyone had a grim face, and in the front was an old man holding the fire. Rig frowned, staring at the old man as if he had seen him before.

The old man stopped, waiting for the last person of the large crowd to enter the cavern. He looked around as if he was not sure which of the tunnels would lead to the exit. Rig stepped forward, he opened his mouth but the old man saw him first. Instead of shouting out in fear, he just raised a hand towards him, like he was reaching out to a long-lost friend.

"You survived the shimmers," he said.

Thirza told Madgwick and Rig about the broken enchantment and that he was leading all these people away from the dungeons, to freedom, before the exits were resealed.

"We have no time to waste then," said Madgwick firmly. He pointed out the correct tunnel, the one they had just come out of.

Thirza motioned the crowd to move down the right tunnel.

"Keep going. Once outside, head straight for the trees. Keep going." He urged.

Once the people were moving, Madgwick spoke with disgust. "All these people were in the dungeon?"

Thirza nodded. "Holka and I were, too. Holka made me lead the people out, their only chance to escape."

Rig looked around. "Who is Holka?"

"Holka was looking after Matt until she was put into the dungeon as punishment. She was taken back upstairs by Wiedzma, the witch. She was going to try and get to Matt, but I don't know how she will get away with that now … especially now." Thirza covered his face in his hands. "I tried to keep him safe but I failed."

Madgwick's eyebrows shot up. "What do you mean, what happened to Matt, is he okay?"

"No." Thirza started to heave, trying to breathe against the dryness and the dull ache in his heart. "That evil witch made him drink a potion that has put him into an irreversible sleep. Holka said she was not leaving him here, sleeping or not."

"An irreversible sleep? Oh!" exclaimed Rig.

Madgwick rubbed his head. "Well, we are not leaving him either. Maybe the elders or Angie could do something to help him."

"That's what Holka said," Thirza muttered but Rig and Madgwick were not paying attention. The last of the crowd passed them.

Thirza turned to go back down the tunnel with Madgwick, but Madgwick put his hand on his arm and spoke. "You need to get these people out. You are their only hope of getting out and past the guards – we will go for Matt."

Thirza slumped and nodded reluctantly. Thirza followed the people down the corridor while Madgwick and Rig wasted no more time. They swooped up the tunnel leading to the dungeon.

Jeff and Rhed climbed the biggest tree the minute Rig and Madgwick were out of sight. They were not taking any chances with shimmers. Rhed kept poking the tree to see if it was awake and that the pongsap root was securely in his pocket within easy reach.

They were sitting on a large branch facing the entrance of the tunnel when suddenly Rhed sat up straight. Someone came out of the tunnel entrance into which Madgwick and Rig had disappeared, not just one, two or three, but a whole lot of people. There were old men and women, children, people of all ages. They were blinded by the bright sunshine and were clearly in a panic, not knowing which way to go.

"Look, Jeff," Rhed said.

Jeff sat up straighter. "They don't know where to go. They will raise the alarm. Let's go, let's go!"

"Madgwick and Rig will be furious if we leave the forest," Rhed protested.

"They need help or those guards will see them, and that could spoil the element of surprise for Madgwick and Rig." He scrambled down the tree.

Rhed matched his descent and within minutes they were rushing towards the people milling around. Jeff and Rhed grabbed the arm of the first person.

"Come, come this way quickly, before you are seen!"

They led the people towards the forest, leaving them inside the tree line before running back to the castle entrance to help some older people that tripped, back to their feet and move them along.

One frail old lady just could not walk anymore so Jeff bent down in front of her, lifted her on his back and struggled back to the forest. Rhed helped the last old man into the forest, all the while anxiously watching the guards. They were sure some of them had seen them but they just turned away, apparently ignoring the escape of the prisoners.

Jeff gently gave the old lady to grateful hands and turned to face Rhed and the old man. The old man was staring at him, his eyes wide. Jeff frowned at him.

"You okay?"

"Ella?" the old man croaked. He could not talk. It looked like he was about to have a heart attack.

"Uhm, nooo." He gave Rhed a sidewards glance to see if he was grinning at him being called Ella. "I am Jeff. But my mother's name is Ella. How did you …"

"Your mother is Ella?" The old man put a hand out to lean against a tree. "Ella … and you are Jeff? Why are you here, Jeff? How did you get here?"

"My brother was kidnapped. He's in there," said Jeff, pointing to the castle. "We came with Madgwick and Rig."

Thirza gasped. He looked from Jeff to the castle and back to Jeff. "Matt? This cannot be happening again! Not again! Matt!" He turned back to Jeff. "Your brother is Matt? Matt is Ella's child?"

213

Jeff nodded, watching with alarm. "What's going on? Do you need to sit?"

Thirza turned on the spot. "I need to get back to the castle!" He rushed about five steps before Jeff jumped in his way to block him.

"You can't go back. Madgwick and Rig will get Matt."

Thirza stopped. His face was grey and his cheeks looked hollow. He grabbed his hair like he wanted to tear it out.

"I knew that they had chosen a child, but I never dreamt it would be one of my own … again."

Jeff flicked his fringe back, raised his eyebrows and asked, "Who exactly are you?"

Thirza sighed with a shudder; "I am your grandfather, Jeff, your grandfather."

"Uh I don't think so … My grandfather disappeared a long time ago."

"I have been here in Drakmere. There is so much to tell you, so much to explain. You look just like your mother. You have her eyes."

He looked at Rhed with raised eyebrows.

"Rhed. Best friend," supplied Rhed, pushing his glasses back up his nose.

The people were not waiting around but started to disappear into the forest in all directions.

Thirza opened his mouth to say something when his eyes went wide and he grabbed his head as he whirled around facing the castle. "I forgot to tell them!"

"What did you forget, what is the matter?" exclaimed Jeff.

"I forgot to tell them that Holka, the slave girl who was looking after Matt, is actually Gwyndion. She is a Sandustian warrior who was captured a long time ago. She is the reason I could not leave

Drakmere. They do not know about her, she will be forgotten. We cannot leave her!"

Jeff bit his lip, studying the castle. "I bet if I run, I could catch them still in the tunnels."

"No way, Jeff, are you nuts?" Rhed's voice was raised.

Thirza was also shaking his head. "You will get caught. You must be a dream catcher too, which means that Wiedzma will do anything to grab you. It's out of the question. I will go back."

Seeing the familiar stubborn look on his friend's face, Rhed frowned until his eyebrows almost touched. "Stop being a hero, you can't go. Madgwick said to stay here."

"Look, I will go as far as the tunnels. If I don't see them then I will come right back. I won't even go inside. But I must try. They're in there to rescue Matt, the least I can do is tell them that Holka is the Gwyn girl … warrior and that she is still in there. I'll stop right at the entrance."

Thirza was scratching his head and Rhed's face was pulled into a deep scowl. Both were shaking their heads at Jeff.

Jeff shrugged, turned and raced as fast as he could towards the tunnel exit, keeping low to stay within the cover of the forest as long as he could.

As he ran he heard Rhed hiss after him while Thirza groaned.

He stopped at the doorway and sneaked a look inside. It looked ominous and eerie. At the far end of the tunnel was a glowing flicker of light that looked like a fire torch.

He crouched at the entrance, hissing Rig and Madgwick's names.

Jeff was met with silence. He bit his lip and glanced over his shoulder at Rhed who was waving frantically at him. Jeff lifted his head trying to decipher what Rhed was signalling. Then it clicked.

A guard was coming around the side. He could not run back to the forest without being seen by the oncoming guard. He had no choice but to go in. Slowly, cautiously, he crept into the tunnel and stopped a few paces inside the circle of darkness. He went down on his haunches and watched the brightly lit entrance.

The guard stopped just outside and then peered in but moved on when he could not see past the wall of darkness surrounding Jeff.

Releasing his pent-up breath with a silent whoosh, Jeff made his way back to the entrance. He was about to peek out to see where the guard was when strange bright orange sparks rippled their way across the entrance like a spider web.

Puzzled, Jeff picked up a twig and tossed towards the sunlight. It bounced back with a loud sizzle and exploded into ash. He was trapped. There was only one thing to do: find Madgwick, Rig and the way out.

38

Matt was flying again, secured in Azghar's talons. He was singing to Azghar at the top of his voice.

"Peanut butter in a big blue jar, got my backpack I'm going far … jam-a-loo, that's right! Jam-a-loo, tripping to the left and tripping to the right … jam-a-loooo …"

Azghar was enjoying this song, although it was just one line. Matt could not remember how the rest of the song went, so they sang that one line over and over again. Azghar sang "jam-a-loooo" with Matt and when they sang "jam-a-loooo," they swayed to the left and then to the right. It made flying in a straight line a little difficult but they were not really in a hurry.

Then the dragon saw something strange coming towards them in the distance. It was flying crazily and looking quite out of control. It came closer at a huge speed, and there was a loud sound, like a motorbike. Azghar was not sure what was coming towards them and his first thought was to protect Matt. The thought of a possible attack made the spines running down his back bristle in anger.

He reached out with his mind, trying to touch the mind of whomever or whatever was coming his way. To his surprise he heard a woman screaming madly.

"Miserable thugs! Mist dung! Haha, call yourselves shimmers, bah, you're nothing but puffs! Tiny smelly puffs! You can't even catch me!"

Chasing her were so many shimmers that the sky was a dark thundercloud behind.

Angie? Azghar thought. Angie under attack!

Azghar growled loudly. A plume of blue fire shot out of his nostrils. He dropped his head and picked up speed. He was going so fast that Matt could not "jam-a-loooo" anymore.

"What's going on?" Matt shouted.

"We're going to fight the shimmers, Matt, it will be fun, you'll see."

He reached out with his mind and touched Angie's consciousness. She immediately responded to Azghar.

Azghar? Is that you? Where the flying thunderbolts have you been all these years? Just look at all these daft shimmers behind me … What a bunch of poppies!

Azghar snorted. *Well, poppies or not, there are just too many for you to handle alone. What on dragon-fire are you flying? What happened to your broom?*

Angie's broom was so taken with Madgwick's dust bike that he had transformed into a splendid wooden version of a Harley Davidson. The broom had even grown a large wooden body with a straw pattern along the side. The exhaust was not visible but the broom was powerful enough, roaring like an animal.

Angie's legs were stretched out in front of her, her large feet resting on foot pedals. Her hands were high up on the outstretched handle bars, which had tuffs of straw flapping in the wind. And on her head Angie had a straw helmet. Her hair was flowing from underneath it. She was certainly a sight to behold.

Angie laughed crazily. Her broom was outstripping the shimmers and was very agile, darting in and out while Angie yelled obscenities to the angry mob of shimmers trying so hard to catch her. She patted the bike fondly.

Azghar heard Angie's thoughts: *"He fell in love with a bike and just grew from there."*

Azghar shook his head. A broom that wanted to be a bike!

I am almost there, but can you take on a passenger? I will keep them at bay while you take Matt to safety.

Matt? You have Matt? When did that happen? Oh my! Yes, I can take him.

She screamed down to her broom, "Are you kidding me? Of course you can grow another seat!"

Azghar flew higher until Angie was a dot below him and Matt shivered. He held the boy closer to the fire within him and stopped the shivering immediately. Then Azghar swooped down on Angie from above her, flapping up a storm while he hovered. Gently he dropped his talons and Matt was deposited into the new seat the broom had just grown. From the side a wooden strap bounced out and secured Matt to the seat, like a seat belt. Angie pulled him so that he leaned comfortably back into her.

"Hello, kiddo," she yelled above the rushing wind.

Matt looked from Azghar to Angie as if he was a little confused. Within seconds he went from flying with a dragon to flying with a lady on a broom bike.

"Hi," yelled Matt. "I'm Matt. I like your bike. How fast can it go? What's Azghar doing? Can we do somersaults like on a rollercoaster? Azghar looks very cool. I have a brother called Jeff. What's Azghar doing?"

Angie's eyes widened at all the questions as if she was amazed that he had survived the castle with such a steady stream of questions. He must have driven them crazy.

She yelled back at him. "I'm Angie. It's a broom that has grown into a bike. It can go fast as a whistle. We can do rollercoaster later, okay? Azghar looks magnificent, doesn't he? See those black thingies? Azghar is going to give them a quick hiding."

"Oh, cool," yelled Matt. "Can we watch?"

They turned to watch Azghar who was roaring and breathing fire on the shimmers. The shimmers had never encountered a dragon before and scattered from the path of the fire.

Azghar relished in the open-air fight, spreading his wings and diving, rolling over and using his huge wings to stop him in mid-air. He opened his jaws to reveal his enormous teeth and gulped the shimmers into his fiery belly. All too soon they were devoured and he had not even used his magic. "Oh well," he sighed. "It was fun nevertheless."

He turned and made his way back to Angie, who was yelling, "Give me an A!" Matt yelled, "AAAAA!"

"Give me Z!" Matt yelled, "ZED!"

Giggling, Angie yelled, "Give me a G!" and Matt yelled "GEEEE!"

Aw, my own cheerleading team, thought Azghar fondly.

Just then his eyes widened. Behind Angie was a shimmer sneaking up on her. She was so busy having fun with Matt she had not noticed. The shimmer rushed at Angie. Azghar yelled out a warning, but it was too late. The broom heard the warning and dived out of the way but not before the shimmer bumped into it so violently that Matt's seat belt snapped, flinging him into the air. They were high up and Matt was hurtling to the ground.

Angie screamed, hanging on to the handle of her broom.

Azghar blew the shimmer apart with a gust of red-hot flame and then dived after Matt who was cartwheeling out of control. Azghar propelled his wings and flew faster than he ever had. This was a race against gravity!

Angie focused all her power and threw it at the little body spinning away from her. She sent a force so strong that the air rippled like a heat wave. Her spell caught Matt and slowed him down little by little until he was suspended upside down by his ankles. She saw the fear on the boy's face. She winked and her magic tickled him and made him laugh.

Azghar got as close as he could to the suspended child and opened his wings. He slowed abruptly and then lunged for Matt, closing his huge mouth over the little body.

Angie had climbed back into her seat. Her broom was shaking in fear as if he was so upset that he had got caught by a shimmer and that he nearly lost Angie. Angie was patting the trunk of the quivering broom, trying to soothe it. She watched with her heart in her throat as Azghar raced after Matt. Then she saw his whole body seemed to stop in a mere second, and just as suddenly she saw Matt disappearing in Azghar's mouth. Gone.

"Azgharrrr," Angie shrieked, "you can't eat him!"

But Azghar was still in a spiral, his mouth closed. Matt was nowhere to be seen. He glided back to Angie who was sitting with her hands on her cheeks in horror.

As he got closer he saw that Angie's eyes were white all around. He opened his mouth to reveal a huge display of shiny white, pointy teeth, and hugging the largest tooth, with his little legs curled around the base of it, was Matt, half the size of the tooth.

221

He was waving his one hand up above his head, and pinched between his two little fingers was a small white object. His face was flushed and his eyes were bright.

"I lost a tooth," he yelled, "my first tooth! I'm gonna get five bucks! Aww that's so cool Angie, let's do that again."

Azghar grinned. If it had been possible, he would have been grinning from ear to ear. Then Angie and Azghar landed in the meadow beneath them.

"Azghar, just how did you manage to get Matt? Was he not at the castle?" Angie was flabbergasted.

"He called me by the ancient word, 'smok'," Azghar said. "I don't know how and I don't think he knows either," he replied when Angie opened her mouth to ask. "But I am bound by it so I came and fetched him away from Wiedzma and Grzegorz. Those two did a lot of damage and I think I will visit them again to teach them some manners once Matt is safe back home."

Angie took Matt's face in her hands and stared into his eyes. Her lips were twitching at the sight of his toothless grin. "Yes, I can see the traces. The magic is all untied except for one thing ..."

"Yes, Amispekus," said Azghar. "I didn't think it would hurt. Makes up for all the heartache he has endured. Besides, did you notice how the magic has already locked? It won't be easy to remove that one. It will do no damage to leave it."

"Oh," said Angie, then she suddenly slapped her hand against her straw helmet. "Oh, oh, oh, oh my drat, Madgwick! Rig! They won't know that Matt is gone. They will be walking into a trap!"

"Madgwick? Rig?" asked Azghar.

"The Sandustian warriors sent to rescue Matt. They should have reached the castle by now. We have got to warn them."

Azghar snorted. "I am faster. I will go to the castle, you take Matt to the doorway, and we will meet you there."

Angie scratched her head under her helmet. "It will be better if I go in. I could sneak in. Besides, Madgwick knows me. You look rather dangerous to those who don't know you. I better be quick about getting to the castle. We may need your help to get the kids through the doorway again, though. There are bound to be shimmers waiting there."

Angie looked around for her Harley broom to find he had turned into another mean racing machine, quivering again, but this time from excitement.

"Oh, you clever broom, you," she cooed.

Azghar sighed, then flapped his wings and waited for it. Frrrruuuupph. Matt's laughter pealed through the air. There was no hope. The more Azghar flapped his wings, ffruuuuppph, ffrruppph, the more Matt laughed. Azghar rolled his eyes and flapped towards Matt who had squeezed his eyes shut and dropped his head back on his neck, helpless with laughter.

39

Wiedzma was walking around in circles again, waiting for the guards to bring Gwyndion from the dungeon. Her cheeks were pink and she was panting: there was a warrior in this castle.

Grzegorz had no idea and she was not going to tell him. No, she would keep Gwyndion's true identity a secret. She would send Gwyndion to her own secret castle without Grzegorz being any wiser that he even had a warrior. He would not remember Holka.

A knock sounded on the door and she flicked her fingers at it. Two guards carried Gwyndion between them. She had put up such a fight that it was easier to carry her than to drag her with effort. Her eyes darted around the room, her face was blank.

Wiedzma stood in front of Gwyndion and studied her face as if she was not sure how much of the warrior's memories had returned.

"The castle enchantment had completed its task with you, unlike it did with the child," mused Wiedzma. "We will have to lift those walls a bit, help you remember your entire past."

Although she kept her face blank, Gwyndion was horrified; she did not have the power to stop her. Her thoughts would be an open book and Wiedzma would know that the castle enchantment was broken.

Please Thirza. Please have all those poor people out of the castle by now, please, Gwyndion thought desperately.

Wiedzma grabbed her face between her hands and muttered a long string of magic words. Gwyndion felt the heat rush through her veins. All her memories were returned, all the blanks filled. As the memory wall came down, Wiedzma had a full vision of her conversation with Thirza.

Furiously, the witch dropped her hands. They were shaking with anger. "Guards!" she yelled, and immediately two guards appeared at the door.

"The enchantment spell has been broken. Check the dungeon. The prisoners have escaped. Follow the tunnels to find them. Then take them back and whip them until they have learnt their lesson about trying to escape from me."

The guards looked back and forth at each other. They wasted no time and rushed out of the room like their lives depended on it.

Wiedzma walked over to the roaring fire in the fireplace. "Well, well, well, Thirza was a traitor right from the start. I never did trust him. I would dearly like to know how he always managed to evade my spells."

She turned around and peered at Gwyndion from under her eyelashes and pretended to study her nails while watching Gwyndion's reaction slyly.

Then she spoke again. "You will never find Matt. He is gone. I knew there would be some sort of a rescue attempt so I had him taken to my own castle far away from here."

The blood drained from Gwyndion's face. She had had no idea how she was going to get Matt out here, awake or asleep. But to now find that he was not here at all, that was a huge blow.

Wiedzma smiled wildly at the emotions crossing Gwyndion's face.

The warrior inside Gwyndion had been suppressed for so long that all her instincts were messed up. She had no idea that she was being lied to. All she wanted to do was to protect Matt.

Wiedzma carried on. "It's in your nature to protect the child. And it was fighting to come through even while you were under deep enchantment. Quite pathetic, really."

"You will be taken to my castle." Wiedzma pointed to a side door that Gwyndion had not noticed before. It was bluish and hazy as if it was behind a rain-stained window.

Gwyndion pushed herself to her full height. "Your castle? Where is that?"

"Diamonds on the lake, the forty-seventh flutter, twirling beneath the prism, as the drops begin to splutter, the whereabouts of my castle are known to no one but me." She looked up with a little smile.

The blue doorway from Wiedzma's castle opened and two guards came out. They did not have a fixed shape but looked like dark smoke in a strange human form. They clamped onto Gwyndion's arms on either side and pulled her through the door.

"Don't do this, please, let Matt go! I will do anything you want, just let the child go."

"Oh, I know that you will do everything I want. Take her."

Gwyndion struggled and strained against the guards but they were too strong. In an instant they were gone and the bluish door vanished without a trace.

Wiedzma smiled to herself, turned, twirled a loose hair into her knot and walked out of the room.

* * *

Jeff reached the glowing torch that was abandoned on the tunnel floor. He lifted it up and looked around. His heart sank. He was in a maze of tunnels and he had no idea which way to go. There were four different exits that branched out from the large chamber he was in and they all looked the same.

He was about to pick one when he heard footsteps coming from one of the other doorways. Hiding in a cleft, Jeff held his breath and waited. Two guards came rushing past and without hesitating went into the tunnel towards the exit from which Jeff had just come. He waited for a half a second, took a deep breath and dashed up the tunnel away from the chamber and the guards.

40

Madgwick and Rig were creeping along the corridor, hands filled with dust, ready to take action at a moment's notice. Then four guards jumped out into the corridor, two in front and two behind them.

Madgwick sighed. Getting so far into the castle undetected was almost too good to be true, almost creepy. They had already searched a few corridors and came across no one, and no sign of Matt.

He nodded to Rig without even looking at him. The two of them were so well tuned into each other's magic and body language that they did not need to look at each other to know what the other was doing.

Madgwick turned sideways to look at the two guards rushing from behind. His dust dropped to form a glittering long whip, which he coiled into his hand. He dropped into a deep crouch and waited until they were in striking distance.

The oncoming guards had their swords out, ready for battle. However, Madgwick could see their eyes were full of confusion. Madgwick did not realise that the broken magic of the castle had an effect on the guards too.

Rig smiled at the two guards coming from the front. He did not have a friendly looking face to start with, so to see him smile was a little disconcerting and made the guards' eyes widen.

One guard frowned, making his small eyes seem to sink deeper into his face. His wide mouth was outlined with a huge moustache, which he started to twirl. The other guard had bushy eyebrows that almost touched in the middle of his forehead. His thin lips were pulled in a straight line.

Rig dropped his dust to reveal a long glittering sword. He spun it around once, twice in his hand almost if he was testing the grip. The fluid movement ended with the sword in striking pose at his shoulder.

"Want to play, boys?"

They pulled their swords and the fight began. The clang of the swords colliding was ear-shattering.

So much for a quiet in and out thought Madgwick as they played with the guards.

Rig made them skip and hop as he advanced towards the guards. His skill outmatched theirs by far. Rig wrinkled his nose as if he was annoyed that the sword play was wasting time.

"Madgwick?" he asked.

"Yes, Rig?"

In a single manoeuvre, he turned the guards around so that they were between Madgwick and himself. With a crack, Madgwick captured two guards in his whip, and he flicked it around and sent the guards spinning into the other two, their heads colliding, knocking them out cold.

"Something is wrong. They know we are coming and these are the only guards we find? We must be wary of a trap," muttered Madgwick as they carried on down the corridor.

They had already searched half the castle and were fast approaching the throne room.

Jeff moved down the corridor, trying not to make any noise on the stone floors. He glanced into each room and sneaked past onto the next. He was looking for Matt and strained to hear any noise of a fight, which would lead him the direction of the warriors.

He was so tense that he hiccupped with laughter when he came across two guards lying knocked out on the floor. At least he was going in the right direction. He raced down the corridor, turned the corner and came face to face with the warriors.

His eyes widened and his arms instinctively pulled up as he yelped and jumped back, his heart thumping hard. "It's me, it's me," he gasped.

The warriors were in a fight stance, ready to attack. Their faces looked like stone and their eyes glowed bright purple.

Madgwick was the first to scatter his dust. His mouth dropped open in shock. "Jeff! What are you doing here?"

"What did we tell you, where is Rhed? Why did you not stay in the forest?" Rig's jaw bulged as if he was clenching his teeth in anger.

"I tried to call you from the entrance, but then a guard came and then I could not get out. But never mind about that, I came to tell you …"

"What do you mean, you could not get out?" interrupted Madgwick.

"The entrance is blocked with orange lightning. Well, that's what it looks like, but I came to tell you …"

"Damn, the castle enchantment is back in place. We are going to have a hard time getting out now," muttered Rig.

"Why did you not stay in the forest? Why are you here?" growled Rig, his face clouded over, a thunderstorm waiting to happen.

"That's what I'm trying to tell you. The old man forgot to tell you that Holka is Quin ..."

"Who?"

"Gwen something, she is a warrior who has been trapped here, uhh, Rig?"

Rig's face went white and he stumbled. Madgwick caught him and propped him up against the wall.

Madgwick searched Jeff's face. "Is the name Gwyndion? Is that the name?"

Jeff bobbed his head up and down.

"She is here and alive," whispered Rig.

"Come on Rig, they're bound to be together. Thirza said in the tunnel that she was going to try and get to Matt. Let's keep moving, we'll find them both and then fight our way out."

Madgwick turned to Jeff who swallowed loudly at the look on Madgwick's face. "I want you on my heels. I want you so close that if I stop, you will be bumping into me, you clear?"

Jeff grinned. "Clear."

41

They continued through the hallways, now hugely concerned that they had not met with any more guards after the four that they encountered earlier. Unknown to them, the guards were also entrapped in the castle enchantment. They had started to remember their past lives and families left behind and when they heard that the tunnels were unprotected, they quickly moved to the exits trying to get out while they could.

The three of them raced down the corridors, briefly checking rooms but finding them all empty.

"There's no one left in the dungeon, so she's not down there," grumbled Rig.

"A whole horde of people stumbled out of the tunnel, so I'm sure they all got out," Jeff answered.

"Well, we have searched all the rooms off all the corridors, and Jeff said he checked all the rooms on the floor below. No Matt and no Gwyndion. It's just this room left. Judging by the double doors, it looks like an important room."

The doors opened to show a huge room with a gaping, blue-sky hole at the far end. The blue beckoned to them, indicating a way out. The exit was in sharp contrast to the castle, the doors broken and the walls crumbled on either side. It was as if someone had forced their way in.

It looked like a rake had pulled up the floor slabs. Standing in the middle of the room was a woman wearing an emerald green dress. A bright yellow ribbon twined around the bodice. Her black hair flowed around her shoulders. She spoke without turning around.

"Welcome, warriors! I am delighted to finally meet you."

Wiedzma turned to face them and Madgwick gasped. Her green eyes were narrowed and he almost felt the cold blast from her stare. Her mouth was twisted in a cruel sneer. Her face was a flawless white with rosy cheeks and a dark mole right in the middle of her chin, like a dimple.

She glanced at Grzegorz and snapped. "Grzegorz, can you please stop your foot from snoring? It's annoying!"

Grzegorz bared his teeth at her and stumbled over to a chair nearby, dragging his foot, which was still snoring loudly.

Madgwick and Rig strode up to the witch but made sure not to get too close. It was never healthy to be in striking distance of a witch. Jeff followed closely behind.

Rig's voice was cold and raspy when he spoke. "Where are they?"

"They? Oh you mean the child and Gwyndion. Shame, until earlier today she did not even know she was a warrior."

Her lips pulled up in a half a smile like she was sharing a secret. "She belongs with me now. You will never find her, and if I am not mistaken, you can't get out of this castle, so ..."

"We will never join you, and nor will Gwyndion," said Madgwick, his dust held loosely in his hands. He dared not blink in case he missed her attack.

Rig was also on guard, half in a crouch ready for the first sign of attack.

"Oh I think you will join me. You can't get out. You see, the doorways are sealed again. Seems I have lost most of my cowardly guards. But I think having two fierce warriors to guard me will be excellent." She laughed and twirled around. "Wonderful for me and my business, keeping people in line. You know, obey the witch or else!" The rest of her words melted away into her cackling.

"Where is my brother?" Jeff's voice was low, his hands clenched in fists by his side.

Madgwick winced as if he was hoping Jeff would make himself invisible while they were dealing with the witch.

Wiedzma stopped as if she had been slapped. Her eyes bulged at the sight of Jeff and she whispered as if she dared not say the words out loud. "The older brother, right here in my castle, a dream catcher!"

Madgwick and Rig did not need to communicate with each other to agree that this was a no-way-in-hell situation. They did not wait for her to attack.

Rig and Madgwick unleashed long silver glittering whips, working in perfect coordination. They flicked and teased Wiedzma, pulling at her hair, her dress, flicking at her hands and making her shriek in pain and fury. A storm started to build up behind her, but Madgwick was not having any of that. Using his whip, he changed the direction of the swirling wind so that her tornado could not form properly. An attack like this was unexpected. Madgwick grinned to himself. He was sure Wiedzma had expected them to have more respect for her as a witch.

Jeff dived to one side to make sure he was out of the line of dust fire.

Madgwick was waiting for the sign that the shock of the initial attack was over. He saw her grimace as she ignored the flicks, the sharp bursts of pain inflicted by the whips.

Wiedzma frowned as if concentrating on her magic. Pulling her power together, she drew her arms in and then shoved them out in front of her, unleashing the energy.

Madgwick was hit with a wave of magic, which sent him flying and rolling on the floor. The force was so great that he could not get back up. His dust was swirling around him out of control. He tried to form a wall to protect himself but could not get his dust to play along. Wiedzma was just too strong.

The pain hit Madgwick like needles passing through his body. It was so severe that all he could do was gasp. Madgwick's magic was quite strong in itself but he was no match for the power of Wiedzma.

As suddenly as the pain hit it was gone again. Madgwick looked up to see he had a glittering barrier around him. Snapping his head, he saw Rig's face twisted in fierce concentration.

Wiedzma twisted around, snarling in frustration and turned her attention to Rig.

Her attention was on Rig but she was backing towards Jeff who was behind a chair.

"Do something, do something," Jeff muttered furiously to himself.

Madgwick flexed his hand and cast his dust to try to help but Rig's barrier was so complete that he could not penetrate it with his own dust. He was protected from Wiedzma but he could not help Rig either.

Rig was considered the best warrior with good reason. Besides his experience, he had immense power and when he was angry that power doubled.

Rig had a furious look on his face. Gwyndion was gone, again, and it was this witch's fault. And where the heck was the child? He did not have many friends. Everyone apart from Madgwick thought he was bad tempered and steered away from him.

Madgwick saw Wiedzma turn her attention to Rig. Her smirk was back and Madgwick did not like that for one moment.

Her power pushed at Rig's wall, seeking a way in, but the wall stood firm and impenetrable. Yet slowly Wiedzma managed to push Rig and his wall backward.

Rig's shoes started to slide on the polished marble floor. He redoubled his efforts but kept sliding backwards slowly.

With a groan Madgwick watched Wiedzma laughing wildly as she neared Jeff.

She taunted Rig. "You can't fight me, warrior. You can hold me back but only so long before I overpower you. You might as well accept that you are mine now."

The witch spoke with a sneer. "If you submit now, you will see that I can be merciful. In time you will forget your old life. It's going to happen, so let it happen now. Save yourself the hurt and pain."

Elder Galagedra appeared in the chamber. Before the dust had settled around him, he was rushing down the aisle towards the brightly glowing globe.

Galagedra's frown was deep set and his jaw stiff from worry.

Jozephus turned at the sound of Galagedra approaching. He appeared just as worried, his normally rosy cheeks pale. He pinched the ends of his moustache and twirled them.

Galagedra nodded and filled him in. "The spell weavers have begun to weave a doorway spell. Most of the elders have gone to assist with their power as we don't have much time."

"How did the message come in?"

"It came through the moon rune door from the great dragon Azghar. How he came to be with the warriors, we do not know." He sighed. "While it is of great relief that Azghar is there, it also means they are in trouble, or he would not have interfered too much. The message was simple: 'Cannot use moonglow doorway, open new doorway at Emerald Pool.'"

Jozephus noticed how Galagedra's blue eyes were shining bright with worry. "How much time do we have?" he asked.

Galagedra stared into the pulsating globe. "We have until twilight, which is the most magical time of the day. This is when the moon shines its first powerful beam. And that is our chance to open the doorway. That is our only chance." Galagedra closed his eyes. "We will only be able to do this once."

Jozephus nodded his head. "We will be ready in time."

"That is not our only problem," said Galagedra. He waved his hand in front of the globe. Jozephus gasped as the face of an old man fleeted across the globe before vanishing again.

"Who is that?"

"Look carefully. It's Thirza. Thirza many years on."

"But ... but how?"

"I think we would like to know that too. We searched everywhere for him. If he ended up in Drakmere that explains why we could not see him or find him. The magic around Drakmere is so strong. It's impregnable."

Jozephus blinked.

"If we manage to get him out now, we need to prepare his family. He has been missing for many, many years. I will go and see the daughter, and explain about the children at the same time."

Jozephus blinked once more. "What about Angie?"

"If I know Angie, she is in the thick of things. As strong and brave as our warriors are, they will need all the help they can get to get all three boys and Thirza out."

* * *

Ella was standing outside the back door, glaring at the darkness of the forest. A mist was creeping through the trees circling each tree before moving to the next. She watched the mist for a moment then shivered. It was creepy, as if it was looking for something, or someone.

"Why do you think they aren't in the forest? You seem quite sure." Jeff's father came to stand behind her, scanning the forest.

"The answer is there, in my head. But every time I search for it, I end up thinking about …" She sighed and felt her cheeks redden before she picked up, "fudge. I end up thinking about *fudge*. I just can't help it."

She looked at her husband, but he stared at her blankly. "They will come home *through* the forest but they are not *in* the forest, which does not make any sense to me either."

"I'll get you something warm to drink while we wait." He turned and went back into the kitchen.

Ella leaned forward as if she could see through the mist. And then she saw a dark figure striding through the mist towards them.

"He seems familiar … like fudge," Ella whispered to herself and slapped her hand against the railing. She took a deep breath and started down the steps onto the damp grass.

The figure stopped a little way from her, his face hidden inside a hood. Ella blinked as glittering silver dust rained down around her. Her mouth opened and her eyes became windows to her past as her memories were returned.

"Hello Ella," the man spoke. "I am an elder of Sandustian and my name is Galagedra." Ella shivered, but his voice was gentle. "You may or may not remember me, but I have come to talk to you about the children."

"The boys? You know where they are? Are they alright?" Ella grit her teeth, fearing the answer.

"I know where they are, and we are working to get them home. They are in Drakmere, they are well and they are not alone."

239

"Drakmere?" Ella gasped. "They have been taken to Drakmere, just like I was? Is ..." Ella searched her memory. "Are Gwyndion and Marigold with them?"

"Gwyndion no, but Rig is with them." Galagedra smiled softly. "Although we don't call Rig by his full name, Marigold, unless we would like to feel his wrath."

Ella smiled weakly. "When are they coming back? Are they coming back tonight?"

"We are working on that now. But Ella ... I have also come to talk to you about your father."

"My father? He disappeared in the forest many years ago. He went looking for me and never returned."

"He is with the children. He is helping to bring them home."

"My father is alive? He is with my children?" Ella swayed and dropped to the floor in a near faint.

With a wave of the hand, Galagedra's dust caught her and lowered her gently to the floor. The dust covered her like a blanket, preventing the damp chill of the grass from seeping into her.

* * *

Rig's wall was starting to lose its sparkle and began to shrink under Wiedzma's force. He needed to stop his slide from gaining momentum, so he dropped the wall around Madgwick.

Madgwick saw the wall come down and instantly rolled away from Wiedzma. Before she knew what was happening he had somersaulted over her and slid neatly under Rig's wall.

Madgwick threw his own power behind Rig's wall, determined to push Wiedzma back. Even with both of them at work, they were still slipping backwards slowly. The witch was just too powerful.

Their dust started shaking in the air and both of them knew it was just a matter of time before it crumbled under her attack.

Jeff was watching with huge eyes. The witch was overpowering the two warriors, and if he did not do something they were as good as finished. He did not know what he could do. He did not have magic or magic dust and he doubted that throwing things at Wiedzma would make any difference at all. Then he glanced at Grzegorz who was on the edge of his chair, his eyes bright as if he was enjoying the show.

In desperation, Jeff rubbed his temple with the tips of his fingers. He pictured a room dark as night, a single spotlight highlighting a filing cabinet. In his mind he was running to the cabinet and flipping through files, oblivious to what he was looking for and worse, not knowing how he was going to use the information in the file.

Just as Jeff despaired that he would never find the right file, he dropped to his knees. From behind his eyes came a blinding light. Flashes flew across his vision like a movie reel and raced across his mind. The images were moving so fast he could not distinguish between them.

Jeff reached out mentally, not knowing what he was reaching for, but at this stage he could not really control what was happening. Without warning, soap bubbles exploded into the air around him. Bubbles of all sizes floated towards Wiedzma. Jeff's mouth dropped open.

"Where is this coming from?" he gasped to Madgwick. His shoulders were hunched up with uncertainty.

Wiedzma was swatting at the bubbles, her face screwed up as she grimaced at the bubbles popping into her face and hair. "Ugh, stop it!"

Rig turned to Jeff, and snarled, "Perhaps something a little more effective?"

Jeff could feel a vein in his forehead jutting out as he strained for the dark room and filing cabinet. It was now or never. By the looks of the warriors' faces, they were reaching the end of their limits. He concentrated on a weapon and grabbed at the next image.

Splat! Splat! Wiedzma screeched in pain. Jeff opened his eyes and dared to look. His eyes stretched wide and he bit his knuckles to prevent himself laughing out loud.

Wiedzma was being torpedoed by a hovering paint-ball gun, shooting paint balls in different colours at her. She was at quite close range so it hurt. Her dress was splattered with orange and then she was hit on the neck and hair with an ugly mustard yellow paint. She was furious as she struggled to hold the warriors but already she had lost focus and Rig and Madgwick had stopped sliding.

Wiedzma, holding her one hand towards the warriors, turned toward Jeff. He gulped at the furious look on her face.

"What the heck is this? It hurts! You're worse than your brat brother, and what did you shoot me with? Is it a potion?" She staggered back a bright blue paint ball hit her in the stomach.

The gun pelted her again and she yelled in anger and pain.

43

Madgwick was racking his brains for an alternative way out of this mess. It was unbelievable how Jeff was using his dream catcher ability. He was a natural. But the fact was that they still had not found Matt or Gwyndion and that they were trapped here with Wiedzma. Their powers against her would not last forever.

Then Jeff heard a high-pitched whining sound. At first it just seemed like noise, but then it started to sound like a high-powered superbike. He turned to Madgwick and saw hope flash across his face.

The sound came closer and closer until it seemed to be right on top of them.

Angie flew in over their heads, tumbling through the door. Thanks to the quick hover spell she cast she landed nimbly on her feet. But she did not stop. She whirled back around, her face dark with anger as she stormed back to the open door.

Leaning out of the door she yelled, "I said get me in nice and close, not toss me like a bag of potatoes over the handlebars!" There was a pause before she shrieked again. "I don't care if that was the quickest way in. I did not expect to be *thrown* in."

Angie pointed her finger at whatever she was yelling at before turning around to face them with a serene smile on her face.

Wiedzma's mouth was hanging open and Grzegorz was peering around the back of the chair where he was hiding from the paint balls flying across the room.

Jeff's heart started to pound with joy when he noticed Madgwick's wide smile.

Angie glanced around the room, taking in every detail before commenting rather drily, "What nonsense is this? Is this the very best you can do, Wiedzma?" Angie put her finger on her mouth as if she were deep in thought and spoke in a high-pitched girly voice nothing like Wiedzma's. "Oh wait: I am the powerful witch Wiedzma. I know I will just push them around the room and then they will surrender."

She clapped her hands and the incredible force released the two warriors. They stopped sliding. Immediately they dropped their dust, which flowed back into their hands. Madgwick felt the warmth of his power rebuilding.

Jeff's paintball gun popped into thin air and Jeff dropped to his knees in exhaustion. He stared up at this strange woman that had just walked in. Was she on their side or were they in for another fight?

Wiedzma howled. "What are you doing here? How did you get in? Aaaaahgggh."

She made a wild movement with her arm as if she was throwing something at Angie, trying to catch her unawares.

Angie was looking around the room, hardly interested in Wiedzma. Casually she turned to Rig and said, "Toss some dust."

Not sure what Angie was doing, he obliged and tossed a handful of dust in the air. As the glittering dust rained down, it revealed an invisible dagger pointing at Angie's heart.

244

The dagger had stopped halfway across the room. It hovered, not moving forward and not dropping to the ground. It was quivering in its attempt to break free of the invisible force that was stopping it from reaching its target.

Wiedzma gasped. No more than two paces from where she was standing were twenty invisible daggers, all pointing at her. They were not quivering, not held back by some force, they were dead calm, just waiting for the attack word.

Jeff really liked this strange woman. She was calm and radiated power.

"Really, Wiedzma? You need to stop wasting your time with feeble creatures such as … him." Angie nodded at Grzegorz who was sitting in the chair again as if he thought that this was the safest place to watch the fight. "And spend more time with witches. They could teach you a few things. Obviously you still have a lot to learn."

Angie turned to face Wiedzma and yelled, "Like how not to kidnap children! Not to mess with warriors, witches and dragons, and how to stop making shimmers."

Glaring at Grzegorz again, she nodded at him and, whoop, an emerald green frog was sitting on the chair that the king had occupied moments before.

Wiedzma was beyond angry. "You come here, uninvited and you insult me. Then you try to kill me with daggers. These warriors are mine. The dream catcher is mine. They are not leaving here, and for that matter nor are you. The castle enchantment has repaired itself and is complete and flawless! Oh how I am going to enjoy making you suffer."

She clicked her fingers at the frog and whoop, he was back to Grzegorz again. The king looked left and right rapidly, his tongue hanging out.

"Wiedzma, you are so funny. At least you still have a huge sense of humour!" giggled Angie. Then she turned to Grzegorz who was still sitting in his chair with his mouth hanging open, looking from one witch to the other. Angie nodded and whoop he was a frog again. "Ribbit," he croaked.

"Time to go, boys." Angie snapped her fingers at them.

Madgwick reached back and hauled Jeff to his feet in a single fluid movement. They stepped closer to Angie, keeping Jeff between them. Madgwick was not sure what the plan was but he could tell it was going to happen fast.

Rig muttered to Angie, "Matt is at her castle and she forced Gwyndion to go there too."

Angie frowned at this news. "Shooting Stars! We will find her. I promise, Rig. I will help you find Gwyndion, but right now we have to get Jeff out of here."

"Ha!" yelled Wiedzma. "You will never find her, unless you stay. You will never see her again!"

Rig did not say anything. A promise from Angie was worth all the dust in Sandustian. He trusted her completely on her promise.

Wiedzma threw her arms round her head. With her tornado suddenly roaring to life, the room went very dark. They heard the evil witch shrieking at the top of her voice in some strange language that Madgwick could not understand. Furniture lifted off the floor, curtains ripped, loose floor slabs lifted and swept into the current of wind. The wind was pulling everything into its force.

Angie pulled them backward until they were close to the entrance. Rig tried to step past but it was blocked with an invisible wall. Wiedzma was right, they were trapped.

Then, to no one in particular, Angie said, "Now".

"Noooooow." Nothing happened. "Alright already, I'm sorry, you were right! I *did* say 'the fastest way in'. I am not mad at being thrown over the handlebars, not really! Okay ... can we go now?"

Something rustled in the background. "Yes," she screeched, "You are the best! Now?"

Jeff was giving Madgwick a look that said "really?"

There was a loud revving noise that became louder until something shattered behind them. Angie's broom had grown into a Harley with a side car attached and it raced into the room. The broom-bike skidded to a stop.

Madgwick could hardly believe this was the same broom as before. It had evolved from a wooden handle ending in straw bristles into a sleek wooden motorbike with a seat, foot rests and wooden handlebars. The body had a green leaf motif. It was revving, itching to go.

Angie jumped on her bike and pushed Jeff into the side car. "Stay down," she said.

She turned to Madgwick and looked him straight in the eye. Her face was a few inches away from his. "You have to stay! Trust me, Madgwick. Don't doubt me."

Stunned, Madgwick nodded numbly. He understood. It was his turn to sacrifice himself for Sandustian.

She hopped onto her broom and ordered, "Rig, get on the bike."

"But Madg—" started Rig.

"Don't but but me, Madgwick will be fine, I have seen to it. Get on the bike. We have to get out of here now."

"I don't like this one bit," Rig muttered but he climbed on behind her.

The broom-bike lurched forward, so fast that Jeff almost lost his grip. It raced away from Madgwick going in the same direction as

247

the wind. They went around the room gaining momentum from the force of the wind. With a burst of speed they raced for the window. Another shattering noise was to be heard and they were out, flying into the blue.

As they broke out the window, Wiedzma screamed. Her plans to keep her dream catcher had just flown out of the window. She stamped her foot. "Drat that Angie!"

She ran to the window and pounded on the invisible barrier; her enchantment was still in place. Next she grabbed a piece of wood lying on the floor and threw it out of the window. It flew out with a shattering noise. There was the loophole she had not thought about. Objects could go through the barrier. People on their own could not, but objects carrying people could pass through.

Then she noticed Grzegorz was still in frog form. She stilled her breathing, turned around, waved her hand and muttered a few words to change him back to normal. She turned to face Madgwick who was crouched in fighting stance, his dust bouncing in his hands in anticipation of an attack.

"So, they left you behind. So nice of them." She turned casually and then whirled around without warning, throwing her power at Madgwick to knock him out cold.

Madgwick lifted his wall of magic but not quickly enough. Wiedzma's power pushed through his dust and knocked him clean off his feet.

He felt it hit like a concrete block. His vision went dark and he fell to the floor.

Wiedzma punched her fist into the air, thrilled she had overpowered the warrior. She screamed as Madgwick started to fade and ran over to him to try to stop the fade but in a blink he was gone. Wiedzma grabbed her hair, oblivious to the paint on her hands as she screamed.

Grzegorz sat staring ahead, his tongue darting in and out.

She dropped her head and raised her hands.

And that was when she started enchanting shimmers into the room. They swarmed around her, fuelled by her anger and desire for revenge. Soon the room could not take any more and they spilled out into the corridor, flowing until every room in the castle was filled with snapping, evil, squirming shimmers, wanting to rip flesh and cause pain.

They pushed against the windows and doors, trying to force their way through the castle enchantment that was holding them in place. Shimmers flooded the castle and the dungeons until there was no more space and the place was ready to burst.

Finally Wiedzma broke the castle enchantment and sent the shimmers after her fleeing captives. This time she was joining the fight. A large shimmer stopped next to her and hovered while she stepped onto him.

Grzegorz leapt from his chair like a frog and grabbed hold of Wiedzma's dress.

"I am coming with you, ribbit ribbit!" he yelled.

Wiedzma ignored him, holding onto the black misty ropes she had conjured up. Her shimmer flew around the room and then out the door. Around her the other shimmers exploded from the castle doors, windows, chimneys and soared into the sky.

44

A ngie's broom-bike flew like the wind. They went faster than they had ever flown before, making for the tree line of the forest. Rhed and Thirza were waiting in those trees and they had to reach them before Wiedzma and her shimmers did. They had a five minute headstart, no more, maybe less.

Angie was quiet, deep in thought about the shimmers that were heading their way and worried about how everyone was going get to the doorway, which was quite a distance away.

Rig yelled over the rush of the wind. "Angie. What about Madgwick? I know you said you have seen to it but I need to know, how are we going to get him out? We could not find Matt and apparently Gwyndion is also there!"

Angie screamed into the wind. "Matt is not in that castle. That is not our worry right now. We have to get to Jeff and Bloo back to the doorway. I don't know if you noticed but we are going to have a lot of bad company very soon."

Jeff yelled back, "His name is Rhed not Bloo."

They had reached the tree line. Jeff and Rig hopped off the broom-bike while it was slowing, giving it no time to stop, and then they ran onto the trees. Angie stayed on her broom and flew alongside them.

"Rhed!" yelled Jeff and Rig together. Then they heard the scrambling of a quick descent from the trees.

Rhed had reached the bottom branch, lowering Thirza to the floor.

"We could not find him, Rhed, he was not there. We have to run, and fast. The shimmers are coming, they're just behind us."

"Shimmers are coming?" asked Rhed breathless from helping Thirza down. He had not forgotten his last encounter with the shimmers, and he was not keen on another. "What do we do now?"

"We start by running," answered Rig. He nodded to Thirza. "Can you get yourself to safety?"

Thirza squeezed Jeff's shoulder and nodded, "Yes, go, go, get the kids to the doorway."

Jeff yelled, "No way, I am not leaving my grandfather here as well. He goes or I stay."

Rig's head whipped from Jeff to Thirza. "Grandfather? When did that happen? We leave you alone for ten minutes and you end up with a grandfather!" He threw his hands in the air. "Explain later. We don't have time now." He had left enough people behind him. Matt and Gwyndion, Madgwick: he was not going to argue about leaving a grandfather behind.

The air started to ripple next to them.

Angie puffed out the air in her lungs. "It's about time."

"Stand back," Rig ordered the boys, bouncing his dust in reaction to the new threat. Just as everyone was looking at the ripple and backing away, there was a loud pop and Madgwick appeared out of thin air. There he lay, unconscious on the golden pine needles covering the forest floor.

Angie knelt down and passed her hand gently over Madgwick's face while muttering a few words.

Madgwick woke up with a start and looked around. He got to his feet and nodded to Angie. It was the work of the spell she had cast that would appear when he needed it the most.

"If that was the rescue spell, then it was a little late, Angie. It would have been better if it had activated *before* she nailed me."

"You're welcome, Madgwick," Angie snapped.

Rig patted Madgwick on the back and Jeff beamed from ear to ear.

"Let's go," yelled Angie.

Angie waved wildly at Thirza to shoo him into the side car while Madgwick and Rig once again threw dust into the air to form off-road bikes, glittering and sparkling. Once the boys were mounted with their helmets on, they were off dashing through the forest, trying to put distance between them, the castle and the shimmers.

Madgwick shouted over the roar of the bikes. "What happened to all the people from the dungeons, did they get out?"

Thirza yelled in response. "They separated into groups and headed into different directions making their way home. They will be safe. Plenty of guards went with them. I was quite surprised to see so many guards come out. They know what to do."

"What happened with Holka and Matt?" he yelled back to Madgwick.

Jeff answered. "We could not find them. Was that the girl you stayed behind to protect, is she Gwyndion?"

"Fat lot of good that did. She is still in the castle and here I am, running away. She will be tortured for sure now!"

"What do you mean you stayed to protect her?" asked Angie.

They were racing through the forest, ducking under low branches, ramping over tree roots. They bounced over rocks and splashed through brooks. It would have been great fun if they did not have the threat of the shimmers behind them. They looked over their shoulders often but there was no sign of them yet. The trees were so thick that it was not likely that they would see them coming until they were right on top of them.

Thirza answered Angie. "The last time a child was taken, two Warriors came to the rescue, Rig here and Gwyndion. I went through the moonglow doorway and ended up at the castle. The child was rescued but one of the warriors, Gwyndion, was trapped. I was so grateful that she helped rescue my daughter that I could not leave her to the mercy of Grzegorz, not if I could help her."

Thirza paused for breath. "I hid her away until no one would be able to read her mind with magic, or *want* to read her mind, and then introduced her as Holka. As long as she did not remember and as long as no one could recognise her as a warrior, she was safe. It was cruel, yes, but I could not get her out of the castle's enchantment and at least she was free to roam about the castle and enchantment perimeter. She was not home but she was not unhappy."

Angie frowned as she absorbed the story.

Thirza continued, "I was going to stay there as long as she was trapped. I was always looking for a way to get us both out. Then I found out about the plan to kidnap another child. I knew that I could not leave, not just yet."

Angie blinked at Thirza and forgot about the bike controls. It lurched, almost throwing him out of the side car. "Your daughter?" she yelled.

"The dream catcher line. My mother comes from Jeff's world, my father from this world. It makes my children and grandchildren excellent dream catchers. I did not even know that Matt was my grandchild until I saw Jeff, who looks like his mother. I never thought they would target my own grandchildren. When will this stop, will my family ever be safe?"

45

A howl came through the trees. It was the shimmers catching up, and it would not be long now before they would be able to see them. They broke through the trees and raced across another meadow. As they reached the bottom and dashed over the stream, there was a little boy running down the hill towards him. He was laughing.

"Matt!" yelled Jeff, pointing ahead.

Rhed joined in, half standing in his eagerness to point the boy out. "It's Matt!"

Matt fell into silhouette as a huge dragon came over the rise. The dragon seemed to be huffing and puffing, swaying his massive head to and fro. The sapphire scales glistened in the afternoon sunlight and looked like the startling blue waters of a cool ocean. His tail was high above his body and the white spines stood out like daggers. Any minute now he was going to catch the boy and eat him. Rhed and Jeff screamed to Matt to run.

"Do something!" Jeff screamed directly into Madgwick's ear, making him wince.

The dragon reared up and roared fiercely into the air, a high flame shooting out of his mouth, which was lined with razor sharp teeth. Matt screamed and darted left and then right, running as fast as his little legs could carry him. The dragon lifted into the air and swooped over Matt, caught the boy in his talons, flipped him in the air and then Matt disappeared, screeching, into his mouth.

Angie yelled above the hysterical screams from Jeff and Rhed. "Oh, stop screaming like little girls, they are just playing." She turned to Thirza and continued conversationally, "I don't really like their game either. It rather gave me a fright when they first did it, but then who exactly listens to me?"

She turned back to the others and screamed uncontrollably, "Stooooppp iiiit!" Everyone stopped screaming and looked at her.

"They are just *playing*," she said slowly so that they understood.

They looked back at the dragon darting left and right, his mouth opened wide. He turned his head to face them so that they had a full view of his fierce mouth with rows of sharp shiny teeth. Matt was standing with his legs spread, a foot on each side of a tooth, and with his arms he braced himself on two hanging teeth. He was yelling, "Left, right, left, right," and the dragon dipped his head in time with the instructions.

Then they both looked down and saw their audience racing towards them.

Matt yelled, "Jeff! Look Azghar, it's Jeff!"

Azghar lowered his head and Matt wobbled out of his mouth, running towards his brother who had already leapt off the dust bike in his rush to get to Matt.

Jeff grabbed Matt and hugged his brother fiercely. He drew back, and searched into his face, and asked, "You okay?"

Matt nodded enthusiastically, his eyes bright, his face flushed in evidence of the great game he had been playing. Just then Azghar lowered his huge head next to Matt's, staring at Jeff.

"This is Azghar," said Matt simply when Jeff gulped and took a step back.

Azghar stared at Jeff, then blinked slowly and tilted his head towards Matt. "Are you sure he is your brother? He does not look like you," he said.

Matt fondly swatted Azghar on the nose. "He's my brother for sure."

Jeff could not understand a word Azghar was saying, but everyone else seemed to, even Matt. It was quite freaky seeing Matt with a dragon as big as a three-storey house, and they were obviously close.

By now everyone had caught up and was milling around, all talking at once, frantic and looking behind them for any signs of the shimmers.

Thirza bumped everyone out of the way in his rush to get to Matt, went down on his knees in front of the boy and held him by the arms. Looking into Matt's widened eyes, he exclaimed, "Matt! My poor boy, I am so sorry I was so horrible, that I made you cry so many times."

Ignoring Angie's stony glare, he continued. "I had to keep you unhappy, make you cry at least once a day, or the spell that they put on you would have worked and you would have forgotten everyone, and they would have won. I am your grandpa, Matt."

Matt lowered his eyes at the sudden display of emotion from Thirza. He gave a sideways look at Jeff for confirmation. Jeff shrugged at Matt. He was not sure.

Matt looked at Azghar, who was staring hard at Thirza. Azghar dipped his head at Thirza and Madgwick raised an eyebrow when Thirza bowed his head back at Azghar.

"Hello Azghar. How over the years I have wished for you to appear and come to save us. Holka ... Gwyndion and me."

Azghar touched Thirza's head. The old man stayed still, which is very wise when a dragon is breathing all over you. Thirza's face relaxed as his memories flowed to Azghar. Azghar was not stealing them like Wiedzma would have. He was just scanning them to make sure Thirza was not under an enchantment.

Satisfied that all Thirza said and thought was true, he said, "I am sorry, Thirza, my old friend. I have been away. I will explain, but not today."

Azghar nodded at Matt. "He is your grandfather."

Matt tentatively smiled at Thirza.

Thirza nodded, smiled a little, as if not expecting an explanation from the great Azghar, and then said, "Thank you, Azghar, thank you so much for casting that protection spell so long ago. It helped to keep me safe from that castle, and from the witch, which in turn helped me keep Gwyndion and Matt safe. She tried so hard to break through the spell over the years but she never could and she could not figure out why."

Azghar nodded to Thirza and turned to stare at the warriors.

"I know Rig, greetings, Rig," he nodded at Rig. "I don't know you. Madgwick, is it? I don't know you but I like the smell of you. You are young but will be a powerful warrior. Your strength is evident in the magic that surrounds you, and you have a good heart, a strong mind."

Madgwick bit his lip as if he did not know what to say, so he just nodded his appreciation. He had heard stories about Azghar the dragon, but the dragon had not been seen for such a long time that no one really knew whether he existed or not.

Madgwick, nervous that all this chit-chat was costing them time, cleared his throat. "Please don't take offence, but we have quite a horde of shimmers behind us. Can we catch up later with all our hellos and small talk. We have a long way to go to get back to the doorway. We have to leave now."

Angie turned to Azghar with a bright smile. "It's true, they are all coming, as many as Wiedzma could manage!"

Lifting his head so that he could see everyone, he said, "We do not need to go to the moonglow doorway. It's too far, and we will never get everyone there in time. I have sent a message to the elders and if they manage in time then they will open another doorway very close to here. Thirza and," he looked at Rhed.

"Bloo," supplied Angie, grinning.

"Thirza and Bloo go with Angie on her super broom," he said winking at her broom bike with his huge sapphire blue eye. The broom bristled with pride and joy at being singled out by Azghar.

Both Madgwick and Rig said together, "Rhed, his name is Rhed."

"I will take Matt, Jeff, and the two warriors, who can ride on my back, if that's okay with you?" he turned to Madgwick and Rig expectantly.

Still looking at the two warriors, he said, "It will not be easy. You will have to keep the shimmers from my back while we are moving at high speed."

Madgwick and Rig grinned broadly as if the thought of travelling at warp speed on a powerful dragon's back while wiping out shimmers was beyond exciting.

Azghar lifted his head and turned back to face the direction they had just come from. He could hear the whistling of the shimmers tearing through the forest. Time to go. Chit-chat was definitely over.

Rhed had a smile on his face as he held onto Angie. He did not mind riding with her. Being so close to a dragon was just too much like asking a velociraptor to tea. Thirza climbed into the side car and the broom bike was revving to go.

Rhed yelled to Angie, "Why can't Matt and Jeff come with us?"

"With so many shimmers chasing us, they will be better protected by Azghar. He will rip them apart before he allows them to touch a hair on Matt's head, and I suppose Jeff too. They are the ones Wiedzma wants, but I am sure she would use you as a hostage. I will keep you safe." Angie yelled back.

Angie yelled over the noise of her broom-bike revving violently. "Which way, Azghar?"

"Head for the forest in the north. Once you get there, circle the diamond tree twice and once around the ruby bush. Hover over the starlite stone for ten seconds and the emerald pool will be revealed to you. That is where our doorway will be opened. I have already prepared the magic bridge. All you need to do is forge the link and keep it open. Go ahead, we will hold them back as long as possible to give you time to get there and start the process."

"I know the place," Angie muttered, turning her broom in the right direction.

Azghar sighed. It was time to take off. "Here we go again." He flapped his wings, fprrrruuppppp, fpruuppppp. Matt's laugher rang through the air.

Jeff was looking from Matt to Azghar. He started to grin. It was impossible not to grin at Matt's infectious laughter. He was about to say something when Azghar suddenly dropped his head so that his steely eyes were level with Jeff, Madgwick and Rig.

"Be careful what you say right now. I allow Matt to laugh because I like him, and he is little. Let me be very clear. *I am not farting.* The sound you are hearing is my wind chamber, which propels my wings in flight, and if I even just hear a sigh, or a hint of a giggle from any of you, warrior or not, brother or not, I WILL EAT YOU!"

The last three words were said slowly leaving no illusion that Azghar was not serious. The dragon turned away, leaving Jeff's mouth hanging open. Rig had a smirk on his face but Madgwick looked as shocked as Jeff.

Azghar swiftly pulled Jeff and the still giggling Matt into his talons. Jeff was too hyped up about the shimmers to relax but there was no way he could fall. It was like standing in a basket. The heat radiating from Azghar was comforting.

Madgwick and Rig leapt up onto Azghar's back, using their dust to secure them to large spines.

In a fluid movement Azghar leapt into the air. Madgwick shook his head and gasped in awe at the unbelievable power beneath him. He never imagined that he would fight alongside a dragon.

Azghar spiralled up before going after Angie who was ahead of them. Behind them a mass of black cloud burst out of the forest into the air, the darkness bubbling over like a pot boiling over. The shimmers had broken through the trees.

46

They were flying high. Angie was so far ahead of them she looked like a dot. Azghar turned to view the black mass of shimmers still pushing out above the trees. It looked like huge thunderclouds collecting over the forest, and they were moving across the sky after them. Jeff caught a glimpse and gulped.

Matt looked so at home in Azghar's talons. His feet were dangling and his arms hanging over the top. He looked sideways at Jeff and flashed a smile. "I lost a tooth, gonna get five bucks," he yelled.

"Get ready, boys, here they come," warned Azghar.

Madgwick grinned and glanced at Rig with raised eyebrows. "When last were you called boy?"

"Can't remember, but don't mind so much if it's Azghar."

"Here they come," roared Azghar.

Madgwick and Rig were ready. They were tied securely and their hands were full of glittering dust. The shimmers came in behind them. Azghar turned sharp left and then shot up above the shimmers.

Rig threw a handful of dust into the air. It hovered for a split second before whooshing towards the shimmers and exploding like fireworks to scatter them in different directions. The shimmers closest to the fireworks sizzled as the glitter touched them and they fizzled all the way to the ground.

"Good one!" yelled Madgwick. He would have yelled more but Azghar had turned on his back. Madgwick had a perfect view of a cloud of shimmers racing towards them. Still upside down, his dust dropped from his hands and turned into a silver net. It caught the squirming shimmers in a bundle. With the flick of a wrist, Madgwick released the end of the net and the shimmers were hurled to the ground, struggling inside as they dropped.

As his dust flowed back to him, Madgwick formed arrows for his bow. He shot left and right, sometimes catching two or three shimmers at a time. Rig was shooting at the shimmers with a dust gun. A burst of silver dust rushed through the barrel, cutting down the shimmers in its path. Rig howled with glee.

Jeff could not really see what was happening with Rig and Madgwick, but he heard the yells and howls. Jeff was wincing, imagining that each howl was Madgwick or Rig being caught in a shimmer. Around them shimmers were dropping, some of them going down like stone, while others floated down like deflated bags, and some flew around erratically like balloons.

He could not keep his bearings either. Azghar moved like liquid, one minute all he could see was black misty shimmers above him, and then it was green forest beneath.

The dragon was amazing. He turned, dived and rolled as if he knew exactly how and when and where to be to give Madgwick and Rig their shot at destroying the shimmers and destroy they did. It was what they were trained to do.

A cloud of shimmers was heading directly for them, full frontal attack. Jeff opened his mouth to warn Azghar, but he had already snapped his head to the side and had seen the shimmers closing in on them. He did not try to evade them.

A deep rumble came from within the dragon, so loud that Jeff could feel it. Azghar opened his mouth and a sharp blue flame streamed out. The shimmers evaporated within seconds and Azghar flew through the black haze that was left.

"Eeeeeuw," yelled Matt.

* * *

The broom-bike had reached the forest in record speed. Angie knew they had little time. Although Azghar was mighty and the warriors were deadly with their dust, there were just too many to keep them all away.

Angie needed time to start the doorway process. The door had to be open long enough to get them through but not too long to allow the shimmers to get through, or even worse, Wiedzma.

Angie hopped off the broom, patted him fondly and made her way to the enchanted pool. She faced the still water, deep-dark green in colour. She dropped her head and raised her arms, palms facing out. She opened her magic and let it flow towards the pool.

Azghar had already forged a magic path for the doorway, so the groundwork had been done and all Angie had to do was reach across with her magic and create the link. She felt the tentative touch of what she recognised to be spell weavers. The link was there. The elders had received Azghar's message and had made it on time.

Now they just had to wait for twilight and the first moonbeam and then the link would be forged. After that the doorway would open and they would be able to cross. Angie had to concentrate and work hard to keep the link strong from her side. It was not easy. The spell weavers had many hands lending strength from their side.

Thirza was standing, half watching the skies for the moment the magic would start. He was also watching for Azghar. He held onto Rhed tightly, squeezing his arm now and then to reassure him and to keep him quiet. Angie could not be distracted right now. All their lives depended on her keeping the link until the doorway was formed.

The forest was dark and the shadows were creeping together as twilight approached. It made the forest seem mysterious. The trees were large like the ones in the forest surrounding Little Falls.

The emerald pool was circular and seemed sunken in as if the forest had grown around it over the years. A little stone wall covered with moss lined the banks. The sides were steep, encasing the deep green water. The water lay very still, looking cold and ancient. Trees huddling over the pool kept it well hidden.

As the first hue of pink entered the sky and the moon could be seen rising, the pool started to bubble and the waters slowly parted to reveal a narrow stairway leading down the side. Round stepping stones rose slowly to mark a pathway across the pool towards the dimly lit outline of a doorway. The moon's first full beam suddenly struck the doorway and it lit up brightly.

Angie lifted her head towards the skies, using her magic to ensure that Azghar heard her. "Azghar, the doorway has been revealed."

Angie heard the dry response from Azghar. "A little busy right now. I will bring a huge load with me if I come down now. There's too many to keep away from the kids and away from the doorway. Drat that Wiedzma for making so many. They just keep coming."

The doorway opened and Angie turned to see cloaked men standing on the other side of the doorway. The elders were there in full force, ensuring the doorway stayed open and also making sure shimmers could not pass.

Their heads were lowered, hidden in their hooded cloaks. They formed two lines and softly started to hum and very lightly tap their left feet. The trees started to dip in time with the rhythm. It felt like the air was pulsating with their chant, pushing through the door in waves. The ground trembled as their feet directed the song.

"The elders are here," yelled Angie to Azghar. "All of them!"

47

Azghar roared in approval of Angie's message, his fire evaporating a host of shimmers. The more they destroyed, the more there seemed to be.

"Madgwick, Rig!" Azghar called to the two warriors who were fighting their hearts out above him.

"The doorway is open, it is time. There are too many shimmers to land without taking them with us. You are going to have to each take a child and drop. I will keep them busy up here."

Madgwick gasped, "Azghar! There are too many to handle alone."

"I know, but we don't have a choice, the doorway has been opened now, it must be now. So do it!"

Madgwick and Rig loosened their dust ties and made their way to Jeff and Matt.

Azghar spoke to Matt gently. "Matt, it's time for you to go home. You have to be brave and go with Madgwick and Rig. It will be exciting, you will see."

Matt's bottom lip started to wobble. "Can't you come with me, Azghar?"

"Matt, can I fit under your bed?" he waited until Matt giggled at the image before continuing. They did not have much time to say goodbye. "You belong with your mother, father, with Jeff and your grandfather. I belong here."

"Will I see you again?" asked Matt in a sad little voice.

"Very soon!" answered Azghar. "When you go to sleep, wait for me at that big tree by the entrance of dreamland. We will go in together, and have some fun and exciting adventures together. We will fly all over the place."

"You're my best friend, Azghar."

Madgwick and Rig swung around the front. Madgwick reached for Jeff, using his dust to bind the two of them together, ignoring Rig's disgruntled glances and waiting for the right moment to release.

Rig reached Matt, looking into the boy's eyes, which were bright with unshed tears.

Rig rolled his eyes at the thought of a crying child and a running nose. He tied Matt to himself and nodded to Azghar. They were ready.

"Are you crying?" he asked Matt.

"Nope," sniffed the boy.

"Do you need to wipe your nose?" asked Rig.

"Nope," sniffed Matt again.

In a sudden twist Azghar roared and released the biggest flame ever. "Now!" he yelled at the warriors. Both instantly dropped away from Azghar, taking the two boys with them.

Matt screamed as they dropped, nearly giving Rig a heart attack.

"It's okay!" yelled Rig, panicked by Matt's bloodcurdling scream.

"Funnnnnnnn," yelled Matt. "Let's go back and do this again."

Rig was speechless. He liked this kid!

Madgwick watched Azghar as they dropped away from him. The dragon had shimmers all over him. He twisted and flamed them away but he could not reach them all. Madgwick concentrated really hard, keeping his dust binding him and Jeff together in place.

Then he stretched out his hand and released the biggest spray of dust he could. The dust attacked the shimmers like a storm, driving them away from Azghar, finally giving the dragon time to turn and gain a little space from the shimmers.

48

The dust flowed back to Madgwick just in time. He could not risk a chute, as descending would be too slow and the shimmers would be over them in no time. He followed Rig's lead and formed a cushioned ball around them, hitting the ground a few seconds later, bouncing around until they rolled to a stop.

Madgwick released the dust and glanced around to see where Matt and Rig were. They had landed a little way from them, Matt still tied to Rig but his eyes were gleaming. The child was begging Rig to go back up and jump again.

Rig had a grimace on his face as if he was trying very hard not to look like he was in any way enjoying the boy's enthusiasm.

Jeff grabbed Matt's hand and hurried in the direction of the forest. They had landed in an open space not far from where Thirza was waving his arms, showing them where to go. They started towards Thirza when a wind came up behind them with such a force that they were all blown over. They were shielding their eyes from the dust and grass. Jeff held onto Matt tightly as they rolled in the wind, trying to see the cause.

Jeff's heart lurched when he saw it. The evil witch Wiedzma had arrived on a shimmer with her windstorm, causing chaos around her. She landed in front of them, blocking their way to the doorway.

Grzegorz rolled off the shimmer and hobbled to the side towards the trees.

Rig and Madgwick pushed up off the ground and stood in front of Jeff and Matt.

She looked calm and gleeful, her black hair flowing freely behind her and her mole was back in the middle of her forehead.

"You won't get past me, so you might as well give up," she said to Rig and Madgwick. "I want a dream catcher, either one or both, I don't really care. I also want a warrior or two. My darling shimmers are not just normal shimmers. These are full nightmare shimmers, quite capable of overpowering the dragon. He may be powerful but there are too many of them to fight at once. That leaves you and me and your dirt." She laughed a deep, eerie laugh.

She turned her head slightly to stare at Jeff. Her green eyes were piercing, "You shoot me with that potion gun again and I will make you eat it." She smiled to lighten her words and continued, "It's obvious you don't know how to use your skill but if you come with me then I will teach you. You will have everything you ever wanted and more. You would be the prince of Drakmere."

"I don't think so," Jeff snorted, his lips curling.

Wiedzma stared at Jeff, slowly nodding. "Then it will be with force, and so it shall be."

She waved her hands and Jeff felt a tug on Matt's body. She was trying to reel him in with magic.

Jeff locked his arms around Matt. Grass tufts and dirt shot up as he dug his heels in, trying to stop the silent pull towards Wiedzma. "Madgwick! Rig!"

Both Madgwick and Rig threw a shield up at the same time, their magic combining to create a wall in attempt to repel

Wiedzma's spell. Madgwick's lips were pulled in a sneer as he concentrated.

The frown on Rig's forehead was deep and his lips pressed together. "We are so close; the doorway was just there, the kids are just steps away from the doorway," he grunted to Madgwick.

"This evil old hag is not going to stop us now." Madgwick's magic dust increased in magnitude as his scowl grew.

Jeff felt the pull ease and hauled Matt to his feet.

"When I make my move, you run with Matt. Don't stop, don't look back. Your only mission is to get across the path and through that doorway." Rig was firm.

'But ..."

"No buts," he said.

Rig dropped his head and did a half turn before leaping into the air to land on one bended knee, his arms spread out, releasing his dust forward towards Wiedzma.

The force of his battering ram knocked Wiedzma backward. He did not stop. He twirled and stretched his arms and legs out, sending another blast in the shape of a cannon ball at Wiedzma.

Watching Rig was like watching a ninja pulling off complicated moves. Wiedzma was screeching and tried to counter the dust with her wind, so Rig had to hold it in place with sheer force, his face fierce with concentration.

Madgwick grabbed Jeff by the arm and Matt by the collar, propelling them forward as he ran. Madgwick turned his back on the boys and threw his hands out in front of him, his dust plunged forward and he joined the fight against Wiedzma and her shimmers.

Jeff and Matt ran as fast as Matt's little legs could take him. They closed in on the trees and were close to the pool where Thirza and Rhed were beckoning them to hurry.

A leg shot out and caught Matt's foot causing them to stumble and fall. They rolled on the moss-covered forest floor, making the landing soft and spongy. Grzegorz limped out from behind the tree.

"You sneaky brat, you are not going anywhere. You will not destroy all my planning."

49

Grzegorz reached Matt first, pulling him up and away from Jeff. Matt kicked his shin hard. Grzegorz threw his head back as he laughed.

"Did not even feel that kick. Thanks to you my foot is asleep, asleep forever. Didn't even feel a thing."

"Kick his other leg, Matt," yelled Jeff.

Matt kicked Grzegorz's other shin as hard as he could. This one he did feel. He lifted his leg in pain and hopped about but his snoring foot could not support his weight and he went crashing down taking Matt with him.

Jeff dashed to Matt trying to pull him away from Grzegorz's grip.

"Stay away from my brother," yelled Jeff, his eyes bright and wild.

Some of the potions and marbles that Matt had stored in his pocket rolled out. Jeff helped Matt gather his marbles and miniature bottles.

Grzegorz screamed, high-pitched like a girl, "Eeeeeeiiiiiiiii my gems, you little thief, Wiedzma, he has my gems!"

Wiedzma's eyes widened. Some of her potion bottles were rolling along the ground. The little brat had taken her potions. Her hand flew to her mouth, she dropped her guard and Rig's dust attack knocked her to the ground again. Rig and Madgwick used this time to race past her, blocking her from Jeff and Matt.

Madgwick looked up from his mad sprint. Angie was standing there just behind the boys. Her face was serious, not angry nor smiling in her usual crazy way but just calm, not good.

"Take the kids through the doorway," she said to the warriors.

Looking at Wiedzma, she said quite calmly, "I have had about enough of you."

Wiedzma's eyes narrowed. "I am sick and tired of being knocked down!" she yelled wildly. "Give my potions back, you deranged old duck!"

"No, I don't think I will give them back, thank you very much, duck indeed! I have been called many things but never a duck before. A goose, or a pigeon, even a pheasant, but a duck, that is a first." Angie looked at the ground. A bottle of potion was still lying there.

"Wiedzma, Wiedzma, Wiedzma," she said, flicking her wrists so that the bottle flew into her hands. She held it up to take a look.

"Fancy letting this out of your sight. Your witch license should be taken away for that alone, but then, you don't really care about the witch order."

That just did it for Wiedzma. She clamped her jaw and hurled spells at Angie. Angie blocked them and sent back some of her own. You could not really see the spells going back and forth but each time a spell or enchantment was blocked there were colourful sparks. Soon both witches were surrounded in circles of pink, orange, green and blue sparks as each witch tried to catch the other off guard.

Madgwick and Rig backed the boys up so that they could not get hit by anything. They moved them around inch by inch, leading them towards the stairs that ran down to the pool.

Madgwick's foot nudged something and he saw one of the potions that had rolled out of Matt's pocket. He swooped down and put it in his own pocket.

Rhed and Thirza were standing on the bottom step. Madgwick motioned for them to go through the doorway. They could hear the chanting from the elders who were holding the door open. They had to go through, and soon, the elders would not be able to hold the door open for too long.

Jeff watched Wiedzma's face. Her eyes and smile, previously bright with wild glee now looked troubled as if she knew she could not win against Angie. It was just a matter of time before Angie would wipe the floor with her as easy as peanut butter on toast.

Wiedzma glanced up at her shimmers fighting Azghar. Her face darkened as if their rage flowed into her mind. She smiled as she calmly told them to kill the dragon.

Angie's breath caught. She screamed, "Azghar!"

A terrible, high screeching roar came from the skies, sending shivers of fear down Jeff's back. Everyone immediately looked up, trying to catch a glimpse of Azghar screaming in pain.

Angie stamped her foot and put her hands up sharply, palms outward as if she was pushing Wiedzma away. As Angie's spell hit her, Wiedzma was lifted off her feet. She twisted in mid air. A shimmer appeared out of nowhere, embracing her like a blanket and they vanished.

"Azghar!" Angie screamed again. She started to run for the clearing.

"Get through the doorway now," she yelled over her shoulder at the warriors.

"Broom!" she called while running towards the clearing. Her broom came up behind her, having transformed from a bike into a rocket. His bristles were blood red with power and he swooped down beside Angie. After two sideways looks, Angie leapt on.

As they shot into the sky they could hear Angie screaming. "How am I supposed to hold onto a rocket? No, never mind about that, just go."

She and her rocket-broom disappeared over the trees in a red flash.

Madgwick, not wanting to waste any more time, turned and urged everyone down the stairs. The chanting had reached a climax. It was time. As they were about to step onto the stone steps, Galagedra came through the doorway. He almost glided across and stood by the stairs, smiling a welcome at the warriors and Thirza.

"We have to go one at a time. Rhed, you go first, then Thirza."

Rhed went down the last step and crossed onto the stones. The pool was still bubbling like a Jacuzzi, and he was not keen to touch the water. He went through the doorway, and the minute he passed through, a warm cloak was draped over his shoulders and he was led across the remaining stepping stones to the bank on the other side. Rhed looked up into the face old a smiling kindly old man.

"You are safe now, Rhed."

Rhed smiled and looked back at the doorway, watching for the others.

On the other side, Thirza was stalling. He had been here for so long, there were so many what ifs going through his mind.

Galagedra touched his hand. "She is waiting for you," he said. Thirza nodded and answered simply, "I will not go before my grandchildren."

Jeff led Matt down the stairs and they started to hop from stepping stone to stepping stone.

Then Wiedzma appeared on the grass bank, her hair still gooey and yellow from the paint ball. She screamed a spell to enchant a vine, which grabbed Matt around the chest and dragged him away from Jeff and towards the side of the bank where she was standing.

"You are *not* stealing my child."

The shimmers were streaming towards the doorway.

Rig flipped backward and landed on the bank in front of the shimmers, his dust sword in one hand, his dagger in the other.

Madgwick turned and started his own dance with the shimmers, using his dust as a whip in the one hand and a net in the other. The shimmers screeched and squealed as he made them evaporate around him.

Jeff scrambled over the stones towards the bank, racing for Matt who was dangling in a vine that was swinging him closer to Wiedzma.

He felt the blood run out of his face. He was angry but calm, his mind very clear.

"I told you to leave my brother alone." Jeff did not yell. He was not in a panic. He was beyond those emotions. Jeff stared at Wiedzma, his face smooth like he was in total control. He was going to make her regret that she ever picked on his brother.

Jeff reached into the darkened room in his mind. It was so natural that it was like flipping a switch. He saw dreams passing like a movie trailer but not fast and uncontrollable as before. This was so easy he could not understand why he had battled before. He clearly pictured what he needed and forced it out of a dream that he did not even realise was passing.

His palms were pushed out in front of him to face Wiedzma. He felt a tingling, like a current passing through his body. He took all that energy and directed it out of his hands.

Out of his palms shot glittering magic dust, like a jet of water from a fire hose. The power was so strong that Wiedzma was blasted off her feet and held against a tree by the pure force of the dust. She screamed and splattered as she got a mouthful of it.

Grzegorz limped towards Matt. Jeff turned to him and raised an eyebrow, "If you think you can get to him before me, try."

Jeff closed his fist and the violent stream of dust was cut off. As he pushed his hand at Grzegorz, the dust flew from his palm and tumbled Grzegorz like a soccer ball into the forest. Grzegorz, squealing, faded as he rolled over moss-covered rocks and roots.

Wiedzma was panting and looked like a drowned rat. Jeff shot his hand at her again and thin glittering strands spun around her like a spider web, binding her to the tree that she was leaning against for support. She screamed as she strained against the web.

Jeff had reached Matt who was lying on the floor. A dust dagger shot out of his hand and sliced a vine, which started snapping like a live electric cable.

Jeff pulled Matt up. "You okay? Let's go home, Matt. Give her a serious attitude salute to say goodbye."

Jeff struggled to his feet, carrying Matt in his arms and staggered to the stairs.

Madgwick somersaulted in front of him and took Matt out of his arms, pushing Jeff down the stairs and across the stones in front of him.

"How did you do that?" Madgwick gasped.

"I don't know. It was just there and it was easy." Jeff was staring at his hands as he hopped over the stones. He was expecting to see them seared with heat but they looked normal, like nothing out of the ordinary had happened.

"Go," yelled Madgwick. They did not need to tell Galagedra twice. The elder pushed Thirza towards the doorway. Thirza was still yelling for Matt when he went through the silver doorway to the other side.

Matt looked over Madgwick's shoulder and gave Wiedzma the commander's salute Jeff had taught him for serious attitude situations.

Wiedzma's eyes widened.

Rig had somersaulted to the bottom step and was waiting with open arms for the next attack.

Jeff reached the doorway. It was starting to brighten, a clear sign that they were running out of time. The doorway was starting to close.

Holding Matt tightly against him, Madgwick hopped onto every second stone. He looked up and saw Jeff standing at the doorway, his arms open, face fierce with determination. With all his power he threw Matt into Jeff's waiting arms. "Take him through, close the doorway," he yelled.

Jeff caught Matt and hugged him tight. Matt's little arms closed around his neck.

"Come on, Madgwick, Rig, come on!" begged Jeff, taking a step back towards the doorway rim.

"No, Jeff, we're going back for Gwyndion, Azghar and Angie! Go Go!"

The chanting intensified and the door was so bright that it started to flicker. Jeff smiled at Madgwick and then with Matt still tight in his arms, he stepped back. The doorway closed in a blinding flash.

Madgwick stared at the place where the doorway had been shining brightly a few moments ago. Feeling the stepping stones start to sink, he quickly hopped back to the bank, where Rig was standing watching Wiedzma. Jeff's dust, which had held Wiedzma tied to the tree, had disappeared when Jeff stepped through the doorway.

She was staring at them. Her face was red and her hair looked like yellow, sticky snakes. She raised her shaking hands, intending to finish them off once and for all.

Madgwick pulled the potion out of his pocket and uncorked it. The blue liquid swirled around, pleased to be escaping. He threw it at Wiedzma. The potion splashed all over her.

Wiedzma howled and started to bat at the blue that was spreading all over her body. She was starting to fade into blueness. She lifted off the ground and swirled away like a breeze on a summer's day. She screamed obscenities at them as she hovered over them before floating away, soon disappearing into the blue skies. She was gone but not for good. Sooner or later the potion would wear off and she would be back.

Rig turned to Madgwick. "Did you see Jeff? That was our magic dust. He was using our dust as if he was a warrior, but how?"

"I don't know. He must have taken it from one of our dreams. I don't know how."

"He is a strong dream catcher, stronger than any I have ever met. Maybe Galagedra will be able to explain."

Madgwick was silent, then said, "Sorry, Rig, I made them close the doorway without us. We can't leave just yet. We have to find

Gwyndion. I am not sure how we will get back but we will deal with that when we have to."

Madgwick spoke very matter of factly and did not sound sorry at all.

Rig was grateful Madgwick had chosen to stay with him and find Gwyndion. He looked at Madgwick's face and saw that his friend did not need words.

Still fearful for Azghar, they both raced through the forest in the direction of where Azghar's horrible screams were last heard.

50

The elders walked the children through the forest. They were all very quiet. All of the elders were wearing dark cloaks with hoods. Their hands were wrapped inside their sleeves and they seemed to glide over the forest floor. Only Galagedra had his hood down and seemed to be walking next to Thirza.

Jeff and Rhed were very upset that Madgwick and Rig had not come back with them.

"They said they were going to help Azghar and Angie," said Jeff quietly.

"What about Gwyndion?" asked Rhed. His tone was flat and tired.

"Gwyndion? What is this about Gwyndion?" asked Galagedra. His normally low voice rose slightly.

"She's a warrior and was at the castle with Matt but they could not find her," answered Jeff.

"Gwyndion is alive! The whole of Sandustian will be in celebration. I am stunned, we watched for years but found no trace of her! They will find her, they will not fail. We will watch Drakmere through the globe for any signs and be prepared for an exit doorway." Galagedra shook his head at the unexpected news.

"And there is always Azghar. Never underestimate Azghar," added Thirza.

"And Angie," said Jeff.

The trees started to sway and made a swooshing noise, so loud that Galagedra stopped short and tilted his head.

Jeff anxiously turned around, looking for a shimmer or mare-mist, but Galagedra laughed softly and spoke to Rhed. "The trees welcome 'Twigwig' home."

Rhed tried to grin in response but his smile looked weak, as if he was not sure how to take this welcome. He checked his pockets for his pongsap root.

The elders fell away until it was only Galagedra who was walking with them. Thirza was carrying Matt who was worn out from all the fun and adventures.

"How long were we gone?' Jeff wanted to know.

"Time flows differently in Drakmere, so although it will seem you were away for a long time, you were only gone a few days. Everyone thinks you were lost in the forest," Galagedra explained.

"Except for your mother, Jeff, she knows the truth."

Jeff's brows rose and he made a mental note to ask her about it.

Soon they saw lights through the trees and Jeff recognised his house.

Galagedra stopped. "Until we meet again, young dream catcher." He bowed to Jeff.

Galagedra nodded at Thirza before retreating back into the forest, the darkness knitting together around him.

They watched until they could not see him anymore before finally moving towards the brightness of home.

Breaking through the trees, Jeff yelled, "Mom! Dad!"

The back door flung open and his parents rushed out. The next thing he knew he was gripped in a bear hug.

Rhed's mother was also there, hugging Rhed so tightly and sobbing so loudly that he could not get a word out.

Thirza handed the sleepy Matt to Ella while the boy tried to tell her that he had lost a tooth, that he had flown on a dragon and that he had found a grandfather.

She hugged Matt and turned to Thirza who was standing quietly to the side, the sorrow of all the lost years etched on his face. She grabbed his hand and then hugged him.

She whispered brokenly. "Mom told me you'd come home if you could, when the doorway was open, and if you could, you would come home. And here you are, home at last. I did not know what she meant until tonight. Thank you for bringing my boys home."

Jeff and Rhed exchanged looks. There was something more here, something to certainly investigate.

A little while later Jeff sat by the window in Matt's room, staring at the moon, wondering where Madgwick and Rig were.

Thirza leaned against the door frame. His eyes were misted at the sight of his family.

Matt snuggled into his bed. His eyes were half closed, and his mother was sitting on his bed crooning the poem that she whispered to Matt every night when she tucked him in.

Moonlit beams and sun-kissed dreams

Await you in dreamland,

Meet me at the big green tree,

We'll go hand in hand.

But if I'm late and you get scared,

Mischief runs amok,

Raise your voice, stamp your foot and shout

smok, smok, smok.

What if Jeff went back to Drakmere to find
a cure for his best friend Rhed?

Visit

BerniceFischer.com

to find out more about Jeff's next adventure.